GW01157289

THE BOOK OF PAUL

Copyright © 2022 by Paul Stewart

All rights reserved. Published by Armida Publications Ltd.

No part of this publication may be reproduced, stored in a retrieval system, or transmitted in any form or by any means, electronic, mechanical, photocopying, recording, or otherwise, without permission of the publisher. For information regarding permission, write to
Armida Publications Ltd, P.O.Box 27717, 2432 Engomi, Nicosia, Cyprus
or email: info@armidapublications.com

Armida Publications is a member of the Independent Publishers Guild (UK),
and a member of the Independent Book Publishers Association (USA)

www.armidabooks.com | Great Literature. One Book At A Time.

Summary:
The events of *Of People and Things* behind him, Paul begins to write again. Part journal and part imagination, he tries to wrestle new events into stories to make sense of it all.

Paul is supposed to be starting a new life in an inherited modern mansion. Used to being poor and alone, he struggles to come to terms with a fresh host of people who demand his attention. They seem friendly enough, but what do they want from him? If only Mr Samuels – the kindly, enigmatic private detective who had saved Paul before – were on hand to sort things out, but he is nowhere to be seen. Instead, Paul imagines what he might be up to as a mysterious woman, and a near fatal encounter, plunge Mr Samuels into what might be the most dangerous, and most personal, case of his career.

[1. Humorous / General 2. Mystery & Detective / Private Investigators
3. Literary 4. Contemporary British Fiction 5. Family Life / General 6. Psychological
7. Social Themes / Mental Illness]

Cover images:
AXL II by *Laszlo Moholy-Nagy*
This artwork is in public domain in its country of origin and other countries
and areas where the copyright term is the author's life plus 70 years or less.
Source: WikiArt.org

Additional background images by *rawpixel* and *Vincent Burkhead*
Source: Unsplash

This novel is a work of fiction.
Any resemblance to real people, living or dead, is entirely coincidental.

1st edition: October 2022

ISBN-13 (paperback): 978-9925-601-21-9

THE BOOK OF PAUL

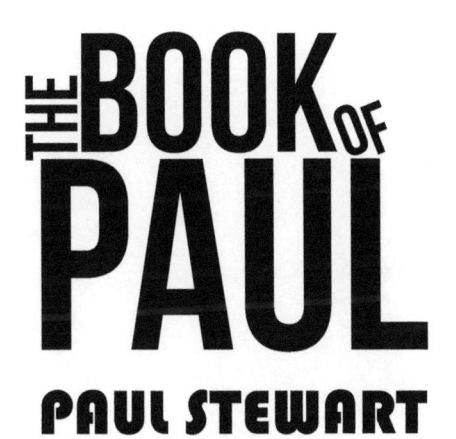

PAUL STEWART

ARMIDA

For Dad

one

I am alone in the house. At least I think I am. I hear the odd noise now and then echoing from beyond my walls but whether these are human noises I don't know. No one lives with me. That is what I mean by being alone in the house; that no one lives with me. There could be a vagabond lying doggo in one of the innumerable rooms for all I know, but I doubt it. Or a stray, cast off dog. Or just rats, for even the most modern of houses is prone to the odd bit of vermin. No doubt there are a fair few cockroaches eyeing me right now, their antenna twitching. They can stay. The rats can stay too, if there are any, but I would regret there being another human.

I gather this was meant to be a new start. It is not. People can intend things all they want; it doesn't mean it is going to happen.

I got rid of the carpet. The shag annoyed me. Beneath that and the underlay was a perfectly decent slab of concrete which is cool in summer and warm in winter through some mechanism or another that I don't really understand. I ripped up the carpet and rolled it up and dumped it in the corner of the garden in the dead of night. Ditto the underlay. I don't know why I did it in the middle of the night. If there was any witness they might think I was disposing of a corpse, and then a second corpse. Or delivering a couple of Cleopatras. But there can have been no witnesses. No one overlooks this gated garden.

Yes, I have made some changes. In that flush of the early days I roamed the house a little, to get a proper lie of the land. In the old days, I had only really had access to the living room and this office, and the necessary spaces in-between. And the necessary house I think on one occasion at least. So I roamed around this realm that was suddenly apparently mine, or partly mine with conditions attached that I never really bothered about. The décor was hideous. Even I could see that. Lots of flashing marble and chrome and stairs that spiralled or swooped and threatened a dangerous fall. Lots of mirrors.

Two rooms I remember well. They were bedrooms. The first was dominated by a gigantic oval bed, with black sheets. I am still not sure how one is meant to lie on or in an oval bed. There is no natural direction in which to lie. You could lie anyway you wanted, it seems to me, or rotate yourself on a daily basis as if the bed were a clock face and you the hour hand. If you were systematically minded. But I rather think that the point of the oval bed was that you could toss yourself around with abandon. This room had a preponderance of mirrors too, or rather one huge mirror, almost floor to ceiling but a trick had been missed, because this mirror did not arc about in line with the bed. Instead it was just flat against a facing wall. And I think it a trick missed because if the point of an oval bed is to toss yourself around with abandon and the point of a mirror is to see yourself in reflection then surely bed and mirror should be in alignment otherwise you could wake in the middle of the night – sweating and panting from a nasty nightmare, let us say – and you wouldn't immediately be comforted by your own reflection. Instead there would be a further panic as you cast about to find your reflection, that face to let you know where you are and who you are.

I think I only remember the bed and the mirror in this room because there was nothing else to remember. I don't like casting about in memory, but I have just done so to the best of my ability and have drawn a blank. There were no pictures on the walls. No objet, d'art or otherwise. If I trawl again, I can see no bedside tables – on what side would they be of an oval bed I don't know – no chest of drawers with nic-nacs on the top, no chair in which to sit, no armoire. I don't know why I have come over all French today, but there you go.

Wouldn't the mirror have been better on the ceiling? Another missed trick.

And when I say that one would be comforted by one's own reflection I am merely saying that there must be people out there who would find such a thing a comfort. I have no more love of a mirror than I have ever had, which is precisely none.

Cass showed me the second bedroom I recall. Yes, she was still here back then. The early days, as I said. She took me by the hand one day, dragged me out of this room, along the mirrored corridors, up the most treacherous of the swooping staircases, and presented me with a door. It was white.

'Need your advice, old thing,' she said. Really, she was forever the optimist.

She threw open the door. This is not an exaggeration.

'Ta da!' She said.

Back then I was not quite sure what she was ta-da-ing, but now I think it might have been an introduction to the volume of clothing that was strewn around. The bed was at least bed shaped; more so, in fact, for its four corners were accented by four posts which supported a white canopy from which white curtains fell. Not that I could see the bed in all its glory as it was covered with a mountain of clothes, as was everything else in the room; the two chairs were buried under clothes; clothes hung from the stand-alone, full-length mirror and from the screen behind which one dresses, from the curtain rails and from the frames of the pictures. There were a lot of clothes, but not a lot of colours, thankfully. Lots of black and grey, lots of white, and I think a few dusky pinks or salmons thrown in.

'I'm having a clear out,' she announced as she ushered me in. 'But how is a girl to decide what to keep and what to throw?' She took me gently by the arm. 'I need a man's eye.'

Apparently she had in mind this man and this eye.

'Pop yourself down here,' and she cleared a little space for me at the end of the bed. She may even have patted it. I sat. The bed gave beneath me. 'Memory foam,' she said. I have no idea what she meant by this. I understood the word 'memory' and recognised the word 'foam' but that was as far as I got. Which is why I remember them now. She knelt before me for a moment and looked up at me, necessarily. This man's eye could not read that woman's eye. She patted my leg and leapt to her feet.

'So what is needed is a little fashion show, a little parade. And you; you are the discerning eye.'

She grabbed a small black dress from a pile of small black dresses beside me and made for the screen, casting me a look over her already bared shoulder as she did so.

I left.

Now what I remember about the room, besides Cass, the bed, the four posts, the canopy, the bed-curtains, the curtain rail, the two chairs, the screen, the stand-alone, full-length mirror and the clothes in black, grey, white and salmon, was the pictures. There were pencil and charcoal sketches, there were oils, there were collages, there were water-colours, there were even photographs in black and white and sepia, but they were all of the same thing. They were all of Cass. I admit, some might not have been as they were too obscured by a twin-set or dress hanging from their frames for me to get a clear sight of them. Either way, Cass had a lot of pictures of herself. And she appeared to have sat for a lot of artists over the years; for futurists, and Dadaists, surrealists and cubists; for Expressionists, and social realists, neo-classicists and brutalists.

Her clearing out was a preparation for her clearing off.

So now, those early days behind me, I confine myself to this room, the necessary house – complete with shower and two sinks – and the kitchen. And the corridor connecting same, of course. If one is to get from A to B there always seems to be an A2, if not an A3, A4 and so on. Luckily, there was but one corridor from this room to the kitchen. I admit the kitchen took me some time to negotiate, so used was I to my kitchenette and the stained Formica of the old days. It took me the best part of a week to find the fridge. It was disguised as just another cupboard in the same egg-shell grey. Egg-shell every which way I looked, as if I were a chick; an unpleasant feeling on a number of levels. But who am I to shy away from an unpleasant feeling, no matter on how many levels? And is not one sink in the necessary house enough? But there was a kind of architectural mania for sinks, for again the kitchen had not one but two, with an elaborate set of chrome taps that swung between them. And a hose. Oh, not a garden hose, but a much shorter one with the hose proper wrapped about with a flexible stainless steel coil. At rest, this hose disappeared into the counter between the sinks. It seems to me that everything in this kitchen was trying to disappear in one way or another.

How did I survive those early days when the fridge was hidden from me? I survived, that's all I know, and it doesn't much matter how.

Algae quickly overwhelmed the swimming pool once Cass had gone. A rather pleasant green, I must say.

Cass didn't say goodbye, as such. One morning I went into the kitchen to find two linen suits, a Panama hat and assorted shirts piled on top of the central counter – an island, if you prefer – and beside them a letter.

'Old thing,' she said, or rather the letter said.

'Old thing. I'm off to pastures new. Try not to miss me too much. I will miss you terribly. Horribly terribly, but it's time for me strike out and take the bally bull by the horns. Still some life in the old dog yet! I need to see if the grass is really greener, or perhaps I just need a new piece of grass to nibble on. I know that this will all seem beastly of me – dashing off into the sunset and all that – but I know it is for the best for you, and for me. You don't need this old crow hanging around like a bad smell.

'Can't say cheerio in person. I'm welling up just thinking about it and a scene is the last thing we need. No more wailing and gnashing of teeth! That's what I say anyway. Who knows how things will pan out, but shoulder to the wheel and all that.

Cass.'

There was then an imprint of her lips in a livid red. Plus several Xs.

'PS. Bought you a few rags so you don't look quite so much like a scarecrow.'

My head is an optical illusion. It looks large, but is tiny. I don't know how this is achieved, but it is. You would look at my head – should you ever have the chance – and think, 'There is a man with a medium to large head; a medium to large hat size would be best', and then you would err on the side of caution and go for a larger size. You would be wrong. You would not be wrong in general principle, for a slightly large hat is always preferable to a slightly small one, but you would be wrong in my specific case. It would swamp me and fly off at the slightest hint of a breeze. Yet Cass had got my size about right. Oh, there was a bit of give in it, but near enough. An inscription inside the hat told me it was a Montecristo. This information left me unmoved.

Why this need to buy me clothes and a hat? I wondered then and I still wonder. The desire for a parting gift I can understand well enough, but I cannot understand this gift. Was she imagining me sallying forth, hat on head, into the world, feeling fresh in my linen suit and shirts even on the hottest of days? Well, not the hottest, but almost the hottest. Perhaps she did. But if she was imagining me sallying forth, why did she not throw in some shoes too? Some nice brogues or some such, rather than leaving me with the collapsing canvas things I occasionally feel the need to press my feet into. Well, there you go, she didn't. On reflection, perhaps she just saw me sitting by a well-maintained pool, here in this place I am told is home, sipping on an iced bracer of some sort whilst contemplating the funny old world and how it had come to this. Whatever this might be.

I have no idea where Cass went.

Needless to say, but say it anyway, that I did not sally forth. I remain here, in this book-lined room.

So, I live by proxy. I send my man out and he reports back. This is not true. My man is not my man and nor do I send him out. I wouldn't know where to send him out to, in truth. But I get bulletins from the front; despatches brought to my bunker. He sits with me here from time to time and he tells me things of what goes on in the world; that portion of the world with which he comes into contact, for although his range is broader than mine I know it is narrower than some. So, I get a slice of life, as the phrase used to be.

His reports are very dull. He sits opposite me, on the other side of this desk, takes out his notebook from his inside jacket pocket, and gives me the particulars, as he likes to call them.

The particulars go something like this.

17 August. Weather as previously.

Proceeded by car to the vicinity of target. Reached 10:17.

Target as described previously in location previously ascertained.

Delivered package as instructed.

Returned to and briefed client.

Client satisfied.

It varies from time to time. He might go by scooter or on foot, rather than by car, for example. He might not deliver a package but merely follow the target for some little time. The weather never varies, nor the client's satisfaction. It has always been client's and never clients'. An oddity, perhaps. The date changes too, obviously. Perhaps it has always been client's satisfaction and never clients' because he prefers to work for an individual, or perhaps individuals only ever seek him out as if one person alone recognises another loner and trusts them on that basis alone. These things could be cleared up, I'm sure, if I were to ask. I could merely say, 'Mr Samuels, do you only ever work for individuals and is that your own choice, or a matter of circumstance and coincidence?' That is far too complicated a question. I would have to re-phrase it, or create a series of questions that could only be answered yes or no. But for that to happen, we would have to talk, and we do not talk in the sense of have a conversation, if my memory of what a conversation might be still holds true.

'My dear man!'

'Good morning! Are you well?'

'I am very well, thank you for asking. And you?'

'Oh, you know.'

'No, my dear man, I do not know.'

'The same niggle in the knee.'

'Oh I am so sorry. Have you not applied that new unguent I recommended?'

'I have, but with little success.'

'Well, I am flabbergasted.'

'But why?'

'I was assured that the unguent would cure all knee related complaints. I myself benefitted from it greatly.'

'And yet I have not.'

'And yet you have not.'

'Curious.'

'Most strange.'

'Odd.'

'Odd indeed. Will you take a seat?'

'I will, thank you.'

'If nothing else than to relieve the niggle of your knee!'

'Ha, ha, ha!'

'Ha, ha, ha!'

That sort of thing. That is the sort of thing we do not do. To avoid confusion. Instead, Mr Samuels ploughs through his notes with his customary monotone, his notebook open before him although he knows it all by heart. When he finishes, he places the notebook back in the breast pocket of his brown suit and adopts an attitude as if open for questions. I might have that wrong. He adopts an attitude, but I'm not sure what it means. He does the following: rests back in his chair an inch or two, inhales, exhales, then crosses his legs, right over left. And might I add that he crosses his legs properly. He does not rest his ankle on his knee, spreading open his crotch area for all to see. No. The cup of the right knee sits snugly on the left and the right foot threatens for a moment to tuck itself behind the left calf before declining to do so. Crotch and environs safely stowed. I don't ask any questions, save one: 'Were you satisfied?'

'Within the parameters of the case I can say that I was satisfied,' he would say.

We would sit on a while, he on his side of the desk, me on mine, and consider satisfaction with some satisfaction. Then he would leave.

He has not been here for some time. How long, I'm not sure. When Cass left, he seemed to also, after a polite period to save face, I suppose. So even my limited window on the world has been shut, or at least pulled to.

Where do you wander, Mr Samuels? And what, Mr Samuels, do you wonder?

two

Mr Samuels woke before dawn in order to supervise the coming of the day, as always. The morning star and others still pinpricked the purple of the night. All was hushed as he took to his small patio, a china cup in his hand to watch the brightening sky. It was already hot. Yet there he was in full pyjamas, sipping a cup of tea. Mr Samuels swore by tea and thought highly of pyjamas. They were brown with a pin-stripe in orange. The tea had a drop of milk and no sugar. The milk was always first into the cup.

A lesser man, I think, would have perhaps heaved a sigh, or let go a yawn, but not Mr Samuels. He simply stood, drank his tea and stared at the sky. The stars faded as the East asserted itself. Day would soon be upon us all.

Ablutions done, suit donned, Mr Samuels tapped on the door of the boy. He tapped again, and added 'Morning.' He tapped again and further added, 'Time to get up.' Something groaned from behind the door.

There was time for an egg to be properly boiled – so that is ten minutes with the water starting from cold – and for bread to be toasted, buttered and soldiered before the boy emerged. He sloughed into the kitchen, his feet splayed and his head hung. He did not favour pyjamas, despite the two fine sets he had been bought, and instead wore only a baggy pair of boxer shorts, under which an erection of sorts suggested itself. His blonde hair flopped into his face down to the level of his full lips, which were firmly set. No sign yet of hairs on his chest and, in truth, his armpits weren't making much of a showing either; a fact not lost on Mr Samuels as the boy thrust his arms in the air, stretched and yawned before sitting in front of his egg.

At least the lesson about breakfast being the most important meal of the day had taken hold. The lesson about not eating with your mouth open had not. He mashed and masticated noisily, prodding the egg with a soldier and then crushing it mercilessly between his teeth. Mr Samuels sat opposite and watched the pulp of the bread gather in the boy's mouth before being swallowed. On principle, Mr Samuels always ate before the boy got up, reasoning that the sight of him eating his muesli would not be one to arouse respect. He ate muesli and not eggs because of past trouble with haemorrhoids. It had been a long battle with those, but Mr Samuels felt he had now won it and was not keen to go back to the days of taking salted baths and shoving piles back up his anus with a carefully inserted index finger. Not to mention the creams that had to be applied. Nor to mention the straining over the toilet, blood splashing into the bowl and the shock of pain racking the whole body. No, those were days best not revisited. He did miss his bananas.

'Stop staring at me,' said the boy.

'Please try to keep your mouth closed while you eat.'

'How am I gonna get the food in then, huh?'

The boy had carefully deployed his 'gonna' and 'huh' in what I believe is called a dead cat strategy. Mr Samuels was on the brink of remonstrating, but thought better of it. Some battles need not be fought, especially not when the foe has chosen the field.

'Where is the belt I bought you?' asked Mr Samuels as the boy once again emerged from his room, dressed for school. His shorts were somewhere south of his hips.

The question was apparently not worthy of reply.

To the mind of Mr Samuels, the school uniform left a lot to be desired, namely: a proper shirt with a proper collar; a tie; a blazer. The blazer he could live without, reluctantly, given the heat, but a tie never hurt anyone. Except for that one occasion, of course.

Nor did a long-sleeved, pressed white shirt, rather than this short-sleeved polo variety that aped at being a shirt and only succeeded in showing how far short of a real shirt it was. And here Mr Samuels was torn, for on the one hand this uniform was clearly lacking in many crucial aspects, but on the other it was as the school rules laid out. If the school stipulated that this was an acceptable uniform then it was an acceptable uniform, even though it quite clearly wasn't.

'Where you going?' asked the boy at the door.

'Walking with you to school, of course.'

'God! I'm not three!'

'Nevertheless.'

So they walked to school, the boy lagging behind all the way. Thankfully it was not far and the hazards were well known, cars parked on the pavements being the most frequent. When there were pavements, and there were often none. Packs of cats eyed them as they picked their way, Mr Samuels striding with quiet purpose and the boy slouching along, scuffing his feet as he went. Mr Samuels did not rise to this.

'Goodbye,' said Mr Samuels at the great, green gates, and the boy disappeared into the throng of children, adolescents and what looked like young adults. Some slightly older young adults were teachers, but one could only tell this by the lack of uniform. Ties were not to be seen.

Was there something wrong with Mr Samuels? On no less than three occasions – the mouth open, the shorts, and the scuffing feet – he had not risen to the bait but preferred to largely ignore the challenge. And they were a challenge, clearly. Yet Mr Samuels had let them slide. This was not a thing he liked to do as he was wary of where such a slide might end. Was he a little defeated that morning? A little weary of the daily struggles?

But there was nothing wrong with Mr Samuels' professionalism. He was well aware as he left the school gates that he was being followed.

To the untrained eye and ear the first signs would have been too subtle. But the eyes and ears of Mr Samuels were trained to a very high degree. His ears were the first to cotton on. Through the roar of engines and the wailing of children and the loving goodbyes and the plaintive cries of sullen schoolboys, Mr Samuels noticed a set of footsteps was matching his own. How, one might wonder, could he filter everything out to focus on this one thing? But, there you go, he could. As he walked beneath the plain trees that shaded the street, he experimented a little to test his hypothesis. He slowed; the footsteps slowed. He sped up; the footsteps sped up. He stopped to let a large car mount the pavement to disgorge its contents and the footsteps stopped too. This was when his trained eye came into play. In the wing-mirror of the car he caught sight of a woman dressed in running gear and consulting her mobile telephone. Not an uncommon sight, but as he resumed his walk the mirror gave him a sufficient view of this woman resuming her walk too.

He admired her technique. She did not look up to check if he were moving. She merely moved too, looking at her mobile telephone all the while.

Thinking of it, I have underplayed Mr Samuels' extraordinary skills, for was not the woman wearing running clothes? She was. It would follow, therefore, that she was wearing running shoes as well. It would have been odd indeed if she were to wear a pair of high heels, or heavy boots, when the rest of her wardrobe spoke of a fitness regime, or a marathon to be trained for, or a visit to the gymnasium. Now, if one accepts that running shoes were worn, then one must further accept that running shoes make less noise than high heels or heavy boots. They barely make a noise at all. Yet

Mr Samuels could detect even this slightest sound, measure its speed and direction and estimate its distance.

Mr Samuels had another sense; one of which he never spoke. When he spoke of it to himself, not out loud of course, he called it his antennae, his radar, or his attunement. He never called it his sixth sense, or his gut feeling, or his gift. In fact, he barely spoke to himself of this thing at all, but he relied upon it nevertheless, sometimes without knowing he was doing so. It was a sense dependent on something shifting, almost imperceptibly, amongst the clatter and clamour of all else rushing about.

Now, being followed was not unusual for Mr Samuels. It came with the job. It is only reasonable that if your job entails, as it often did, following people then at some stage you too will be followed. You might even encourage the person you are following to follow you in turn. All grist to the mill. So he was not alarmed; merely a little curious. To assuage his curiosity, he detoured to the park that ranged behind the school.

The time has now come to choose a month. If we are going to the park, we need a month. Schools are open, so that rules out the end of June, all of July and August, and a fair bit of September. How do I know this? I have lived amongst the living, and that includes the younger varieties, long enough to pick up things, as if by osmosis. Perhaps Mr Samuels' other sense was a form of osmosis too? It's worth a thought.

Anyway, given the state of the schools, it shall be late September.

Ah, the season of dust and dried grasses; of scentless air, of grit at the back of the mouth, of ever-weeping eyes.

The park had long since given up as a park, for the year, or until the weather cooled, which ever came first, and there was no knowing. Shoes ploughed through thick mounds of dust with each step; Mr

Samuels in his brogues, his follower in her gym shows. Clouds of dust around their ankles, billowing and falling.

Oddly, Mr Samuels chose to make his stand not in the shade of the trees, but beside a defunct pond, of the man-made variety. It had been drained, and the fountains at its centre were just metal stumps. Oddly, but reasonably. If he had taken to the trees a tiresome hide and seek might have ensued. No doubt the shade would have been welcome and staved off sweating for a while, but the added effort of any now-you-see-me, now-you-don't nonsense would have only accelerated waves of perspiration. Mr Samuels is not immune to sweating. No one is immune to sweating, but our sweating is a sweating of such severity that it is best to be avoided. Anyway, Mr Samuels was making a stand, not trying to gain an advantage, so the clearing about the pond leant itself. He took himself off to the further side, turned about and had a clear view of his pursuer in her act of pursuing.

The woman took up her own position beside the pond, opposite Mr Samuels, and pushed her sunglasses onto the top of her head. She too was taking a stand. So, there she stood, looking at Mr Samuels, and there Mr Samuels stood looking at the woman. If it were possible, the air became more heavy and more still.

The air didn't do anything. It didn't care.

But for these two, the park was empty. Too early or too late, no matter.

The woman. Young, thought Mr Samuels. But what Mr Samuels considered young might not be young at all. Younger than Mr Samuels, certainly, although he had always looked older than his years so was younger than himself, as it were. Older than his years throughout the years, that was Mr Samuels. Had he sown his oats in wild abandon in this teens and twenties? Imbibing and snorting and popping and fucking? Rolling out of strange beds in the late morning, little knowing where he was or who he was with? Little knowing who he was, if it comes to that. Staggering from one hangover to another, aiming for that sweet spot – enough drink consumed to overcome the worst, but not enough to slide back down again – but never hitting it? Taking his breakfast straight off of the mirror?

Young, thought Mr Samuels, but not so young as all that. He calculated 37. His calculation was based on the following:

The woman had long red hair, tied back but dangling free here and there. The hair was very red, so it was most likely dyed, to cover up an odd unwanted root, or to just give an impression of lustre.

The woman had applied make-up with care, but with taste. A natural look had been sought, and been achieved. Her eye brows were her own and well maintained. The need for the make-up suggested the odd line or blemish, because there is no look so natural as the natural look itself.

The woman had a figure which spoke of years but also of maintenance. She was slim, without being emaciated; thin in the hips, slight of bosom, long of leg.

In truth, the figure of the woman made him hesitate as to an age, but he reasoned thus: she exercises on a regular basis and has not borne children. He even let himself intuit a woman devoted to her vocation. The exercise and the childlessness allowed Mr Samuels to increase the age rather more than her figure seemed to suggest, but this brought it more in line with the lessons of the hair and face.

Of course, this was provisional, for was she not quite possibly in disguise? Disguise was not something Mr Samuels indulged in, but he recognised it as having its proper place in the resources of his profession. So, the hair could be a wig, the bosom could have been strapped and a strict corset donned. But, on the whole, he thought not.

She eyed him too, from across the empty pond.

It was she who made the first move. She raised her telephone to her face and aimed it at Mr Samuels. Having done this a second, she lowered the telephone, looked at it, looked at him, smiled, waved, turned on her heel and exited the arena.

Well! What it was one to make of that?

three

Yet there must be people, it seems. You can't get by without them. People have tried, I know. Where are they now, those people who took themselves off to the desert or shoved themselves up a column to be far from man and closer to God?

There's a little bit of knowledge I have retained over the years; the fact that there were such people. I have no idea why I have hung on to it, and even less of an idea as to whether holding on to it has done me any good. Still less what it says about me. If anything. I have also retained the fact that all the continents were once one big land mass. Everything jammed together, surrounded by a broiling sea. I have also retained the fact that necessary is one C and two Ss, and the reason for that is this; I can still hear a little rhyme in my head — en-e-cee-e-sus-sus-ary. I don't know where this little gobbet of inner-noise comes from, but, there you go, I've always had it, rattling away in the mansions of the mind until it is called upon and I hack it up. Like an owl gobs up a ball of fur and bones.

They come with the house. That is how I reason it out, for they didn't come with me. I became aware of them only after Cass had left. She must have dealt with them beforehand, saying, perhaps: 'Let the poor chap alone; let him get used to things first'. Ever the optimist. So maybe they came with her rather than the house, but when she left they remained so the house was the prime mover in all of this after all. Otherwise, why didn't they shuffle off with her when she bolted for pastures new?

But just to be clear — although god knows why — the people are not of the house but somehow attached to it. That could be clearer, but never mind. The things of the house demand there be people. Yes, it is the things that demand the people, and not the people the things. That seems to be the way of it. I have no need of the people, and yet there they are from time to time. So it is the things that are to blame.

'My friend!' said the man I had never seen before. He threw open his arms as if I was meant to rush into his embrace. I didn't, for the obvious reason. But also for the less obvious reason that by throwing open his arms the man had revealed large sweat stains in his pits.

This was in the kitchen. I made sure the island-counter was between the two of us. The kitchen seemed a lot smaller with him in it.

'There you are,' which was undeniable. 'I've been told all about you so don't worry!'

I worried.

'I'm sorry,' he said, 'I am George. You'll have heard of me.'

I hadn't.

'Mrs Johnson didn't say anything?'

She hadn't.

'Never mind,' he said, but it looked like he minded. His open face shrank into itself a little, just for a moment. When I say open, I mean it looked like it had been hit by a shovel. His nose sprawled across his face, and his mouth seemed far too big. I now realise why. The nose being flat to the face, or thereabouts, meant that he had to breathe through the mouth, so the mouth was perpetually open, and never more so than when at rest. When not talking, he exuded snuffling sounds. Breathing, I assume.

Let's get it over with. We've done the face we might as well do the rest. His hair was undecided. Where there was any, it was thick and black. Bits of it were then scraped over the top of his head. In fact, the top of his head was the least hairy bit of him. His eyebrows were bushy and his ears sprouted thick tufts. From the top of this open shirt, a verge of dark material swarmed and glistened with sweat. If I had seen his back, which I did not nor hope ever to see, it too would have been thickly matted in dank hair. In this climate too! I should have pitied him, but I didn't. No doubt hair swathed his stomach, although at a stretch, for it was very large and hung over his belt. I assumed the belt; it couldn't be seen.

His legs were short and bowed.

His feet were large and splayed.

Now all this is very miraculous. To have seen so much and remembered so much! Are my powers increasing? I mean those of observation and recall? Perhaps. But perhaps also George was of a slight build, to the point of being wispy, with luxurious blond hair swept back in dramatic fashion, with a pinched face, sharp nose, slight freckles and unsettlingly light blue eyes. Perhaps he had a dainty foot shod in patent leather.

It doesn't matter. Strange man in kitchen calling me friend; that is what matters.

There was a silence for some time. There had been a silence on my part throughout, to be fair, so now this George man was joining in. He didn't like it.

'I am here to help,' he said.

I said nothing.

'With whatever needs to be done.' His eyes cast about looking for things that needed to be done. Nothing that I could see. Yes, a small sign saying 'fridge' where the fridge was might have been a help, but if I was that bothered I could have done it myself.

'Little things. Or big things.' He demonstrated the meaning of his words by bringing his thumb and forefinger into the closest possible proximity before squinting at them, and then throwing his arms wide with such force that I feared the buttons of his shirt would burst. It was then I confirmed my suspicions about his stomach.

'Outside,' he gestured. 'Or in.'

I took this to mean outside as far as the boundaries of the property, for outside is an awfully big thing to be responsible for if not. Similarly, I took in to mean between the walls of the house and definitely not any spurious depths, his or mine.

'The pool,' he said. 'You'll need a man to do the pool.'

I had no idea that a pool came with a man attached.

'My cousin, he's a great pool man, I can have a word and it will all be sorted.'

'Leave it.'

'Leave the pool?'

'Yes.'

I could see he was struggling with the concept of leave.

'Leave it to nature.'

Nature was here the conceptual difficulty.

'You mean, do nothing to it? With it?'

'Yes.'

'But it will stink!'

'Then it will stink.'

He shook his head and sighed. Poor man. Perhaps he had promised his cousin a nice little earner, or perhaps the thought of a pool going to wrack and ruin disturbed him.

'You'll need a gardener,' he said. 'My cousin, he's a good man, he could come and do the garden.'

Now a garden and a pool are two completely different kettle of fish, in my mind. I'd never had a pool and have a general dread of water, whereas I have had a little patch of dirt that I called a garden in the past and I had been quite fond of it, if I remember correctly. The garden that surrounded the house was very far from being a patch of dirt. There were fruit trees of various sorts, lots of palms and succulents and whatnot, I am not a horticulturalist. But most of all, there was a lot of grass and I knew, given time, the once pristine lawn would become more of a mess of undergrowth and weeds and invasive species of all kinds. I pondered. The invasive species, so called, would no doubt just have been indigenous species that weren't wanted; the ugly ones, in effect, or the troublesome ones. There was good reason, I had to concede, for a man to come every now and then and do battle with all this. But was not I a man? Could not I do battle just as well? Obviously not as well as someone more practiced, but well enough when all said and done. When will that day come? The day when all is said and done? Each day means more to be said and more to be done; the more saying because there is more to do; the more doing in order just to say more. That doesn't quite work. Saying and doing, doing and saying, it doesn't matter which way around, they have some sort of connection that is beyond me at the moment.

'I would like a goat, please,' I said.

'A goat?'

'Yes. A goat.'

'A goat goat?'

I was not aware there were any other kinds, but there you go.

'For the garden,' I said.

His already wide face widened still further.

'To eat the grass. The weeds.' I was growing expansive.

He sighed again and shifted his weight from side to side. He even stuck out his tongue a little, the better to concentrate.

'So, my friend, you do not want a gardener, but you want a goat?'

I nodded. He nodded back. Then puffed out his cheeks, exhaled and let his lips ripple.

'A goat! Well, well!' He got a large mobile telephone from the back pocket of his trousers – at least I hope it was from there – and consulted it at length, dabbing and swiping at it from time to time. 'I don't know,' he said. 'Men I can do, but goats! Ha ha ha!'

It wasn't an honest laugh, but it was passable.

He kept repeating the word goat over and over again as he stared at his phone, rubbing the back of his neck with his free hand when the need arose, flicking at the phone screen with his thumb. Lord knows what he was doing but it seemed to be a necessary process – nailed it once again – so I let him get on with it.

It may have been a necessary process, but it was not a successful one. He gave up after some little time and merely said that he would see what he could do.

'Goat! That's a new one! Ha ha ha!' He threw up his hands the better to laugh. 'So, that's me with a job to do, isn't it!'

It was. I hadn't meant to give him a job at all, but he had said he was there to help and so I had asked him to help. It might not have been the sort of help he had wanted to give, but it was the sort of help I needed.

I thought that our interview was at an end, but I was wrong. He now introduced a silence. Yes, the silence definitely came from him and as we stood there in the kitchen, I eventually understood that the silence was designed to get me to recant, to say 'My dear chap! The goat! Ha ha ha! What was I thinking? No, no, of course I must have a gardener and your cousin sounds like the very man'

— but I held my peace and let the silence gather until it proved too much for him.

'Well,' he threw up his hands again, 'I'd best be off! Gotta get a goat!'

He was on the verge of the exiting the room, when he stopped, turned and said, 'Of course, Marina will be in on Friday as usual for the usual.' And he was gone.

Of all this, only the word Friday made any immediate sense. It would have made more sense if I had then known what day of the week it actually was, but, there you go, I did not.

four

To say that Mr Samuels was discombobulated by this encounter would be false. He stored it away in his mind for future clarification. I'd like to think of the mind of Mr Samuels as a sphere, perfect in its way yet not so perfect as to not allow the occasional addition, through whatever means one might imagine. But I can't. No, the sphere of mind, or mind as sphere, I don't know, will not do justice to the man.

So let us think of his mind as an office, albeit a well-run office, overseen by some faceless manager who has a cubicle all to themselves. Themselves! Honestly! I don't know; man, woman, it doesn't matter. What matters is that this person is entombed in a glass-walled cubicle from nine-to-five. From there, the entire office is open to view, with a little twisting, admittedly, or a little wheeling about on a well-oiled chair mounted on casters. Nine-to-five doesn't work. Never mind. Anyway, the manager overlooks this well-run office, and sees neatly arranged desks and chairs and the necessary employees sat at them doing their jobs, checking documents, cross referencing one piece of paper against another piece of paper, making notes on a further piece of paper, and then storing this third piece of paper in a small filing cabinet to the right of the desk before returning pieces of paper one and two into two separate small filing cabinets on the left of the desk. A man, and it is a man, pushes a trolley laden with documents up and down the aisles, distributing new documents to left and right to be checked, cross-referenced and stored.

When the time comes, and come it does on occasion, another man strides the same aisles, goes straight to the correct desk and secures a piece of paper from the cabinet on the right hand side of the desk. No words are exchanged. He does not say 'Morning Janice! How is Bert these days?' and Janice does not say 'Oh same old same old' and he doesn't say 'Still, mustn't grumble' and she doesn't say 'Try telling Bert that!' and he doesn't say 'Ha, Ha! Document 24a slash 06 slash 1971' and she doesn't say 'Here you go love. All my best to Bernice!' No. Both know which document is required and it is duly handed over.

Such is the mind of Mr Samuels. Until it is not.

I wish Mr Samuels was not called Mr Samuels. Hell to pay with the possessive apostrophe.

So the encounter in the park was stored away in its proper place for quick, efficient recovery when needed. Who knows when.

The day was still young, or young-ish. The boy was safely stowed at school, although Lord only knows what they taught him in there for he had seemed to retain nothing that Mr Samuels could discern. His mathematics, to name only his mathematics, was appalling.

This would seem to make Mr Samuels free, but he was not. Things to do, to get done, things I cannot imagine. He spent his days doing these unimagined things, now on his brown scooter, now in his small car, now in conversation with a client, now in silent, solitary vigil under the glaring sun. So, slightly imagined.

It was the dusk of the day when he returned home. The house was already beginning to creak as it gave up its heat to the cooling twilight air. Not cooling enough, obviously, but cooling. They boy was already at home. Mr Samuels didn't just trust to routine to tell him this. As he entered the front door, his senses told him that the cooling air had been disturbed not long since and on that air was the whiff of sweat and rotting feet that was a sure sign of the boy.

For the sweat and the feet, Mr Samuels blamed the school. He had tried to get a grip on the situation some time past, at least as far as the feet went. The boy and he were together at the kitchen table. A rare occurrence, but one Mr Samuels had arranged by summoning the boy to him with the promise of something to be seen.

'What is it?' Shouted the boy from his room.

'You'll have to come and see, I said,' said Mr Samuels. 'In the kitchen.'

When they boy finally lurched into the kitchen, Mr Samuels once again regretted that he had not bought the child a new belt into the bargain, but, there you go, he had not.

'What?' Said the child, but stretching out the single syllable to such a length that it creaked.

On the kitchen table was a shoe box and inside the show box was a nice pair of black leather brogues. Mr Samuels carefully placed the shiny new shoes on the no less shiny table.

'God!' he said. 'You gotta be kiddin' me! No way! No way am I wearing those. What are you trying to do to me, eh? What? I'll get pummelled, I'll get battered, I'll, I'll get... marmalised. Do you want that, eh? Do you? I'll get ribbed for ever. I'll get laughed at! Do you know that? Is that what you want, eh? Do you want me to be laughed at, do you? I'll look like a right twat wearing those! No one wears shoes like that. No. One. God.' And he was gone.

Such was the boy's verdict, so why then did Mr Samuels blame the school? He carefully placed the shoes back in the box, folded the tissue paper gently over them, and sat down to mull. He blamed the school because the school had been woefully ambiguous in the specifications for shoes in the list of what they claimed amounted to a uniform: black. That was it. No mention of material whatsoever, which meant he had not a leg to stand on. The boy's school shoes – which barely qualified as shoes in Mr Samuels' thinking – were undeniably black but they were made of such stuff as sweat is made in, leading no doubt to the athlete's foot from the which the boy suffered and yet Mr Samuels had no recourse to a set of rules that prohibited such shoes, which he mentally scare-quoted as he mentally said it. The inadequacy of the rules had led to all sorts of things appearing on the pupils' feet, so the boy was no doubt right that he would have been ridiculed, mercilessly if Mr Samuels' recollection of teenagers was anything to go by. In addition, the school had previous history in its lack of thought concerning the uniform, vis-à-vis, the school shirt which was not only barely a shirt but again made of some mad man-made fabric that seemed almost to pool sweat in the armpits to there let it fester.

None of this had gone to the plan that Mr Samuels had laid out.

'Now,' he had planned to say, 'although leather might seem like a counter-intuitive choice given the extremities of our climate, I can assure you it is the best material to allow the feet to breathe and thus assuage the fungal problems from which you currently suffer. I have bought you cream to apply that will bring the situation under control, but prevention is always better than cure and these shoes will prevent reoccurrence. You might not thank me now, and the leather might chafe before it relaxes, but you shall thank me later. Cream; night and day.' He was then planning to smile, benevolently.

What happened that day, we will never know. The present calls.

It was perhaps with a slight memory of that benevolent smile that he had never bestowed that Mr Samuels went to the boy's room on this day of what might be called The Mysterious Lady.

Can one remember something that never happened? Silly question. Of course one can. Don't know why I even raised the issue. In this example, for example, Mr Samuels might have remembered not only the idea of a benevolent smile but also what a benevolent smile might look like. Head of a pin nonsense that I must guard against. But why? Who cares if I wibble on about the inconsequential or write a philosophical tractate of the most profound and piercing lucidity? There's a whole host of them in this room. A blue, leather bound collection of 'The History of Western Philosophy' arranged chronologically. Seven volumes in all and all the spines unsplit and no doubt many a page uncreased. A job lot bought as a job lot, no doubt, their attraction being the blue leather and the very pretty gold lettering. Very handsome. Ditto the complete works of some bloke or another, but in a deep purple which might even be prettier than the blue. Dickens, perhaps. Another nightmare for the possessive apostrophe.

The boy's room.

Hang on. All this is nonsense. The shoe business just does not work at all. Flawed from start to finish, and for this reason: who bought the shoes that the boy actually wore to school? Mr Samuels is the only answer, surely, but would Mr Samuels so debase himself and his principles as to buy a pair of shoes that were barely worthy of the name? Mr Samuels buying a pair of brogues is one thing. Mr Samuels knowingly putting the boy's feet in fungal danger is quite another. What possessed the man? What possible reason could there be for such a thing?

Fuck knows.

The boy's room was pitched in gloom, lit only by a screen on a desk at which the boy sat. The screen flashed a host of garish colours at rapid speed which played across the boy's face which in turn improved and then disfigured his features, such as they were.

Did Mr Samuels feel a pang of disgust? He did.

Did he then feel a wince of pity? He did indeed.

He fixed the benevolent smile upon his face to ask 'How was school today?'

The boy didn't answer.

'School? Today?'

Again no answer.

Mr Samuels coughed. Nothing. He knocked at the door, even though it was already open and he was standing on the threshold. Nothing again. The smile was beginning to fade, so he reset it firmly, approached the boy and tapped him on the shoulder.

'Jesus!' said the boy, snatching something from out of his ear.

'Look what you made me do,' he said, jabbing at the screen. It was not at all clear what Mr Samuels had made the boy do, but it had been some calamity of sorts. The boy harrumphed back into his chair.

'What?' he said.

'I just need to have a word with you, if I may.' Mr Samuels would have liked to follow this up by taking a seat somewhere in order to establish the proper aura of a chat. There was no other chair and the bed – the sheets rumpled and Mr Samuels thought quite possibly stained – was not inviting, so he was forced to remain standing.

'How was school today?'

'Fine.'

'Fine?'

'Yeah; you know.'

'Nothing out of the ordinary?'

'Fat chance!'

'Nothing at all?'

'Zip.' Mr Samuels maintained his smile despite this.

'So, a good day, then?'

'Good!'

'Satisfactory, then?'

'S'pose.'

'Did you talk to any strangers?'

'What?'

'Strangers. Did you talk to any?'

'Oh yeah! This bloke took to me off to the woods to see some puppies! Jesus!'

'So no strangers at all? A woman, say? A redheaded woman?'

'Fit?'

'Healthy.'

'No. Fit fit. As in good-looking.'

Mr Samuels did not know how to answer, so he did not answer. To his credit, and amusement, the boy noticed.

'Nope. No fit, strange woman.'

'Are you sure?'

'Yeah.'

Mr Samuels examined the boy in the gloom. He looked sure enough but was there not just a little hint of something around the mouth, a little suggestion of a hint of a smirk, supressed but still just visible. Perhaps it was the effect of the screen which was once again flashing away.

'Very good,' said Mr Samuels. 'Have you finished your homework?'

'Not got any.'

Mr Samuels, letting the grammar and the blatant lie slide, left the room the better to think. What he thought was this: why had he intuited a connection between the strange woman and the boy? True, she had appeared at the school so there was a connection born of proximity, but surely the woman might well have just known that he sometimes walked with the boy in the morning and that this would be a fine opportunity to pick up his trail and even reveal herself, as indeed she had done. There was no necessary connection and Mr Samuels knew full well that he alone was sufficient cause. Yet still. He didn't finish the thought, but let the 'yet still' hang in his mind.

five

Friday came.

At least I assumed it was a Friday. I wasn't about to change the habit of a lifetime and start counting the days, not at this late hour. If the hour is late. I think it is.

So I assumed it was a Friday, knowing all the time that it was just an assumption based on some very dodgy information, that is, that this Marina woman would come on a Friday as usual for the usual. Of course, this itself came from a man I had never met before. Oh, he seemed to know what he was talking about, roughly speaking. Yet I had no way of knowing whether he was dissembling, mistaken or incompetent, or whether he could be all three by turn; now dissembling, now incompetent and now mistaken. Or indeed that these three might not combine in a single moment, so whilst he thought he was being a cunning dissembler he was in fact being incompetent and mistaken. Maybe, beneath that comb-over he was thinking 'I will say she comes on a Friday, when she really comes on a Saturday' when unbeknownst to him she in fact always came on a Friday. Now why he would have dissembled in such a way, I cannot imagine. Well actually, I can. Perhaps I had hurt his feelings when I had refused a pool-man and a gardener. Yes, perhaps preferring a goat over a gardener galled him. I admit it was an irksome request. He had been all primed to deliver a gardener and I had asked him for a goat. That would have been reason enough for a little revenge. Add to this that perhaps he was receiving a little kick-back from the gardener for securing the work and you have a man not only slighted but also out of pocket.

But had he not said he would help in any way he could? He had. If memory serves. So why would he have felt the need for revenge when I had told him how he could help? Because the way I wanted help and the help he wanted to give had not matched, obviously. That must annoy. You offer help and the help requested is not the help you had hoped to give. Or perhaps you had hoped that the offer of help would have been declined. 'Oh, no,' you had hoped, 'I couldn't possibly impose upon you! I am fine, although I thank you for the thought, for the kindness.' Yes, being thanked for a kindness that was never actually delivered, I can imagine that would be a satisfactory state of affairs.

Two things trouble me. Oh, innumerable things trouble me, but two will do for now. One: when had I become so attuned to the nuance of thought, and Two: why do I care what he thought or why he thought what he did, because the result would be the same – Marina would come on a Friday or she would not – regardless? He could think what he liked and it was no business of mine. And if she didn't come on a Friday, and if she didn't come at all to be fair, it little mattered to me. She had been coming, or not, without my knowing, so knowing would again make no difference.

I was wrong. I wasn't attuned to the nuance of this thoughts. I was just making it up. All this is just made up. For example, kick-backs. What do I know of kick-backs? I know of them, but nothing about them, so there you go.

How did I fill my days before that Friday, if it was a Friday? I filled them. They were filled.

Some time was filled with my feet. More time than perhaps necessary. And when I say my feet, I actually mean my toe-nails. From time to time, I become aware of them, if aware is the word. Most of the time, they are just there, and then they are too much there and so I become aware of them. Yes, that about nails it. I happened to catch sight of them on one of those days and thought to myself, in my innocence, 'they could do with a cut', and I was not wrong. The big toes in particular. Great slabs of pearl-grey nail, curling in on themselves. Back in the old days I would have attacked them with a pair of rusty nail clippers, gouging beneath them to get purchase and then chomping at them with as much force as I could muster. The results were ragged, but they were results of a kind, at least. Now, I have no idea what has become of those clippers. They were left behind when I moved, no doubt, along with so much else of my meagre hoard. So little, but so much of it lost. I went to the bathroom next to the office in which I sleep but could find nothing of use. Ditto the bathrooms of the upper floor. I did come across what looked like a promising pair of small scissors, with a gentle curve to their edge as if designed precisely for the contours of a nail. Worse than useless. They failed to make an impression at all. Worse than useless because they had promised to be useful and then utterly failed. A flicker of hope dashed, again. So, I went to the kitchen – I knew my way around the house better than I had thought – thinking that if small scissors designed to cut nails failed then big scissors not designed to cut nails might succeed. I looked through each hidden drawer and cupboard and found nothing. I found lots of things, in truth, but not a pair of scissors. I found lots of things, in truth, that defied description and for which I could not imagine any possible purpose. Oh, I admit I got lost contemplating some of these objects from time to time, I'm not immune to a bit of novelty. Perhaps I will go back there one day and contemplate them again. Yes, that is a little resource I should not lose sight of. Don't kitchens need scissors? I thought so, but this kitchen had none, so there you go. What this kitchen did have, and around which I rallied, was a very small grater which, if it had been larger, would have been a cheese grater. Its size meant I couldn't think what it was meant to grate and yet it was undeniably a grater. So, I reasoned, if it is meant to grate, let it grate! So I took grater in hand, put my foot on a chair, and began to saw at the big toe nail. I soon tired of this position, so sat on the chair and placed my foot on the floor and began again to saw at the big toe nail. This soon made my back ache, so I put my right leg over my left, exposing the crotch necessarily, and one again began to saw at the big toe nail. Saw is not the word. More of a grind. I did this for no little time until the grater started grating flesh and there was a small heap of powdered nail on the floor. I put my right leg down, lifted my left on top of it, and applied myself again until the result was the same: slight grating of flesh, small heap of powdered nail.

I sat on for some time. Nails are dead, yet they grow. The base is living and the end dead. Is there a zone in-between, a dying section? Or is it living, and now dead?

No matter how long I spent contemplating, it was not enough to fill up the time until Friday, if Friday it was.

Oh, yes! I trimmed my hair. The very next day, in fact, at least I think so. I was sitting at this desk, this bulky relic, and in an absence of mind started to rummage in the draws a little. I've no idea why I had not done this before but, there you go, I hadn't. Maybe in a darker recess of my so-called mind I had thought: 'don't go rooting around in the desk drawers just yet, because there will come a time when you will be glad of the distraction.' Or perhaps: 'don't go rooting around in the desk drawers because who knows what might be found that cannot then be unfound'. This second option was obviously not taking into account my ability to forget. Maybe, at bottom, I just don't like rooting at all. So, in an absence of mind, I rummaged. Oh, there were all the usual bit and bobs, paper-clips and a stapler and some bull-dog clips and some little gadgety things that escaped me and some pens and pencils and pencil sharpener and a notebook – not mine – that I did not read, obviously. There was also a pair of scissors. Now, when the need for a pair of scissors had gone, a pair of scissors appeared. Things are really rather badly arranged, are they not? I looked at them with something like awe, as if a miracle. So pleased was I to have finally found a pair of scissors at last, and so miffed – if the word is not too strong – that I no longer had a use for them, I soon cast about for something to do with them. A bit of origami, perhaps, or make little paper-doilies, or just tear to shreds the unread volumes on the shelves to then scatter them about like the dead leaves they were. Apart from the latter, these things were beyond me. So, I must have reasoned a little to find a use for them, and what I must have reasoned was, if my toe-nails had needed a cut then surely my hair would similarly be in need. Now, I am a lot more aware of my hair than of my nails, so I knew that this was indeed the case.

What can I say of my hair? It's there, it grows, it loses a little of itself every now and then without intervention. It has a variety of colours, I now know too: brown, beige and grey and even white. It serves its function, whatever that is. Sweat pools at the hairline from time to time. Dandruff descends from it once in a while. Cobwebs get tangled in it. It needs a scratch every now and again. So, I know quite a lot about my hair, all told, and so knowing it needed a cut was added to the store of my knowledge.

And how I went about it was this: I hacked at it. I hacked at the top, the front, the sides and the back as best I could. Did I mention I cannot bear to look in a mirror? I think I did, long ago which might have been last week; long ago when people came and went and did things and talked and argued and I was witness to it all, in a way. If I didn't, I do now. I cannot bear to look in a mirror. So I hacked at my hair sitting at the desk and went at it blind as it were, great tufts of my pelt flying about. I can't deny there was something satisfying about it, probably the feeling that with each snip a little bit less of me was left. I ran my hand over my head when it was all over and noted, again with satisfaction, that there were not any great tufts sticking out or any bald patches or any blood. Yes, the whole thing had been very satisfactory indeed.

I slipped into my cot beside the desk and went to sleep, the better to feel satisfied.

Anything else?

I faffed with the Mr Samuels malarkey, a little.

Oh yes! I took a tour of the grounds. I popped my new hat upon my newly shorn head and sallied out into the garden, for a shufti. It was either early-ish in the morning or sometime in the early evening, because the shadows were long and gave some relief. Not twilight, though. Definitely full-blown day. I don't trust twilight. All sorts of nonsense gets done in the twilight and I won't countenance it. Give me day or give me night and none of this shilly-shallying.

I pause to note 'shufti' and 'shilly-shallying'.

So it was day and I went for a decko of the garden. There was a lot of it. The lawns around the pool, which had a nice greenish tinge, were ankle high already and punctuated here and there by spires of the more aggressive weeds, and by aggressive I just mean better at growing. The trees were laden with fruit, most of it rotting on the branches and where not rotting on the branches, rotting on the floor, covered in a fine gauze of minute flies. One particular orange was doing a grand job of decomposing, chivvied along by some insects no doubt. It must have split open when it fell to the ground and this scar was already fetid. The rest of it was doing its best to catch up, especially where it touched the earth. Yes, the earth was composting it as quickly as was reasonable and the orange of the orange was already turning black, or grey, or a green vermillion. Red in tooth and claw, my arse. Black in rot and mould.

I beat a retreat to the house when I started sneezing, uncontrollably.

I miss my old creaking house. This place doesn't creak at all, as far as I can tell. Impervious to heat and lesser heat, it doesn't groan its way into the evening. I more than make up for the lack. I groan when I sit. I groan when I stand up, lie down, sleep, wake, walk.

And I know I groan in my sleep because my groans wake me and then I groan some more. I've also started to make up for the lack of creaking. Oh, early days I think, but a start is start and what is starting to creak is my ankles, the right in particularly. A creak is not as crack; they have cracked before and I hope they will crack again, so I know the difference, as far as one can know such a thing. Other bits of me crack still, for example the knuckles. Not that I go out of my way to crack them – lacing the fingers of two hands together and thrusting them forward – but the they crack nevertheless, from time to time. As do my shoulders. No, the ankles creak and do not crack. A little, high note of complaint. You can't blame them. And I rumble, well my stomach does. Now, some people might think that a rumbling stomach is a sure sign of hunger, but the reverse seems to be the case for me. It rumbles only after I have eaten. Rumbling doesn't really capture it, to be fair. It is more of a great gurgling mass of internal explosions shifting from right to left and up and down as if squeezing from the small to large colon, or vice versa. So maybe it is not my stomach at all, but the intestines that are to blame and no doubt they are not to blame either, but I am; I am to blame for whatever I shove in my mouth hoping that it might sustain me. Hoping is not the word. But, and this is the odd thing, I don't fart. These explosions remain internal as far as I can tell when they would be more likely to herald some great trumpeting of wind. Such a mighty wind is beyond me, sadly. It must just quietly escape from my fundament when I am unaware. But if it does, it doesn't smell, unless my sense of smell has gone for a burton.

So I crack and creak and groan and rumble my days and nights away.

I made no foray into the world beyond my walls.

I dreamt of my goat. Yes, that was another thing I did whilst waiting for Friday. A proper dream, at night, whilst asleep. I never remember my dreams, but this one I did remember and maybe I remember it because it seems to signify nothing more than the acquisition of a goat. I dreamt that I walked into the garden, fully clothed I might add, and there was my little goat waiting for me already chomping down on the grass like a good little soldier. A pretty thing it was; all white with a little beard and little nubbins for horns on its head, white ears flopping down on either side of its face. I approached and it raised its head, still chewing, and eyed me a while, as no doubt I was eyeing it. Yes, they we were, eyeing each other before it applied itself to the grass again, with something like relish, I hoped. All was still. No birds sang, no insects thrummed or chirruped and no traffic noise could be heard. There were just the gentle sounds of a masticating goat and of my breath.

I woke with a start and in a sweat. I always wake with start and in a sweat.

I rearranged the bookshelves. It didn't need doing, but I did it anyway. What irked me about the way it had been organised was that size hadn't been part of the thinking at all. Of course, given that most of the shelves were taken up what I assume were multiple volume works, or collections of some sort or another, then there was a nice degree of uniformity. But when one of these collections came to an end, all hell broke loose. The books would be pootling along in their matching liveries and consistent heights and then, without a by-your-leave, the level would plummet or rocket up, or, most annoyingly, slightly alter. So, I set about arranging them by height. I took all the books off to get a clean run at it and then set a level with a rather nice green set of five books, with titles down the spine in white. I then tried to find books of the same height to fill that shelf. I did this by eye and trial and error until I realised that there were no books of the same height. There was a hiatus of some time. I might have slept on it, the books scattered around me. I rallied and decided that a slow decrease in height from left to right would be the way to go, so I took down the five books in green and replaced them with the tallest books I could find, which were a set of seven in a rather disgusting yellow. These were followed by a set of some twelve books in purple; that Dickens bloke again. He keeps cropping up. Anyway, the discrepancy in height was one I could live with, but what I could not live with was the clash of colours. The yellow and the purple side by side screamed at me in a way I have never been screamed at by colours. So, still clinging to the idea of decreasing height, I cast about for a set of books that wouldn't clash so badly with the yellow. I tried a brown set which were rather shorter than I would have liked but at least didn't make my eyes bleed. Then I looked for another set to set against this brown lot which were of acceptable height and colour but the nearest thing in terms of height was another set of yellow. Nothing wrong with that, I thought in my naiveté, and indeed there was nothing wrong with that as long as you only looked at the shelf from close up. For then, there was quite a calming swoop down from yellow to brown to yellow. But if you had chance to look at them from a distance, as I did on returning from emptying my bowels, they just looked like a flag of some dodgy country or another, I don't know, one that specialised in bananas and cocoanuts and wanted to capture their love of bananas and cocoanuts in the symbolism of the nation. Now I have nothing against bananas, cocoanuts or the nations that produce them, but I do have something against the effect produced by an arrangement of books in yellow, brown, yellow when even the principle of descending height had already been compromised. So, I rallied once again and thought how wrong I had been to think the height discrepancy was the worst of all evils when all along the colour clash was the thing to be avoided. So, I put the books back as they had been at the start, or as near as damn it.

Why so many yellow books? Oh well, there you go, because there were.

Do goats eat books, I wonder? Time will tell. Or I could just burn the lot of them, or just leave them scattered about the garden and watch them warp, crack and rot into the earth.

Friday came.

Oh, yes! I sharpened the pencils! Some of them needed sharpening and some of them did not but I sharpened them all the same. I took them out of the desk drawer, lay them on my desk and counted them. I forget how many there were; less than a dozen, but more than eight. I then arranged them by degree of use, or height if you prefer, with the most used to the left and the least used to the right. I didn't have the same difficulty as with the books in this regard as they were all the same colour – grey. I toyed awhile with arranging them according to hardness, for B to H left to right, but they were all HB I quickly discovered. I didn't know I knew so much about pencils. I suppose I have been around them for a good deal of my life and so had picked up the odd hard fact here and there. I took out the pencil sharpener which was silver and metal, thank the Lord. True, what I really wanted was one of those bulky, cylinder jobs with a handle to crank the round jaws. The sort that was clamped to the edge of the table. I have no idea when I last saw such a thing, or indeed when I ever saw such a thing, but I know they exist, or did, and that was what I truly wanted. Needs must, I slotted the least used pencil into the sharpener and it was a very pleasing fit indeed. Snug. Holding the sharpener in my left first and I applied my right thumb and forefinger ever so gently to revolving the pencil, feeling the blade bite it ever so slightly as I did so. A feeling of great gentleness all round, in fact. If I had an aim, it was to make as long a continuous shaving as possible. The shaving spooled out of the sharpener and curled about itself, the inner shaving become a little brighter, a little cleaner with each passing rotation, until it broke. I moved on to the next least used pencil, and I wonder why I did. I had no need to actually use the pencils and if the aim was just to create the longest shaving then one pencil sharpened to a nub would have had the same effect as several pencils sharpened just a little. So, maybe there was something else going on. The snug fit of pencil and sharpener never palled.

What did pall was the gentleness of it all. By the fifth, the pencil was gripped in my full fist and ground into the sharpener and the length of the shaving be damned.

So that happened.

six

Time passed, as it does. It passed for Mr Samuels too in a myriad of diverting ways that will be forever unknown. No doubt he went about his business, which, after all, was the business of others.

Must I imagine? May as well. Nothing better to do.

Let's say, then, he had a job. One of the normal ones, but a job nonetheless. He roamed strangely empty streets, attuning his senses to the new noises and scents that must have always been there but had been masked by the more ostentatious noises and scents. His job took him back into the old parts of town, the decay and renewal cheek by jowl. He had scouted the scene before so went straight to the necessary alley and in a half-opened door that led to stone stairs arching up into gloom. All this was expected. Smells wafted down from above. Human smells and cooking smells, body odour and fat frying. Rather, odour of bodies once present and fat once fried, because the small flat, or room to be frank, was empty, as Mr Samuels knew it would be.

Yes, a room. Little light came from the shuttered window, but slices of sun shone through enough to pick out what little there was to be seen. There was no bed; just a mattress on the floor with a stained sheet rucked across it. The sole chair was losing its wicker seat but still passed near enough to being a chair. In the darker recesses of the room, a small electric hob and sink made a stab at being a kitchenette. Flies milled about the plates and left over food piled into the sink and the sole tap protruding from the wall hadn't been used for some time. A plastic demi-john next to the hob surely said that such was the only available water. There was a scuttle of hidden insects.

So many signs, so much to read, but Mr Samuels took it all in and understood it all with a single glance.

Mr Samuels took a brown, well-stuffed envelope from his left inner jacket pocket, placed it on the mattress, and left.

Job done, he was a free man, until the next job came along.

His way back into the alley was blocked by the form of a woman in silhouette. Now this irked Mr Samuels, and the reasons were these. First, he wanted to exit the property as quickly as possible and without being seen. This had not been part of any explicit instructions, but Mr Samuels was a master of inference if nothing else. Second, he didn't for a moment think this was a chance encounter. Over the days and nights he had scouted the place, not once had a woman been present. Indeed, from his other preparations he knew that any female presence was not to be expected at all in any connection to this case, as he called it. That was one of the reasons Mr Samuels had been happy to accept the job. Oh, it wasn't the only reason he was happy, but it was one of the reasons. He had quickly assessed what was necessary for the job to be completed and no less quickly assessed what complications might be expected, and women had not featured among them. Nor had men, to be fair, by which I mean other men. Nothing complicates a case more than people. So he had expected neither man nor woman. Yet here was this undeniably female form in front of him, which led to his third reason for being irked. He had been followed. Followed without him at all suspecting it. Of the reasons to be irked, this irked him the most. He was used to being followed from time-to-time and even took a little pleasure in it. A quiet, rather subterranean pleasure, but a pleasure nonetheless. Sometimes the pleasure was in assessing his opponent, or his colleague, and his or her mastery of the art of following. Knowing full-well he was being followed, he could relax a little part of his mind and enjoy the techniques employed or mentally tut-tut at miniscule failures. In either case, he would often then take it upon himself to test his opponent's skills or improve them by leading them a merry dance, or a subtle one, or an instructive one. Yes, in his quieter moments, perhaps over a cup of tea in his garden at the close of day, Mr Samuels would allow himself to consider a life after retirement from active service. He imagined himself passing on his knowledge and skills to some willing pupil – male or female, it didn't matter – who would metaphorically kneel at his feet and take it all in. Was there some vanity in these imaginings? Yes, there was. But there was also a wish to uphold the honour of his profession into the future, to ensure that things would be done well now that he could not do them himself. The fourth reason for being irked naturally followed on from the third: was he losing his own faculties or was this female so skilled in the art of following that he would have to admit that he would have to up his game? Now the reason that this reason irked him a little less than reason three was that it disquieted him more than it irked him.

'Walk with me,' the silhouetted figure said.

So now this figure must have a voice. Chocolate and steel.

As she stepped away from the doorframe, the silhouette revealed herself to be the same woman Mr Samuels had encountered in the park. There were differences – she was now blonde and dressed in a very smart light grey linen trouser-suit and the sports shoes had been replaced by a pair of vicious high-heels – but she was the same woman for all the changes in what Mr Samuels thought of as the incidentals.

Mr Samuels had come to be ambivalent about the question of disguise. He called it masking. He recognised its place but no longer went to that place himself. As a callow youth, learning the ropes and taking his first faltering steps, he too had been attracted to the art of the mask and even considered himself quite adept. He had a collection of wigs of varying lengths and colours. He had an equally fine collection of facial hair, from the subtle moustache to the full beard. He had a wardrobe full of clothes from the tatty to the casual to the smart. He had even dabbled with fake noses. Yet he had come to realise that all his energies were going into the art of masking when really he should have been honing the more basic skills to perfection. It was then he adopted the mask that he had worn ever since; the nondescript.

But each to his own, I suppose. Or her own.

If I cast my mind back, then an invitation to walk with someone usually means that you walk side by side, the better to converse, I suppose, to share the moment, to commune on some level or another. Why one would want to do this is another matter. Mr Samuels didn't interpret the invitation in quite the same way. Instead of walking side by side, he stayed approximately two metres behind and slightly to the right of the woman. This also seemed to be what the woman intended, because she didn't turn around or urge him to catch up or any such thing. When they turned out of the alley and headed south, Mr Samuels switched sides to be on the woman's left, so that he was in the shade whilst she was in the sun. This was itself a form of masking for if the woman had turned back to get a good look at him she would see next to nothing for brief seconds as her eyes shifted from the glare of the full sun to the gloom of the deep shade. This was a masking of Mr Samuels own devising. It also allowed him to admire the woman's technique. To the untrained eye, she would seem just to be walking with a little urgency; a business woman perhaps on her way to a power-lunch, whatever that is, or just a meeting, a plain old ordinary meeting. But, to the slightly more trained eye, here was a woman who had a little time to herself, in her own head, as it were, for she glanced at the shop windows from time to time. To the fully trained eye, the glances at the shop windows were a means of assessing where Mr Samuels was and in what attitude and the somewhat urgent gait was a clear sign that she would disclose whatever it was she was about at a place and time of her own choosing and that Mr Samuels should keep her in sight but keep his proper distance.

She stopped at little way from the bustle of the old town. She had chosen some monument or another – all white marble and line upon line of black lettering – for reasons best known to herself, although comfort could not have been one of those reasons, for there was no bench on which to sit, nor any shade to speak of. Yes, the municipality had once again missed a trick. Here was a perfectly fine monument, no doubt doing a fine, silent job of memorialising whatever it was meant to be memorialising, yet the citizen could not take his or her ease in its vicinity. They could not sit on a shady bench and consider the line upon line of black lettering and come to some sort of understanding as to what the hell it was all meant to be about. Instead, it was shunned and sloughed in ignorance; all for the want of a bench and a bit of shade.

Mr Samuels knew what the monument was in aid of, and he had no doubt that this woman did too. They stood with their backs to the marble, still keeping their distance.

'Mr Samuels,' she said. This was not a question.

'You have me at an advantage,' said Mr Samuels.

'Yes,' she said. This was not quite the reply Mr Samuels had hoped for but, there you go, it was all he got.

For reasons that were not entirely clear to him, Mr Samuels felt the need to take the lead in the conversation.

'Here we are, then,' he said.

She said nothing.

'Might I enquire,' Mr Samuels enquired after a long pause, 'why we are here?'

She said nothing, again, if one can do nothing again.

'Or,' after some little time, 'perhaps more pertinently, why are we meeting?'

She did not turn to look at him, but said, 'You work alone, Mr Samuels.' This was not a question. 'I work alone, Mr Samuels.'

'It is the nature of the work.'

'As you say, the nature of the calling.'

Having established that working alone was in the nature of the business they were both engaged in, they fell silent, both looking dead ahead, like two stone sentinels. Unlike two stone sentinels, however, they gauged each other in this stony silence regardless of not actually looking at each other. Over the small distance between them signals were passed and read. So less like sentinels and more like bats. Or sharks. What a testament to their years of service! So honed were their skills that language could be put aside and the electric nuances of proximity could be sensed and appreciated.

Whatever was sensed, he of her, she of him, it allowed for a return to language.

'Yet,' she said, 'now we must work together, if you agree.'

'I cannot agree without knowing more.'

'What you can know, you will know.'

'And when might I be able to know?'

'In time,' she said.

'In the fullness, or at the right?'

'Both.'

'But not in advance?'

'No.'

It was now that Mr Samuels broke his reserve and looked at the woman. She kept her cool, and so he only saw her in profile. An admirable nose. A clear complexion. A hint of rouge on the cheeks. Five fine lines cutting out from the corner of her eye. A full mouth with lips slightly glossed.

'So on what basis can I agree?'

'On the basis of my competence.'

'On that alone?'

'No.'

'Then at what else?'

'On your own too.'

'Then I agree.'

She turned on her vicious heel and headed south, leaving Mr Samuels alone again.

seven

I have been forced to read again. Forced is not the word; obliged, perhaps. Don't think that I have been reading this drivel as I have been going along because I haven't. No, Cass has obliged me to take up the practice again. There was that letter when she left, which I had indeed read, and now a post-card, on what I took to be that much anticipated Friday. The reading of the letter she had left I could have just passed off as an anomaly, a momentary lapse of judgment, and that is how I consoled myself at the time. 'Do not worry,' I had told myself, 'a single read letter does not mean that you will start reading again. Relax,' I had told myself, 'all will be well and now this is read there will be no more need to read.' When I say that I told myself I don't actually mean that I told myself anything at all. I had a feeling that remained silent, but the effect was very much as if I had told myself something, for I relaxed in this regard if no other. It was with a calm eye that I could then look at the bookshelves and know that the books would stay where they were, unopened and unread.

But then a post-card from Cass arrived. I had no idea how it managed to find its way on to the island in the middle of kitchen, but that is where I found it. The front was a very pretty picture of palm trees shading a long white and empty beach lapped by clear, azure waters. All very nice, if you like beaches, which I don't. As to where in the world this might be, the post-card made no mention. I looked at the stamp and was none the wiser as it was just some plant or another. The franking mark over the stamp was blurred. Cass didn't feel the need to say where it was. But it was a real place, I am sure of that. Somewhere in the world is a white, palm-fringed beach devoid of people. The reverse, well the side opposite the address, was packed with a dense, neat hand in puce ink.

Her card read as follows:

'How long has it been? The days ebb and flow, the moon waxes and wanes and the only time I know is how my body moves with these tides. I have sloughed of my old skin and emerged anew. A butterfly from its cocoon, a phoenix from the ashes. The stars move me and I move with them. Cassandra-Gaia.'

Rather than a kiss, or an X standing for a kiss, Cass had drawn a six pointed star. The hand was hers, but were the words? That's what I found myself wondering. The words didn't match with the Cass I knew, or had known, or had thought I had known. Not a single tickety-boo or old thing or chap to be seen. And what was this Gaia business at the end? Perhaps she has remarried, I thought, but who was this Mr Gaia? Of course, she could hitch up with whomever, it was no concern of mine, but you'd have thought she might mention it, if only in passing.

One of the things I have not missed when it comes to reading, is that it is not enough just to read the words but you also have to make some sort of effort to understand them. Now, the words of this post-card were simple enough, but I struggled to understand what they meant. If she was now a butterfly, what was the cocoon, and what had happened to the caterpillar? This particular life-cycle must have been drilled into me at some stage, and I have kept hold of it, perhaps because the bit that always interested me – the word is too strong, but never mind – was the cocoon. What goes on in there? At what stage is the switch made and one can say, now it is a butterfly and no longer a caterpillar, whereas prior to that tipping point one would have said, here is a caterpillar on the way to becoming a butterfly?

Now if I was confused by the butterfly, I was no less confused by the phoenix. Here, I think I might not be alone. That's the trouble with myth; so many versions going about the place that stories merge and contradict. Maybe all stories merge and contradict, but it seems to me that myths are more prone to this than other stories told. Somewhere in this ramshackle mind, the phoenix is an immortal bird, but also one that raises from the ashes of the fire, rejuvenated, reborn or some such. Am I confused? Can something be immortal if it has to keep being reborn? Sounds like cheating to me, but I am no expert. I could have sworn eggs were also in the mix somewhere or another. Still, it has been a symbol for one thing or another for a good long while, so who am I to quibble?

Yet I quibble. What would I be without quibbling?

So, Cass was now somehow immortal or reborn into immortality or utterly changed. This last one doesn't really fit the phoenix myth at all, in my mind. It is not like the phoenix goes into the flames as one thing and emerges as another. Not like the butterfly business at all, when you think of it. It is not burnt as a bird and reborn as a bear, or a lizard, or a rhinoceros. Other animals are available.

Despite all this, I got the gist. A transformation had been made, at least Cass believed that such was the case. Perhaps that Gaia chap had helped.

So, credit where it is due, my little foray into reading had given me some information, after I had struggled for a good while, it has to be said. But it is one thing to gain information, and another to know what to do with it, and I had no idea what to do with this little gobbet. What it did matter to me if Cass was a phoenix or a butterfly? Nice to know, but useless to know, so I was glad I had been told, at least.

'Aha! There he is!'

Finally something, sadly, incontrovertible. Quite where else I could have been I am not sure. I don't go anywhere. In another of the cells in this mansion, I suppose, rather than in the kitchen, as I indeed was. And so was George. I should have been taken by surprise, but I wasn't. Even before he declared himself, I knew he was there. The air must have ruffled, or buckled, as he entered.

It must have been yet another hot day out there, judging by the look of him. He made straight for the fridge, yanked out and downed a bottle of water. Extraordinary Adam's Apple action. Sweat gleamed amidst the dark pelt of his raised forearm. He gasped and asked, 'So, who's it from?' It was only the jerk of his head that let me know what the hell he was on about. 'Thought I'd better bring it in for you.' So that little mystery was solved. I said nothing. Not that because it was none of his business, which it wasn't, but because I knew he knew who it was from. That is one of the properties of the post-card; a quick glance and you know what is what. There is no need to steam an envelope, open it with the most delicate of touches, read the contents and then slip it back in and re-seal. Perhaps give the letter a quick going over with an iron, just to be sure. No, there is no need for any of that and all of that would have been beyond George, I think. He didn't have the fingers for it. His fingers, though, were good enough to flip over a card and clock the signature, if nothing else.

'Anyway,' he said, seeing that I was not going to divulge what he already knew, I suppose, 'I was just passing, so thought I'd see how my friend was doing.'

'Is it Friday?'

'Thursday.' He got his mobile telephone from the back pocket of his trousers, consulted it and then confirmed. 'Yep, Thursday.'

'Do you have my goat?'

'Ah!' This was quite different from his earlier 'Aha!' He wiped the back of his hand across his mouth, and sat himself on one the stools arranged about the island. It gave out a small hissing noise and appeared to sink a little beneath his weight.

'Now,' he said, 'this goat. Are you sure you still want one?'

I nodded.

'Right, goat it is. 'Cause I was thinking, that maybe a donkey might be better? I can do you a donkey, no problem. A goat, not so much.'

'You can't find me a goat?'

'No, no, no. I can find you anything you want.' He tapped the side of his nose with his index finger. 'There is nothing George cannot find. But a goat? Well, that is gonna take a little more time. No, hands up,' he put up his hands, 'a goat is giving me some bother. No doubt about it. But if you want a goat, I'll get you as goat. Just,' and here he leaned across the island towards me, 'donkey might be the very thing you need. No, no, hear me out, hear me out! I was talking to a friend of mine, cousin actually, and I told him about the goat. He has a farm, you see, well, a bit of land, and I thought he might be able to get hold of one for me. Eager to please, that's me! Ha, ha! Anyway, this cousin of mine, well more of a second cousin, he says to me "Goat! Nah, you don't want a goat. You want a donkey. Much less bother and it'll do the job no problem. As it happens", he said, "I've got a donkey you can have right now if you want." So I played it cool and I said to him, "I don't know, I'll have to talk to the head honcho." So, here I am. Apparently, this donkey – and he's a good natured beast, he told me – this donkey will keep the garden munched down no problem at all. As good as a goat, but without all the goat hassle, you know?'

I didn't know.

'Here,' he fiddled with his telephone a little and then slid it over to me across the island, 'have a look at least. See what you think. Where's the harm, eh?'

On the screen of the telephone was undoubtedly a donkey. He or she, I don't know, was pictured in three-quarter face, which must be a good angle for a donkey because it looked to be a fine animal indeed. Its sad countenance was appealing, no doubt. It was a face that said, I have been a donkey all these years and I have been a donkey long enough. The flies that were attached to it were no doubt irksome too; a minute-by-minute, second-by-second reminder of all that flesh is heir to. Yet still the eyes, hooded by lashes, looked on, having no choice in the matter. If the times had been different, if I had been different, a donkey would have been a fine thing to have. I could have wandered the world on its back, going wherever it willed, stopping whenever it needed, each of us flicking away the flies, it with its tail, me with my hand. Or perhaps the flies would not have mattered in time, and we would both have suffered them, if not gladly, then perhaps patiently, as we ambled along dirt tracks under a merciless sun.

'It is not a goat,' I said, pushing the telephone away from me.

'But I can get you a good deal!'

'I'm sure. But it is not a goat.'

'Best deal, I swear. And my cousin – well he is more my wife's cousin really – says I won't find a better deal on a donkey in a month of Sundays. So, don't look a gift horse in the mouth, you know!'

'A goat,' I said, 'or nothing.'

'Right, right, right you are,' he held up his hands and puffed out his cheeks.

Another bit of mythology I don't understand. Surely, you want to look a gift horse in the mouth because then you'd see it was chock full of Greeks intent on murder, pillage, rape and arson? But, apparently not. Perhaps it is best not to know that your violent end is near.

I don't recall how he left, but he left. Must I remember everything? Think of everything? What matter how he left, as long as he left, which he did.

I was sad it was not the Friday. But, there you go, you have to get through Thursday first before the boon of a Friday is granted.

Hang on. He didn't leave. Well, he did, eventually, but not right then and there with the donkey matter concluded. He made to leave, and therein lies my lack of recall.

'Right,' he had said, 'If you don't need me for anything? No? Nothing at all? Suit yourself. I'll be off, then. Busy, busy, busy.' He slapped his gut with both hands. He plonked himself to the floor from the stool, which hissed again and grew a little. 'Back on the goat trail!'

He gave me a broad smile, with his mouth at least; I'm not sure how much of the eyes were involved. I gave no response, so he patted his gut a second time and left the kitchen, whistling a tune of some sort.

Now, that sounds like a person leaving. The whistling, tuneless though it was, faded as he made his way to the front door. But this cannot have been the case, and the reason why is this: sounds reached me as I sat on in the kitchen. They were the sounds of a man trying not to make any sounds. A distant clatter, for example, followed by harsh whispers. Were there two of them? George clattering and another whispering?

I could not make out quite where the sounds were coming from, but they were in the house somewhere or another. Now, they sounded as if from upstairs; later as is from the basement, if this house has a basement, and I think it has; then from the ground floor. Now, I know this could all just be a matter of acoustics with this massive shell of a place echoing. All that marble and chrome bouncing the sound around, dispersing the point of actual noise into a host of other points. What does it matter? One place, or multiple places; one man or two? What matters, if anything, is that George had not left but had instead made to leave and then snuck into the rooms of the house with a purpose I couldn't imagine to make supressed noises I couldn't identify. But, frankly, it didn't matter all that much, for I almost forgot the whole thing. If he wanted to go rooting around the house, who was I to stop him? I didn't want to root about the place, but that doesn't mean the desire might not arise in someone else, so root away, I say, root away, for all the good it will do you.

Poor Echo, when you think about it. Poor, poor Echo.

eight

The priest was dead.

Or sleeping. Or in gentle repose. Or in a state of quiet commune with his god.

Mr Samuels didn't like art. In particular, he mistrusted portraiture, as this thing appeared to be. What he stood in front of was a large, full length painting of a priest, with his tall, black block hat, flowing grey beard and equally flowing robes. His arms were held to his side, but without tension. That much was reasonably certain. The eyes were closed, that was certain too, but Mr Samuels couldn't read what all this added up to, if anything. Death, grace, sleep, prayer, it could be one of these or none of these. Frankly, the painting failed to call a spade a spade, and Mr Samuels did not like this at all. Now, put Mr Samuels in front of a photograph or indeed a real person and he could read off all the signals with a single glance, or thereabouts. Unless the photograph had been doctored in some way, but Mr Samuels was a keen student of the dissembling of the lens and the darkroom so he could quickly spot any fiddling with reality. Painting, though, gave him trouble, because he never felt comfortable with the relation between the real, the painter, and the painted. Was the painter merely following the dictates of the real, and being as faithful as possible given the constriction of material and, no doubt, of talent too? Or was the painter applying a subtle, small twist to the real, consciously or not, and so the painting was another thing altogether?

So, this priest. Was the painter aiming for an image of him asleep, but the mark been missed, overshot indeed, and ended up with a dead priest? Or vice versa; aiming for death but hitting sleep? Or grace, or prayer, or whatever. Was the painter a bad painter and just got it all horribly wrong, allowing in all kinds of confusion? Now, the fact that the painting was in a gallery suggested that at least someone thought this painter was a good thing in some sense. Money had been exchanged; a frame applied; a place for it to be hung selected. All that suggested that this painter – Mr Samuels looked again at the name and saw it was a man, dead – was supposed to be a good example of the painter's art, and more, given the speciality of the gallery, that he was a good example of the painter's art as conducted in this neck of the woods. This didn't exactly increase Mr Samuels' confidence. This neck of the woods is small and so the usual problems arise. 'Look,' say the citizens, 'look what we can do, well what one of us can do, and isn't it just as good as anything else from anywhere else? In fact, is it not better than anything else from anywhere else, because it is from here? It shows our genius, our native brilliance, our national je ne sais quoi.' This meant little to Mr Samuels. If a painter couldn't paint a dead priest to look like a dead priest then it didn't matter where he was from. He was also more than aware that just because money had been exchanged and a gallery wall selected didn't mean the painting was actually any good. It just meant that a certain coterie of people had thought it good. But, at bottom, the biggest problem was that Mr Samuels didn't really know what the word good meant in any of this business. Good drifted free, loosed from whatever moorings it might once have had; a situation for which Mr Samuels did not care.

Mr Samuels, then, was not in front of this picture for anything other than work. The place and time had been set by a simple, typed message slipped beneath his front door and found that very morning. The code used, which really was a very fine example of the art indeed, had been so fine, so well constructed and so well conceived, that he immediately took it to be from the woman. She still had no name. She had impressed him, there can be no doubt of that, and she had asked him to trust her competence and here was another display of just the sort of competence he could trust.

This little message was a thing of beauty about which once could marvel. It was to be admired and when examined from every angle, as if turning a diamond in one's fingers to catch the light, not one flaw could be seen. A perfect thing.

I have no idea what the coded message looked like.

I do know that it led Mr Samuel to be in front of this particular picture on this particular hour of this particular day.

Did Mr Samuels find himself sucked into the picture, perhaps just a smidgen? The hands – painted in a palette from grey to beige, colours of which Mr Samuels approved – were too long, anatomically speaking. They went on for far too long, by design or fuck-up, Mr Samuels did not know, although he didn't say 'fuck-up', he said 'error'. Actually, he didn't say anything. He thought 'error'. Possibly. But Mr Samuels had to acknowledge that this quirk of the hands meant one looked at them rather more than was warranted in the normal run of things. The question, for him, not only came down to one of artistic competence, but now also of degrees of tension. He declined these as: active-somnolent-dead. For a moment, although he mentally regretted it in the same mental breath, Mr Samuels was prepared to think the artist knew what he was doing. That left the issue of tension. Active? No. But at rest or at rest for all eternity? He couldn't decide.

It was at this point that Mr Samuels was stabbed.

Not that Mr Samuels knew at this point that he was stabbed, because he did not. He felt a slight wince in the area of his right kidney, it is true, but he thought nothing of it. He winced from time to time and from place to place. It was a natural condition of ageing, and he had been standing for some time. When he started to feel a slight, sticky discomfort in the same area he was a little concerned, it is true. When he then crashed to the floor it was too late to feel anything whatsoever.

A small old lady in wide-brimmed hat first tutted and then gasped.

A bulky gallery attendant in an ill-fitting, polyester shirt, chuntered 'Oh, for fucks sake'.

A retired army officer of a foreign power in a cravat and linen jacket exclaimed 'Goodness me!'

That evening, a busy day behind him, the retired army officer of a foreign power told his wife, Mabel, all about it.

'Oh yes,' he said, over a gin and tonic, 'I'd almost forgotten! The most extraordinary thing happened. I was in that gallery. That new one. With the funny name. Some local chap or another, I don't know. Wonderful air-conditioning, but shocking art, really quite shocking. I could do better, and you know what a duffer I am with pencil and paint. But the air-conditioning is really top-notch and they do a decent G&T in the café, I have to say. Bit too swank a place for my liking, but credit where it's due. None of the optics nonsense; just a good no nonsense pour and splash of the anti-malarial. Anyway, that place. There I was taking a shufti at some local dauber – can't remember his name. All these women moaning and groaning and the like. You know the sort of thing. All headdresses and wailing like banshees. Not my cup of tea at all, but I had to hunker down until 11 o'clock. Standards, my dear. Anyway, there I was not making head nor tail of the whole kit and caboodle, when this chap goes crashing to the floor. "Hello," I said to myself, "this looks like a rum do." But he didn't look like the type, and it wasn't even eleven, not that that would stop those types for a second. No standards. So, I make a recce of the situation and size up this blighter and think perhaps a heart attack. You know, a stroke or something. Or what's that thing they have nowadays, when the brain just goes pop all of a sudden. One moment, not a care in the world, the next dead on the floor. Like getting hit by a train, but in your head. Mind you, not a bad way to go. You'd know nothing about it at all. Better than going all gaga for years and crying to nurse for a bedpan. No; short and sweet; that's the way. But the thing is, this chap hadn't bought it at all. Looked to me like he had gone to join the choir celestial, but no, he was still twitching around the eyes. Always look at the eyes, Mabel, they are the last to go. That's how I knew Fred had slipped from me. Poor Freddie. Guts all over the sand, but it was the eyes that were the last to go. You remember Freddie? With us just after Margaret was born. Wife knew her way to a Vodka bottle a little too well. Freddie. Dragged me out of that scrap that time. Splendid fellow. Wife a lush. Did she sleep with the Captain? I would not put it past her, or him for that matter. He had an eye, at least until his foot was blown off. Rather put the kibosh on the Don Juan business. Still, he kept himself dapper and you know how far a bit of sympathy can go when it comes to a bit of how's-your-father. So, who knows. Footless and fancy free. Ha, Ha! So there was this blighter stretched out and the old training kicked in. Yes, that's still very much there, happy to say. Like that time I had to patch up that Cockney chap. What was his name? Corporal something or other. Rough diamond sort. Scar down his cheek and a tattoo of the flag on his forearm. Always ready with a funny story in the mess. You know the one. Got skewered up in the mountains that time when we were on night patrol. Lovely night it was. Nightingales singing away under a full moon. Taking a break with him on post when he yells out, which wasn't like him. Good discipline that man, so we all knew something was amiss. Never saw it coming, he said. Some local nips out of trees, shoves it in him and disappears. Bloody cowards, the lot of them. Never a stand up fight. Always a knife in the dark, some sniper from the rooftops, bloody bombs and whatnot. No way to behave. Anyway, he'd been spiked in the back, one-two, just like that. So pressure on, quick bandage and a drop of morphine did the trick until we got him off that mountain and back to barracks. Up and about in no time. Good man. What was his name? Johnson? No. Jackson? Something-son in any case. Anyway, so when I got up close

I knew exactly what I was looking at, whipped off my cravat and put pressure on the wound. Just oozing, but at quite a rate. Making a right mess of the floor. Guard was no bloody good at all. Just running around like a headless chicken. Had to tell him to call for an ambulance. Can you imagine. "Call a bloody ambulance," I had to tell him. Some just crumble under a bit of pressure. No training. No standards. Some old dear looked like she was about to have a fit herself, so I said, "Madam, don't be alarmed. I'm fully trained." That did the trick. So, all was under control, everything in good order when this young woman – elegant type, red-head, bit like Barclay's wife, Anne, before she went cuckoo – this young woman – extraordinary thing, really – she taps me on the shoulder and, cool as a cucumber, says "Sir, step away. Step away and then walk away." And this when I'm applying pressure to the poor sod's wound! "Madam, please leave this to me, I know what I am doing." That's what I told her. But you won't believe what she said! She said, "You might think you know what you are doing. But you do not. Now. Step away and walk away." That's when she took off her sunglasses and looked straight at me. Let me tell you, Mabel, there was something about the way that woman looked at me that sent a chill right up my spine. Me! Never spooked in my life until his bloody basilisk gives me the eye. So I stepped back. Surprised more than anything. But did I walk away? No, I did not. I wasn't about to leave him to her without a by-your-leave. She kneels down to him – putting pressure on the wound, so that made me feel a little better – and just whispered in his ear. I swear the man was on the edge of passing out, but whatever she said to him got him on his feet and out the door. Extraordinary. So when the ambulance and the police showed up – they took their bloody time – there was nothing to see but a blood stain on the floor and this old duffer left utterly flummoxed. I gave my report, every little detail, but I couldn't tell you what it amounted to in the end. Hadn't seen him stabbed; never seen the man before; never seen the woman before either for that matter. I gave a description of both but that was about all I could manage, because that was all I knew, really.'

He took a long sip of his gin and tonic.

'What bothers me, though, is why did I abandon my post? Because that is what I did, in the end. You can dress it up however you like, but when that woman said step back, I stepped back and just let her take over. Amounts to a dereliction of duty, when you think of it. Maybe I'm just rusty. Yes, just a little rusty. That'll be it. Don't you think, Mabel? Mabel? That I'm a little rusty?'

Mabel didn't reply. She had been dead for thirteen years.

nine

Finally, Friday.

All caveats aside now, because I don't care. It was the day of Marina's arrival, and that is enough for me. What does it matter, anyway? A day like any other bloody day, time out of mind.

She was in the fridge. Not entirely, of course. It was a hot day, I admit, but not hot enough to want to crawl into a fridge which, come to think of it, is not a bad idea. Now that I have such a voluminous fridge I could hunker down amidst the perishables.

Her legs necessarily protruded from beneath the fridge door. Small, slender legs, shod in sandals. She only knew I was there when she shut the door and, after folding up a canvas bag, caught sight of me. Neatly folded, the bag proclaimed itself to be 'fo if' in nice, calm green letters. The fridge whirred a little, struggling with the sudden, late influx of warm air.

It was not a scream. I have heard screams in my time, in the dead of night more often than not, and I know a scream when I hear one; deep down and yet high pitched, uncontrolled and uncontrollable as if disgorging the heart, ventricles and all. I've even heard men scream, I think, I mean men other than myself. My own screams, if there have been any, I don't recall. Unimaginable to me now. And I don't mean screams of pain. I'm not sure I have even heard a scream of pain, the physical type at least. Never seen or heard a woman giving birth – spared that – for example, but I'm reasonably sure a fair bit of screaming is involved. First the mother, then the child. The first in pain, the second in pain, surprise or indignation, who knows. Maybe it would just save a lot of time and bother if we were never to let that first scream die in the throat but keep it going instead, howling our way through the inexorable days. No,

I don't mean screams of physical pain, but of the psychic variety, if the phrase is not ambiguous, and, in truth, I don't care if it is ambiguous, it is what I mean to say. Howling screams from the psychic gut.

No, it was more of an involuntary shriek. The canvas bag went flying into the air, all its neat folds unfurling and the next thing I knew she was disappearing through the door. Bag for life, apparently.

Had I acquired some hideous growth, unbeknown to me? A massive, suppurating carbuncle in the middle of the forehead? Maybe my nose had rotted away, revealing the septum, and chunks of skin were sloughing off my face, disgusted finally at being part of the farce. Was I to understand that now I was a true leper at last? Or had the mark of Cain finally been revealed?

Her sudden absence gave me some time to gather myself. Proudly, I surmised that this strange female was Marina, in on Friday as usual for the usual, all caveats aside. I know, I know; shaky foundations on which to build a conclusion, but I worked with what I was given, and I was not a little proud of that too. I further surmised that the mystery of how my fridge was stocked without my ever raising a finger was now answered. To be honest, the question hadn't bothered me but I admit it could be seen as bothersome. How, one might ask, is this man keeping body and soul together when he never goes anywhere, not even to the shops? Yes, the days of the shops were over for me. A blessed relief, all round. But I can see how that question might nag; a thread from which the whole tapestry might unravel. But, to me, it was just a fact. Fridge stocked, fridge depleted, fridge restocked. Mysteries abound, so why bother with the mystery of the fridge? And even this mystery was not fully solved, if you are of a certain bent of mind. For who stocks a fridge is one thing, whereas who pays for the fridge to be stocked is quite another. Seeing this woman put things in the fridge only opened up further questions, if you really want further questions. How was fridge kept going, by which I mean, how was electricity paid for, be it quarterly or monthly, or by putting coins in a meter, although I doubt that last one. With my patron gone – not gone gone, but gone enough – how was all this managed? By whom? Who cares? It was done. If it had not been done I would have muddled through all by myself, but it was being done and that was enough for me.

So, Marina was a cog in the wheel of this machine. One of the many cogs, if you prefer, I don't much mind.

I was working all this through, or something very much like it, rooted to the spot when her head poked back around the door. A small head. Was she a child, forced into domestic servitude? No, she was a small woman. They exist. Her features were small too, except for her eyes which were too large for her face. Great, startled, grey eyes, like a naked owl's.

'Sorry,' this face said in a whisper.

'Your bag,' I said. 'You dropped your bag.'

She didn't move, nor took her eyes off me – so maybe my face wasn't all that bad after all – so I stooped down, picked up the bag, folded it neatly, but now it said 'ba fe' I'm afraid, and placed it on the kitchen island, just by the sinks. She looked at it. I looked at her looking at it. I should have left, but I didn't. Free from my presence, she could have reclaimed her bag as she wished. It would have been the thing to do; a gesture of delicacy, a ceding of the ground to her to do with as she would. She looked at me, and I at her. I nodded towards the bag and she stared at it before looking back to me. I may have smiled. Normally, I would poo-poo the idea, scoff at it, dismiss it out of hand, but on this occasion I rather think that I did actually smile, or made an approximate attempt. What state were my teeth in? I may even have had the presence of mind to keep them hidden, just in case.

'I can't,' she said.

A pause of some duration.

'Can't get it.'

'The bag?'

She nodded. Her ash-blonde hair was pushed back with a broad grey band.

I went to get it for her, but this only meant that she ducked her head back behind the door. Not seeing me made her a little more able to speak it seemed.

'I can't see you,' she said.

'The door is in the way,' I said.

'No. I mean, I can't see you.'

This clarified little.

'I mean, not meet you.'

'Is that what we are doing?'

'What?'

'Meeting?'

'On no account should the employee be in presence of, converse or otherwise engage with, here fill in the name of person. Failure to adhere to these precepts will result in the termination of the contract of, here fill in name of person, without recourse to tribunal or mediation and with immediate effect.'

'I see,' I said, but I didn't. Nor did I see her as she kept the door open but safely between us. 'So that means not meeting?'

'No.'

'Does handing you a bag mean engaging with, do you think?'

'I think it does.'

'Hmm,' I said. 'Is this conversing?'

She did not reply for a moment.

'Does it mean talking?'

'I think so.'

'Then, yes.'

'And I suppose you are present?'

'Seem to be.'

'And I'm over here being present.'

'Yes.'

'Does that mean in the presence of, then?'

'Hmm,' she said.

'Even with a door between us?' I said, just to paint the fullest possible picture.

'Well,' she said, unsure.

I then had something like a brainwave. I wish I could report more fully what this felt like, in the interests of anthropology or psychology or any other ology, but it was a surprisingly underwhelming feeling. No sooner had a thought dawned than it dimmed. Oh, the thought itself was good enough, but the elation of first thinking it soon passed.

'When I came in,' I said, 'you were in the fridge and I was over here, so we were in the same room and that must mean in the presence of.'

'Oh no!'

'So, you have already been in the presence of, so being in the presence of now doesn't really matter.'

'No, it makes it worse!'

'And we have conversed and are still conversing, so that doesn't matter either.'

'Of course it matters!'

'Why?'

'Because, failure to adhere to these precepts will result in the termination of the contract of, here fill in name of person, without recourse to tribunal or mediation and with immediate effect.'

'There you go!' I said triumphantly.

Did I detect a small sob from behind the door?

'Might as well be hanged for a sheep as a lamb. Or hung, I'm not sure.'

'What?'

'In for a penny, in for a pound.'

'Please,' she moaned, 'what are you talking about? I'll lose my job!'

It was now my turn to say 'What?'

'That's what termination means.'

'I thought it meant something else.'

'What? What did you think it meant?'

'I don't know.'

'Well, I do,' accompanied by the sound of snot being sucked back into the nose, if I was not very much mistaken.

We mused together. She on her side of the door, me on mine, our presences adjoining.

I rallied.

'But what I said still holds true! If being in presence of means immediate termination without faffing or whatever, then the moment you and I were in the same room then from that moment the termination comes into effect.' Yes, I was proud of this, I don't mind saying, and I wasn't going to give it up without a struggle.

There was some sniffling from her side of the door. I can't judge a sniffle: resolution, unable to stop crying, the start of a cold; I've no idea.

'But,' she said, 'no one knows. Do they?'

'Well, I don't claim to a legal brain or anything, but I stand by my interpretation.' I was a little affronted, if truth be told.

'No. I mean there is only you and me here so who can tell we were in the presence of?'

'Me and you.'

'Yes, but no one else. There's no one else here.'

This was true. I said as much.

'But I know,' I said, 'and you know, so we witness each other.'

'Yes, but…'

'Are you saying that I'm not here?'

'No!'

'Thank goodness! Are you saying you're not here?'

'No!'

'Thank the lord! Then…?'

'All I'm saying,' she said, 'all I'm saying is that we know we are here but no one else does, so it will be alright, as long as we are alright.'

'Are we alright?'

'I'm alright,' she said, still from behind the door. 'You alright?'

Her last question brought our rather impressive back-and-forth to a shuddering halt. On the few occasions when I have been asked if I am alright, I have struggled. This was no doubt because of the sceptical tone that usually went with the question. You ask someone if they are alright only when it is obvious that they are not. But, it also seems to me that you are only asked if you are alright when the questioner only wants the answer 'fine' or 'mustn't grumble' or 'middling' or somesuch, even when it is obvious that the person – me, for example – is not alright at all. The last thing they expect is a catalogue of the myriad of ways in which one is not alright, to assert that far from being alright one is distinctly all wrong. Further, being alright, despite its apparently all-inclusive nature, is actually a very low level of well-being; all things considered, what with the copious amounts of varied shit I am currently caked in, I'm not too bad, thanks for asking. And when someone asks, 'is everything alright?' what can the possibly expect as an answer? 'No. No, because I have a small patch of athlete's foot on my big toe and there has been a case of bubonic plague in outer Mongolia.'

Marina's question was of a different order, though. If I was not very much mistaken, she was asking whether or not I had any problem with her proposed solution and not whether or not I was hale and hearty, body and soul. As it happened, I didn't have any problem with her solution in principle, and she was right that it would only work if the two of us adhered to it, so checking if I was alright with it was probably a good thing.

'I see no one, so there is no one to tell,' I said. 'So it is alright with me.'

'No one?'

'Oh, sorry, yes, that George man. I see him. From time to time. He's getting me a goat.'

'I know George,' she said and cowered a little more behind the door. She took a deep breath — amazing hearing I have these days — and remerged, saying 'don't tell George a thing.'

'Nothing?'

'Nothing.'

'Nothing it is, then.'

I must have said the right thing, because Monica — no, Marina! Who's Monica? — Marina edged herself from behind the door and so we stood face-to-face in the same room and undoubtedly in each other's presence.

Grey eyed and small in feature and form, that is all that is needed, all that will be given.

'I'm Marina,' she said, and extended her hand.

'I'm Paul,' I said, and extended my own.

We shook hands.

'It's lovely to meet you,' she said, and smiled.

'And you.'

ten

Finally, Mr Samuels came to. For a moment, in that wooze of growing consciousness, he thought he was in a helicopter; the whirr of the rotary blades, the rush of air. This turned out to be a ceiling fan. It gradually came into full view, from which Mr Samuels surmised he was on his back in a bed. What bed, he could not yet say, but not his own. The smell was wrong, for a start. The laundered sheets gave off a faint hint of jasmine whereas his own laundered sheets gave off no discernible smell at all. Sounds too slowly came to him which marked this place as somehow other: cooing of doves, the chirrup of insects, distant howls of dogs and further distant braying of a donkey. All this came to Mr Samuels as he stared up at the blades of fan.

As yet, no noises or smells of humans, save himself, his breath and odour of sweat.

He was quickly conscious too of a pain in his side. He looked upon himself – his body seemed strangely distant – and saw a large bandage wrapped around his torso. Apart from this, he was naked. So much of this was wrong, to Mr Samuels' mind, but in a dim way. He couldn't yet categorise and prioritise all the levels of wrong which he felt in this situation that was slowly dawning upon him.

The last thing he could remember was the large hands of a dead or dying priest. Then; nothing. How being in a strange bed with a bandaged torso was connected to a dead divine was beyond him. It will come, he told himself, when the fog clears and signs become decipherable once again.

When next he came to, the fan was still whirring but a sheet had been draped over him, to save his modesty, perhaps. The pain in his side remained. He could now make out a smell underneath that of his own body and his laundered sheets; iodine.

When next he came to, he could see a little more of the room. The ceiling was of rustic bamboo, with wooden beams in support. A dim sort of light came from his left, and to his right he saw that the walls were of a bare, yellowish stone. He trawled his mind for the likely geology and so likely location, but he came up with nothing. Calm, he told himself, that too will return, in time.

When next he came to, he brought his hand to his face. It came into focus after a little while and he saw that his finger nails had grown. Usually, they were cut almost to the quick but now there was a thin line protruding beyond the fleshy pads of his fingers. This was noted but yielded nothing. Deduction, he told himself, will return, in time.

Of those intervening moments between his moments of waking, Mr Samuels knew nothing at all and still the time from dead priest to being in this bed was blank to him. He had no sense, either, of how long those intervals of unconsciousness were. He did know, though, that with each round of wakefulness and sleep, his faculties were crawling their way back. He practiced his focus when he felt strong enough by following the progress of a centipede climbing the wall to his right, tracking its way amidst the rough stone. It was long with a vicious pair of pincers at its tail. It made its swerving way up the wall, the hundred legs rippling as it went and the pincers held up high, as if ready for all that might befall a centipede. Mr Samuels tracked it all the way until it crawled its way into the bamboo ceiling. Good, he thought, the focus is returning. Somewhere the donkey brayed as if in pain.

It was now that Mr Samuels finally allowed himself a deduction.

'I am not at home, nor in the city, but somewhere in the countryside.' It was an obvious conclusion, but it was the first proper conclusion he had come to since finding himself in this strange bed, so he allowed himself to be a little pleased with his progress.

When next he woke, Mr Samuels came to the further conclusion that he was being cared for. By whom, he could not say, for he never saw them. They must come, he thought, when I am unaware. They must wait, he thought, until I am unaware. They must survey the scene to pick their moment. Mr Samuels felt well enough to deplore his use of the plural pronoun, but, he reasoned – so that too was returning – that before any further evidence presented itself it was best to leave things open. It could be a man, it could be a woman, it could be a host of carers, never the same one twice. No, it was better to leave things open until things could be more certain.

He spent some time considering his wound. The dressing was kept clean and fresh, so his carer was, or carers were, diligent. But how could his wound be washed and dressed without him being woken up? Were they, or she or he, sedating him, and if he was being sedated was this therapeutic or malign? Unanswerable questions, for the moment. It took a few rounds of sleeping and waking for Mr Samuels to recall being stabbed. Rather, he recalled events and then deduced he had been stabbed. He had been looking at a painting, felt a sudden sharp pain in the areas of his kidney and had very quickly crashed to the floor. This sequence of events seemed to him to be correct and yet wrong at the same time. Correct, in that each of these things had happened; wrong, it that the interval between the sharp pain, the crashing to the floor and, he assumed, unconsciousness was just too quick to be credible. A piece was missing, he felt; a crucial piece of the jigsaw had yet to show itself. Without that piece, the puzzle might never be finished.

I don't understand jigsaw puzzles. Well, I know what they are and how they work, but I don't understand what drives people to do them. You start off with a jumble of bizarrely shaped pieces, you then spend hours, days even, putting those pieces together to form a picture of a kitten or some such and then you dismantle the whole thing and put all those bizarre pieces back in a box. If you want a picture of a kitten, just get a picture of a kitten. If you want to do something pointless, do nothing. All that work for one brief moment of a complete kitten before scattering the whole thing to the four winds, as it were. And that's if you are lucky. Many must be the time that you spend hours, days even, assembling your kitten only to find that a piece is missing and that a feeling of completion will never be yours, never, never be yours.

'The boy!' He tried to exclaim. All that emerged was a gasp like a wind amongst dry leaves. Should we condemn him that only now, after so many rounds of sleeping and waking, he remembered the boy? It's only natural that you think first of your own body, your own predicament, before thinking of others. At least, I think it is natural. Natural or not, it had taken some time for his unconscious mind to come around to the boy, and I say his unconscious mind because he had tried to exclaim 'the boy" as he woke with a start. What dreams were playing in his mind?

Now if I understand dreams aright, and given that I hardly have any, or remember any, I might not understand them at all, the point seems to be, if dreams have a point, is that the thing one dreams about is not the thing one is worried about. So, rather than my dream of a goat being about wanting a goat, it was about something else entirely. The goat was just a proxy. A moat, for example. By association. Yes, the dream said Goat, but meant Moat, a nice deep ditch around the house, filled with stagnant water, mosquito larvae and lampreys, a surfeit of which is not to be recommended. I'm a mine of information today. Lord knows why. So, Mr Samuels did not wake fresh from a dream about the boy. I don't know, one in which the boy was in some danger or another – on a crumbling precipice, for preference – and Mr Samuels was desperately trying to reach him, to call out to him, but his legs were being sucked into the earth and his voice was stopped by some choking veil. Something along those lines. You see, if he had woken from such a dream, he would not have thought of the boy, but of the real point of it all. He would have woken and cried out 'I've left the gas on!' or whatever, I'm not a psychiatrist. No. Rather his dream would have been about his inability to find his favourite pen.

From this we learn a number of things. First, I seem to be capable of reasoning these days. Second, I must have dabbled in this dream business at some stage, although I can't remember exactly when or how. But seeing as we have a bit of reason to play with let's hold fast onto it, ride the bastard for all it is worth and hope it will collapse with exhaustion. Did I read about it? Possibly. I have not always not read. Even if I had read about it, it wouldn't have been with any real attention, I fear. Just a cursory skim, gleaning little gobbets here and there to be hacked up later. Gobbets are usually enough. But might I have also put those gobbets to some use in some way? Possibly. Yes, I can see myself doing that, not like now, but in a vaguely coherent and perhaps even a sustained way. Delving into some poor sod's psyche via the backdoor of the dream. It is even possible that I was the poor sod I delved into. That might have been possible, once. To what end, though, I cannot imagine.

Of course, it is entirely possible that this dream business is just another bit of shit that has been flung at me as I went on my way, oblivious.

Exhausted yet? If only.

So, Mr Samuels woke from a dream about a missing pen and tried to exclaim 'the boy!' He raised himself a little in the bed, pushing up from the mattress with his elbows, but collapsed back down, exhausted.

He heard a door open and soon saw a face looming above him. The woman. Now, she was blonde and as her face came into view, Mr Samuels got the first good look of her eyes. They were a startling blue. Not pale gull's eyes, but a bright blue, like a clear sky on a hot day. But there was an edge there; a metallic glint.

'Not yet,' she said and Mr Samuels immediately felt a slight pinprick in his arm. Soon, he felt nothing all, once again.

When next he woke, she was already by his side. She put a glass of water with a straw to his lips and he sipped a little, spluttered, then sipped a little more. She was too intelligent a woman to ask if he was feeling better. She had eyes in her head, after all, those bright metallic eyes, and she knew too that feeling better meant little when the baseline was feeling near death.

'There is some damage to the kidney and liver. There has been a degree of neurological damage too, but the effects should be short-lived. The wound itself is healing, although the puncture wound might result in some scaring. We have kept you sedated to ease recovery.'

'So, poison?'

'Poison, administered by knife. Stiletto, I'd say.'

'Why?'

'That's enough.'

She looked a little longer at him, then left.

So much to consider, so much to unpack, so many questions to be answered. Mr Samuels did none of these as sleep once more descended upon him.

Days, weeks, months? Who knows. You are asking the wrong man.

It took sometime before Mr Samuels felt strong enough to leave his bed. He had not seen the woman again. Still, whatever ministrations were done, were done whilst he was sleeping, or sedated.

Water was to be found beside his bed, so that was covered, but what of his toilet, not to put too fine a point on it? Urine was gathered in a small plastic bag strapped to his lag. A tube ran into the eye of his penis. It was the first time in a while that Mr Samuels had taken notice of his penis. So, that was covered too. But what of faecal matter, not to put too fine a point on it? There was no evidence of a method of capturing and removing said matter, and yet he wasn't wallowing in his own shit. Strange, he thought, but then realised that some things are just not worth thinking about. Not every i must be dotted, not every t crossed. Not every shit and piss accounted for. Not every punch and kick and slap and fall noted. Not every thought and sigh and wish and dream unearthed. Not every bruise and cut and scrape and scar detailed. Not every word and deed and hope and loss described. Not every fucking minute of every fucking day of all the fucking god awful months presented.

eleven

I've been mulling. It started incoherently at first. Thoughts flitting like birds hither and yon. Birds were on my mind, perhaps, no doubt because of meeting Marina who struck me as bird-like from the off. A small finch, edging its way into the garden to get at the ball of suet, or nuts in a cage, fearful of the world around it. When we say bird-like it is always those little, timid ones we have in mind, it seems; not some great condor, or bald-pated vulture smeared in blood and offal, or the frankly obscene shit-eating Marabou stork, that stuff of nightmares. And even those little, timid ones are all wrong, with their puffed out breasts making them top-heavy and rather ludicrous as they hop about the place. She was nothing like any of these things.

Best just to say that Marina was a small adult female.

Yes, my thoughts rotated around her, I confess, and the reason for that was no doubt the novelty of it all. I have come across women in my time, don't get me wrong. But mainly, they were just sort of there, like Cass, or enigmatic, like the crazed Pauline, or tangential, like Violet. Cass aside, all these – all! – I had encountered out and about. Marina was the first to find me in my seclusion. If I had a memory, no doubt I could come up with a whole host of women and even girls I have known, from childhood on, and perhaps one or two of these might have impinged upon me in similar ways, but I cannot remember any of them, so there you go.

Are men ever likened to birds?

So, my mulling started to focus on her, and the focus was 'what is to be done with her'. Now, this surprised me. Why would I have to do anything with her at all? I had been happily oblivious of her – well, not happily, but you catch my drift – and that for some time whilst she stocked my fridge and did a little cleaning in what I believe are called the common areas. My toilet I cleaned myself, when necessary. But where did the toilet paper come from, when necessary? I admit I had this thought whilst at stool. I was patient, as I always am on such occasions, letting gravity have a go before applying any muscle to the problem. Gone were the days of using an old newspaper or some other scrap, because right next to me was a pristine peach loo-roll on its holder, ready to be put to use when the time came. Perhaps I am incurious, but I had never before considered where the loo-roll came from. Like so much, it was just there. Stuff is like that; it is either there or it is not. Such is my experience. So, this was the first time I had considered the question of loo-roll since I left my hovel and moved into this arid opulence, at the instruction of my patron, of course. Maybe I had cast a glance at the toilet paper before, marvelled at it a little, then shoved it from my mind, thinking it of no consequence. But what is of consequence, if not the little niceties of life? I hadn't always thought so, and maybe life was better then, but I think so now, for better or worse.

I am changing. A thousand little things tell me so. A slow, unremarkable metamorphosis. Things of no consequence becoming things of consequence, to name but one change. And the need to do things with people is perhaps another one. With, not to; I am not so changed as all that. Why not just let people be? Let them do whatever they will, whenever they want, with no thought of what it might mean and no consideration of some grand scheme, no matter how illusory. Apparently, that is no longer enough. Somewhere, I say to myself: 'something must be done with Marina'. I don't trust this somewhere, nor what it says, but I hear it whether I want to or not. But how dare I think such a thing? It is not for me to do anything with anyone at all, surely? To foist a course of action on someone, to push them in a direction that might not be their own, to coerce, cajole or downright manipulate; to badger, hector, distort and contort, like a mad god shaping a lump of clay into its own image for its own ends.

'Let her be, Paul,' somewhere else tells me. 'Just let her be.'

Must I do something with George, too? The thought doesn't appeal, nor perhaps even arise, apart from just now, obviously.

Must I do something with everyone that crosses my path? If I ever go back out into the world, will every shopkeeper, pedestrian, barber and shopper need my intervention, a nudge or a kick, a push or a shove?

Let them flit like a sparrow through a hall on a winter's night. Bloody birds again. I need a scarecrow. A pumpkin impaled on a crucifix, with a smile and eyes gouged out. Wrap him in a mackintosh, shove a hat on his head and let him flap about as if alive.

'A gift! I've brought you a gift.'

George, again. Lord knows what day it was, but I can give a location: the kitchen. Must I meet everyone in the kitchen? I didn't think I went in there that often but perhaps I do. It is where things intersect, this kitchen which is and is not mine.

'A goat?'

'Sadly, my friend, not a goat.' He sat down on a stool at the island, without asking, I might add. Look at me getting all proprietorial. What do I care where he sits, or if he sits?

'Working on it, believe me. But I tell you,' he wiped his great hairy paw across his brow, 'it is giving me no end of trouble. But what is a bit of trouble, eh? Between friends?'

I think this meant me.

'Nothing! That's what it is. Nothing! But I said to myself, "George" I said, "George, you can't break the poor man's heart again." Joking! I just said, "George, be patient with the goat and it will come, softly, softly catchy monkey, you know? So, George, keep your irons in the fire but a watched pot never boils." That's what I said, but I was worried, I don't mind telling you. "George," I said, "you can't just go in there with a sorry and a sob-story and think that will be that." So, I thought a bit and came up with a little something, just for you. Come.'

He went over to the fridge.

'Come on!'

I went. Getting closer to the fridge meant getting closer to him, but you can't have everything. He swept back one of the doors in dramatic fashion. I thought he might 'ta-da' but sadly not. On the middle shelf sat a large pie.

'It is a pie,' I said.

Apparently, this was hilarious. George burst out laughing, clapped me on the back, clutched his chest, collapsed back on to the stool and wiped his eyes.

'A pie, he says! Ha, ha, ha! Oh, you wait 'til a tell her that one! A pie! Pah! Oh my friend, that pie is the greatest pie you will ever taste. Calling it a pie is like calling… I don't know, calling a something a something. A mountain a molehill. Yes, it is like calling a mountain a molehill to call that pie a pie.'

It took some time for the man to regain his composure. You can never be sure what will send someone over the edge, can you?

'But seriously,' he said, tapping his forefinger on the counter top, 'you will never think of pies in the same way again.'

'I have never thought of pies at all.'

'Well, there you go then! But the pie is not just my gift to you,' and here he put his right hand to his breast, 'but from my wife. She made it, and she thought of it. You see – but sit down my friend,'

I didn't, 'I told my wife all about the goat, all the disappointment, all the trouble I was going to, searching everywhere I could think of, nagging all my contacts, rattling every cage I could think of.

"'George,' she said, "why are you going to all that trouble?" Yes, she cares about me from time to time. I'm a lucky man, and no mistake. "Martha," I said, her name is Martha, you see. Martha the martyr I call her. Ha, ha, ha. On account of her headaches, migraines, whatever. I tell you, when she gets one of those her life is a misery. Noise she can't bear, and light she can't stand. Days they go on for. Days and days and days. Then there's her neck. Pain like you wouldn't believe, she says. Great big knots as hard as a rock. And when the neck's not playing up, it's her back, down in the hollow, aching away like there's no tomorrow. Crippling, she says. Then there's her veins, varicose, you know, like a bloody road map down there, itching and hurting and whatnot. Then there's her allergies, Spring, Summer, Autumn, Winter, it makes no difference. Snivelling and gobbing up phlegm and sneezing and weeping from the eyes. Then there's her stomach, God knows what's going on there, cramps and shits and constipation and all sorts. Then there's me, of course! Ha, ha, ha. Yep, Martha the martyr.

'Anyway,' he said, "Martha, you know me – give me a job and I'll move mountains to get it done." Now, you won't mind me doing this, I know,' as he leant across the counter towards me 'but I told her a little bit about you. Your set up here, I mean. Nothing personal – not that I know anything, 'cause I don't – just how you're on your own here what with Ms Johnson gone and Mr Johnson gone. "Martha," I said, "if I can do that man a kindness, I will, and if it's a goat he wants, then it's a goat he'll get. I can't bear to let him down."

"'You're a fool to yourself, George," said my Martha, "but I tell you what, I'll make him a pie. Your never lonely with a pie." So it was her idea, see? From the goodness of her heart.

'So happens, that there's a little history to this pie of my Martha's.'

Christ on a bike!

George tried to lean even further across the counter but his paunch got in the way.

'Truth is, it was the pie that won me over. Oh, I was a catch back in the day, believe me! Girls like bees around a honey pot, all wanting to get me down the aisle, to tie me down. I had a load of them on the go, blonde, brunette, tall, short, fat, thin, rich, poor, I didn't mind. All grist to the mill, eh? Then there was this one girl, timid little thing, like a bird, or a mouse. Wouldn't say boo to a goose. A strong wind would blow her away, so I didn't pay her no mind, to be honest. Other fish to fry. Anyway, one day – it was a wedding or something, some big do – and this little bird of a thing sidles up to me, didn't say a word, and just plonks down a pie in front of me. Strange, I thought, like you would. But I tell you, one taste of that pie and everything turned upside down! I ran around the place for days trying to find the pie-girl. Just had to have a bit more pie, and as I was running around I must have got to thinking, if she can make pie like that, what else can she make? I'll be set for life! A king amongst men! Well, that girl was my Martha. She was small, she was shy – not my type at all, really – but by god that pie! You know what they say: the way to man's heart is through his stomach, and here I am, living proof!'

He flung open his arms at this point, beaming. The beam faded, the arms fell and so did his face.

'You be careful,' he said, 'it's the little mousey ones you need to watch out for. I still get an odd pie now and then, but by god the grief I get off that woman you wouldn't believe. Morning, noon and night, seven days a week, it's "George why don't you do this?" and "George why don't you do that?" and "how come my cousin has a lovely house and we have to live in this hovel?" and "George, you're bone idle" and "George, I should never have married such a worthless heap of guts" when it was her that gave me the gut in the first place with her pies. I tell you, she is a slave driver that woman. No life to call my own. None at all. Not a bit.'

Now, this Martha didn't make much sense to me, in truth. I had never met the woman, so only had George to rely on, but she seemed a mess of contradictions. On the one hand, George obviously had her down as a shrew of the untamed variety and yet there he was talking about the goodness of her heart and that he was a lucky man. Was his life one of unremitting woe relieved only by the promise of pie? Was I meant to feel sorry for her because of all her afflictions or rail against her as a petite bully?

It also made no sense whatsoever that George was telling me any of this at all. He could have just said, 'there's pie in the fridge if you want it that my wife made' and all the necessary information would have been given. Was I meant to care in some obscure way?

'Yes, my friend. Don't let those little mousey ones get under your skin. Trust me. There'd be hell to pay.'

We were silent for some time.

'What sort of pie is it?'

'Cherry,' and the thought of it seemed to lift his spirits a little.

'Right,' he said, getting to his feet, 'I promised Martha I wouldn't touch a crumb of it. All yours. That's what she told me, and that's what I'm going to do, or I'll never hear the end of it. Now, back to your goat!'

Not sure I like cherries.

twelve

Now, the last thing we need is Mr Samuels flailing around in the all-together with a piss-bag on his leg. But, as design would have it, he found on waking a pair of nice pyjamas – brown with an orange pin-stripe – at the foot of his bed. He donned these with care.

The house he found himself in was well-appointed, as the phrase used to be; rustic, with the odd nod to the arts and crafts of the area in the wooden chairs and various baskets dotted about. A renovation, of course, not the actual hovel to be found in the almost empty villages of the interior. He gained the garden but had to wait for the glare of the sun to subside before he could make out much clearly, and what he did make out primarily was the woman, sitting on a rustic chair beside a rustic table with a blue teapot and two cups arranged upon it. She had the sense, of course, to be in the shade, but this did not stop her from wearing a large sunhat which flopped to right and left, sagging under the weight of its own straw.

In silence, Mr Samuels took a seat on the opposite side of the table, lowering himself with care. In silence, she watched him, then poured him a cup of tea, then adding a drop of milk from a delicate jug. It says something about the thirst of Mr Samuels that he did not mind this state of affairs and fell upon the tea with relief.

'Madam,' he said, 'you still have me at an advantage.'

Her silence let him know that the advantage would be maintained.

He sipped the tea and rallied again.

'I understand, but, Madam, I am afraid I must press you for some details. Of course, which details you choose to divulge I leave entirely to you. You know best what it is best to know at this stage, due to my incapacity over the past days.' He slightly inflected this last word to almost make it a question, but she did not rise to it. 'For this past period of time, shall we say. Now, my mind has not been at its most acute, so forgive me and indeed correct me if I go astray. It seems to me that I was assaulted, stabbed and poisoned on the occasion of your proposed meeting. I received your message, decoded it – and what an excellent code, if I might say – and acted upon it. Rather than meet with you, for reasons you have still not felt fit to tell me, I was met with an unknown assailant who, not to put too fine a point on it, attempted to kill me in a manner I have already outlined. I am aware, Madam, that you, or someone appointed by you, has since been taking care of me whilst I recuperate.'

So far, she had said not a word, raised an eyebrow nor nodded an assent. Remarkable control, thought Mr Samuels.

'So, my first question is perhaps rather obvious, Madam, but must be asked nonetheless. Do you know who attacked me and why?'

'No and no,' she said.

'So, it is not connected to the mission you wished us to collaborate upon?'

'Investigations are on-going.'

'Are these investigations coming to some form of conclusion?'

'Not as yet.'

'But are you hopeful that they will be brought to a conclusion?'

'Hope is not a word I use.'

Mr Samuels thought this very wise indeed. He also thought it wise that she kept her eyes fixed on the garden rather than on him, even if it caused her to squint a little and crows-feet to appear.

'Where am I?'

'A safe house.'

'A safe house, or a safe-house?'

'A safe house.'

'Belonging to...?'

'Irrelevant.'

'Madam, it might seem irrelevant to you, but I'm afraid I do need to know. I do not like to incur a debt without knowing to whom I am indebted. Whether the debt is small or large, as this one is, it needs to be accounted for properly. Even the smallest of debts, if left unguarded, can accumulate in ways that are undesirable or inconvenient. They might be called in at a time when one simply cannot pay, or the payment demanded is too high. I am not talking financially, Madam, as I'm sure you are aware, because the financial debt is often the least of one's worries in our line of work, is it not? It is. No. Debits and credits must be carefully monitored and serviced. So, please Madam, if you can tell me to whom I am indebted I shall be most grateful.'

She turned her blue eyes upon him.

'Shall we say, to me?'

'We can say that, indeed, but would it be true?'

'Would that matter?'

'Would what matter?' Truth to be told, Mr Samuels was flagging. The tea had revived him a little and he had managed a fair stab at talking and reasoning, but his strength was giving out, little by little.

'Whether it is true or not,' she said, leaning towards him a little, 'it is the assumption upon which you must work, for the moment.'

Mr Samuels gazed off into the garden. A paved patio was covered with a variety of pots from which sprang blooms in a host of colours and shapes. Beyond the patio, fruit trees, apple among them, sagged in the heat. All this was logged but not yet analysed, for Mr Samuels knew he had to conserve his strength.

'Where is my boy?' he asked.

'Under supervision,' she said.

'Supervision?'

'As I said, supervision.'

'Whose?'

'Mine, and my associates.'

So now there were associates. This was a development Mr Samuels did not care for.

'Is he,' and here Mr Samuels almost felt all his strength desert him, 'safe?'

'He is safe now,' she said in the most blank tone Mr Samuels had ever heard. He again admired her technique but was soon worried by the word 'now'; did it mean the boy had been in danger but was no longer so, or did it mean that he was not in danger for the moment but might be soon? His mind vaguely reached a formulation of this worry, but his lips did not voice it.

'I'd like to see him.'

'When it is safe and you are well.'

'When might that be?'

'Time, Mr Samuels, will tell.'

She reached across the table and rested her hand on his hand. He noticed she had perfectly tapered fingers and no less perfectly manicured nails. Her touch was cool and Mr Samuels felt a reassurance in her touch. A touch, he told himself, deployed in such a way is not to be trusted. It is a strategy, carefully evaluated and carefully executed. It is not reassuring. But it was.

Urine drained silently into its bag.

Oh, Mr Samuels! Could you have better withstood a full frontal assault? Perhaps if there had been a pool, she could have emerged from it as you came into the garden; water and oils glistening on her limbs and décolletage. She would have poured your tea gazing into your eyes, licking her lips before applying the milk. She would have brushed your arm as she bent towards you to whisper 'feeling better?' Would your pulse have raced as she did so, and more so as her hand stroked your forearm, slowly back and forth? Would your breath have quickened as she said 'I am here for you' and her blue eyes flashed at the ambiguity of it all? Would you have felt a strange surge as this nameless woman looked deep into your eyes and breathed 'Everything will be alright; leave it to me; just leave it all to me'?

Perhaps. Or perhaps not.

In bed again, Mr Samuels worried. He did not like to worry. He preferred to reason things out and this faculty had stood him in good stead for as long as he could remember. Nothing is so big, so complex, so Gordian that reason cannot be brought to bear and results obtained. That had been a watchword, consciously held and repeated from time to time, when the need arose. Now, though, with the fan once again whirring above him, Mr Samuels had to admit he was worried. Inconsistencies haunted him. For a start, the woman had assured him, had she not, that she worked alone. Yet now there was the talk of associates, looking after the boy no less. He felt a surge of discomfort at the thought.

The house in which he now lay seemed to further confirm some sort of organisation and, when he thought it through, the manner of his being there and the fact that he had been brought there at all confirmed this view. Surely, she could not have been the only one watching over him, injecting him, changing his catheter, applying new dressings? Of course, a struck-off doctor, a barred nurse were possibilities. If you slip such people a few quid – well, quite a lot, actually – then their services could be secured and no questions asked. But how had he gone from the gallery to this bolt-hole in the foothills? She could not have dragged him out of there all by herself. She could not have bundled him into a car, bleeding all the while, without raising some form of suspicion. If memory served, he had not been alone in the gallery. Surely, those bystanders would have raised some sort of alarm, called the police or ambulance, even? For it is not every day that you see someone collapse to the floor in an art gallery. Now, the emergency services, so called, might not be the finest but even they would have mustered some sort of competence. An ambulance team would have arrived. They would have assumed a heart attack or stroke but even the most incompetent among them could not have failed to notice the blood on the floor and eventually notice a stab wound. That would have set the police in motion. Mr Samuels avoided the police on the whole. They rarely helped his work and often hindered it.

Hang on. Is Mr Samuels a criminal involved in nefarious activities?

No. He operated in the grey areas from time to time, it is true, but never in the black.

So, Mr Samuels imagined, the police would have first resented being dragged away from the mid-morning coffee but then, when they had realised that here was an actual case not dissimilar to one they had seen on television, they would have gone into full swing. Tape would have fenced off the area. An outline of Mr Samuels in white would have appeared on the floor, until an officer pointed out that that was only for dead bodies and not for the near fatally stabbed. Witness statements would have been taken and documentation checked. A search for the murder weapon would have been launched. Yes, they would have assumed that Mr Samuels would succumb to his injuries, such as had been described, if only because a murder was so much more fun than a common-or-garden assault with a deadly weapon. Back at base, the homicide squad would have been itching to intervene. They hadn't had a good murder to get their teeth into in a long while. Some of their number hadn't known one at all and this one, all agreed, would be a good one; middle-aged white male, citizen of the country, no previous record, homeowner and tax payer: perfect.

But none of this had happened. Somehow, Mr Samuels had been spirited away and the whole thing hushed up. Now, Mr Samuels did not doubt the skills of the woman, but this would have been beyond the abilities of any one person. A team would have been needed. A well-trained team of operatives all skilled in their various roles and duties.

Necessarily this gave Mr Samuels some concern. Two possibilities arose in his mind. First, the woman had quickly assessed what had happened and summoned the team who were remarkably rapid in their response. Second, the team had been there all along and the woman herself had stabbed him or arranged for him to be stabbed.

It is safe to say that Mr Samuels did not care for this second option at all.

He felt a sudden and urgent need to sleep. As he slipped away, he couldn't help thinking that his tea must have been drugged. How contemptible to spike a man's cup of tea.

thirteen

It has not escaped my notice that my existence is scarcely credible. The whole thing is shot through with holes. Contradictions abound, as is their wont. I've known for a while, but the feeling is growing and it worries me more as the days crawl by.

Knowledge, for example. I seem to know an awful lot of useless crap but have no idea how I got any of this. That myth business, for one. You know, Greeks bearing gifts and all that. No idea. No recollection at all of anyone, anywhere at anytime telling me any of that, and yet there it is.

And then the practicalities, so called. Light, for example. When the day finally gives up the ghost, and after the dusk is done and the true dark begins to gather, I might put on a light. It might be a lamp, it might be a ceiling light. Of course, I enjoy the dark a little before I do any such thing and there are times in fact when I don't bother with light at all. I let the darkness gather and then take myself off to bed, picking my way with care lest I knock into something. I brush my teeth in the dark. I shit and piss in the dark, if I need to shit and piss. I then lie down in the dark and look up at the ceiling but fail to see it because it is dark. What do I see, then? What is this thing in the middle distance that I cannot see past? That is what I think sometimes, as I drift off, or toss about. Most of the time though I think nothing and just stare into the gradations of gloom. But there are times, and they might even be more often than not, that I put on a light the better to do whatever it is that I am doing. Now, for however long I have been here, and for however long I have been alone here, the light has never failed. I flick a switch, and on it comes. When Cass was here one might have assumed that she sorted this out. In truth, she was more fond of light than I was, although nothing too harsh. She liked a soft light, as she used to call it. More flattering, she used to tell me. Covers up the bally wrinkles, apparently. So, liking light I had assumed she had taken steps to make sure it didn't get cut off. With her gone, how was this still achieved? Was she taking care of me from afar, from that pristine beach? Or were the measures she had taken to take care of herself still in operation and so would I find myself one day plunged into darkness? If that was the case, how long did I have left? Which rather begged the question: how long is one given? Which further begs the question: how long has it been since she left?

I was tempted for a moment to measure it by toothpaste. Am I on the same tube as when she left, or a new one been opened? But then I don't know how long a tube lasts so that gets me precisely nowhere.

Or let us take laundry. I wear clothes. These clothes necessarily get dirty. More importantly, these clothes begin to smell. The armpits of the shirts in particular soon give off an odour that even I cannot ignore. This happens within the first ten minutes or so of my donning a fresh shirt, given the temperatures and humidity to be endured. But did I not say, way back when, that this house stays strangely cool even whilst everything outside is being burnt to a crisp? I think I said something like that, but I'll be damned if I'm going to check, so, if I didn't say it before, I say it now: this house stays strangely cool in ways that I do not understand. Yet even this doesn't stop the pooling of sweat in the pits and the slow trickle of perspiration down the flanks. Perhaps it has less to do with temperature and more to do with me. A predisposition to perspiration, as it were. Now, this bothered me less when I lived in my old hovel that got hot when it was hot, damp when it was humid. I'm sure I must have sweated just as much then as now, more so, or at least logic would suggest, and surely the odour must have followed too, but I don't remember it that way. Perhaps the new shirts that Cass presented to me do things that my old rags did not. Perhaps my sense of smell is becoming more acute. Perhaps it is getting yet hotter and the cooling system is fighting a losing battle. All a possibility.

So, inevitably, after a week or so, I discard the shirt. After all, I don't want the thing to rot through. Is sweat acidic? I fear it might be. Mine at least. All these nagging questions. When I say discard, I mean leave lying around wherever I happen to chuck it; on my cot in the office more often than not, so when I climb into bed at night I have to throw it to the floor and there it might lie for a while.

Now, all this might be all very well and good if I had an endless supply of fresh shirts, to mention only shirts, but I do not. So, there must come a time when the discarded shirts scattered about the place must be taken in hand and washed and dried and generally made ready to be worn again so they can be soiled again so then they can be washed and dried again. This is what used to happen in the old days, in the old house. The time would come when I was shirtless so I gathered up the stinking garments and washed them in the kitchen sink and then hung them out to dry in the garden, such as it was. Ditto smalls and socks and such like. I'm not saying it happened very often, but it happened. Yes, I remember times spent with my arms thrust into smalls and suds.

But this never happened here. The shirts and smalls and socks and such would pile up and then they would be gone to be replaced some time later by freshly laundered clothes in a bundle on the kitchen counter. I never saw them gathered and I never saw them being washed and dried. They were there, they were gone and they were back again, but clean. I never bothered to wonder how this was achieved, just as I never bothered to wonder how my fridge came to be stocked. It was just the way things were since taking up residence here. Nor did I wonder about money, how it was earned or how it was spent. I knew, and know, that I don't earn but that has not put me into direst poverty, as far as I can tell. There is money, then, unless the whole shitting issue has collapsed beyond my walls and we are back to bartering, but where this money is, how it is spent, and by whom, I didn't care to know. Why pry? I must have thought. Will knowing what is going on make anything any better? Will my knowing make the system any more efficient? Perhaps the system is dependent on my not knowing and never wanting to know? Don't fall into the sin of curiosity, fatal to cats and no less to humans.

In truth, I thought none of these things. Things were as they were and who was I to quibble?

Marina. It was almost as if she were invented to account for some of the deeper mysteries of my day-to-day life. I even went so far as to ask her questions, believe it or not.

'Do you do my laundry?'

'Yes.'

'When?'

'I collect it on Fridays,' she said.

'Like today?'

'Yes,' and I think she might have looked at me a tad strangely at this point.

'And?'

'I take it away and wash it and iron it.'

'And then you bring it back?'

'No.' This surprised me.

'So how does it get back?'

'A man in a van picks it up.'

'A man in a van?'

'Yes.'

'What man in a van?'

'The laundry-pick-up-man.'

'And this man brings it here?'

'I don't know. Maybe. Maybe there is a laundry-drop-off-man who does that.'

I didn't like the way this was heading. Not so long ago, I had believed myself alone in the house. So far, not only George but also Marina had shown themselves and behind them was the possibility of a whole bevvy of buggers trooping in and out, or working behind the scenes, without my having the foggiest.

'Hang on,' I said, 'if you do this every Friday, how do you get the dirty clothes without my noticing?'

'I wait until you are asleep.'

'You steal into my room at the dead of night?'

'No. Your day-time sleep.'

I suppose it would have to come out sooner or later. I sleep from approximately midday until two, every day, without fail. If I could sleep longer, I would. If I could sleep from midday to midnight, have a quick snack to keep body and soul together after a fashion, and then sleep again from midnight to midday, I would. This doesn't seem to have been gifted to me, this time around, but a man can always dream.

I must have looked surprised, because she added, 'I'm as quiet as a mouse,' and smiled; well, raised the corner of her lips a little.

Time rears its head again. This was a Friday. The one after the previous Friday, by which I mean the Friday when Marina and I had first met. Of the week in-between? Nothing. Perhaps I should rather say, first properly met, because here was Marina telling me that our paths had crossed many times before but that I had been unaware. Many was the time, I surmised, that she and I had shared a room without my knowing. I was off in dreams or merciful oblivion whilst she was scurrying around attending to my laundry.

'Hang on,' I said, yet again, 'I thought you weren't allowed to be in the presence of, etc.'

'You were asleep.'

'But I was present.'

'I suppose. But not really. When you think about it.'

She cocked her head slightly to one side. I cocked my head slightly to one side. We thought about it. Personally, I came to no definite conclusion on this point.

'How long have you been doing this?'

'Oh, ages.'

Now far be it for me to criticise other people's grasp of time, but I must admit I found this a little disappointing. I'm a hypocrite, I know, because if you were to ask me, for example, 'how long since Cass has left?' then 'ages' would probably be my reply. But it might have been less than a month, for all I know. I know, I know, I really should keep better track of such things, but I can't. Ages or the blink of an eye, it is all one to me, if I were to have my way. What is a month anyway? Ages in one sense; sod all in another.

Something must have got the better of me, for I found myself asking 'Did you meet Cass?'

'Cass?'

'The lady who lived here. With me.'

'What lady?'

'Cass. She might have been blonde, or brunette; tanned or pale. Slim, though. Always slim.'

'You lived with a lady?' It was her turn to sound surprised. 'No. There was no lady. Just you. They didn't mention a lady.' Was there a mournful hint? My hearing is growing ever more acute and can even pick up nuance these days. My my!

'She's gone,' I said. 'A friend.'

'A friend?'

'After a fashion.'

'Really?' Her right eyebrow arched a smidgen.

'Really,' I said, and the eyebrow fell.

'Right,' she said.

'Right,' I said.

'Well that's nice,' she said.

'Is it?' I said.

'I don't know,' she said. 'Is it?'

'You said it was.'

'Suppose it is then.'

'If you say so.'

'No for me to say, really, though, is it?'

'You just did.'

'Yeah, but, whatever.'

'Whatever what?'

'Whatever whatever.' She flapped her hand at me, whisking away me, it, something; the words that hung in the air, perhaps. 'Best get on.'

I didn't know what 'on' meant, but I did know that she got down from the stool on which she had been sitting – which rose almost imperceptibly as she did so – and left the kitchen in the direction of the garden and, in a little while, as I watched from the window, I saw her cutting a swathe through the undergrowth and exiting through a back gate. So 'on' actually meant 'out'. At least that was cleared up. Or maybe 'away'.

I'd like to say I mulled over our conversation, but it is not the word. Fretted over is perhaps overdoing it, and examined is way off, but it was a kind of wayward, anxious replaying of selected highlights which were highlights in the sense that they were in need of light being brought to bear upon them. High-darks, then. Nothing doing, though. The darks remained darks, no doubt because what little light I had was too little, too diffuse, too weak. But as I replayed things in my haphazard way, some light did emerge. Not a light brought to bear, but a light emitted by events, such as they were. We had sat together at the kitchen counter. She on one stool, I on another, of course, but together for all that. I had not asked her to sit, nor she me. We had just sat. She had not scurried for the door as she had before. She had not hidden her face nor shrieked at the sight of me. No. We had sat and exchanged words, even sentences, in the cool of the kitchen whilst the desiccated world baked under the afternoon sun.

fourteen

Did Mr Samuels consider escaping? Indeed he did. This was hindered by a number of factors. First, and he was very much aware of this as he lay on his bed contemplating the ceiling fan once again, was the catheter. Could he remove it himself? Indeed, how was it lodged up there in the first place?

This led Mr Samuels to have to contemplate his penis, as he never failed to call it. Not for him the infantile willy, or todger or prick or dick or schlong or trouser snake, one-eyed, or little man or john thomas or Johnson or pork sword or knob or tallywhacker or old chap or love truncheon or sausage or thingy or shaft or winkle. He had once flirted with virile member, but this had failed to satisfy. Generally, he did not call it anything as he had no need to do so. It was there and performed its urinary function quite well and that was all Mr Samuels required a penis to do. Now, that function had been supplemented by a tube and a bag. With his pyjama bottoms neatly folded next to him, Mr Samuels sat on the edge of the bed to get a better look at the problem. His penis had shrunk into itself, as if horrified by the invasion of the tube. Gently, with thumb and forefinger, he gave the tube a tug. This extended the penis a little but the tube itself did not seem to budge. Pain? A little. But what is a little pain compared to thoughts of escape. He girded his loins and tried again, but with greater force. Sadly, the end was the same. He grasped the tube in a full fist, took a deep breath, closed his eyes, but then thought better of it. Who knew what might happen if he jerked the thing out? Who knew what damage would be done? Not Mr Samuels, for one. So he sat back on the bed, deflated. Angered too, by the limits of his knowledge. Mr Samuels was a mine of information, both practical and theoretical, but in all his resources of mind there was not a single thing that could help him in his dire need. Somehow, the mechanism of a catheter and its correct removal had passed him by. He took a mental note to rectify this at the earliest opportunity.

A man like Mr Samuels is not deflated for long and he soon came to realise, with the offensive appendage once again sheathed in pyjamas, that the whole point of a catheter was that it allowed one relatively unrestricted movement. Hidden beneath clothes, surely you could just go about your business as the waste drained away without so much as a tinkling trickle. He had been following a red-herring all along. His rational mind had been distracted by a gross invasion, and now he saw that clearly he was once again calm and could consider the further obstacles to escape: two, no clothes; three, no idea where he was; four, no access to transport; and five, no access to money.

The no clothes issue troubled him for two reasons. Obviously, he did not want to roam the countryside in his pyjamas as this would arouse suspicion and might well see him under arrest or sectioned, or both. So, he would have to acquire clothes and this might involve theft. He could creep up on some unsuspecting washing line and bag himself a pair of trousers and a shirt perhaps, but he was conscious that his conscience would be tested by such an act which, bad in itself, did not address the real problem which was shoes. Shoes were a necessity, for if he knew anything about the countryside, and he did, he knew that shoes were indispensible. The ground would be rocky and filled with the most vicious of burrs designed to lodge themselves into the pelt of a goat or the paw of a dog with a tenacity that almost belied their purpose of dissemination. In the foot of a human, they were hell. Clothes might be purloined from a washing line, but shoes were seldom given such an airing.

This was compounded by Three, not knowing where he was. He had a suspicion that once he gained the open road he had no doubt that he could quickly orient himself, but it was hazardous to gain the open road without knowing quite how far that road might lead and to where. He knew, through the study of the stone walls of his room, what region he was in – the mix of yellow and grey was a dead giveaway – but that was no help in establishing quite where in that region the house lay, or whether it was near a village or miles away from one. On that score, more data was definitely needed.

Luckily, this meant that obstacle Four – no access to transport – and obstacle Five – a lack of funds – were irrelevant, at least for the moment. Without knowing where he was, all would be mere speculation and Mr Samuels was not about to do something as silly as speculate.

So, he hatched a plan.

'Dear Madam,' he said, already putting quite a bit of his plan into action. He had thought long and hard about what to call The Woman. In his mind, he always called her The Woman but this would hardly be the right name to apply to her face-to-face. He could not, and would not, go up to her say, 'Woman, what the hell is going on?', perhaps rapping on a nearby horizontal surface for emphasis if one happened to be handy, or placing both hands on hips if one were not. He had already deployed Madam to some effect, so adding 'dear' would, he hoped, have the right mix of gratitude and solicitude to make it endearing. In order for it not the merely patronising, Mr Samuels carefully modulated his tone.

But this was not all. In merely finding The Woman out on the veranda, Mr Samuels' plan had already paid dividends. The shade came from the east and it was morning, so the house was roughly on an east-west axis; an observation confirmed when he felt the slightest of cooler breezes coming from the north which, given the region he assumed he was in, meant the mountains of the interior. Immediately, he realised that if he were to return home under his own steam he would indeed need transport of some kind, if only a bicycle, although something with an engine would be preferable. When the bells of a church reached his ears, he knew that a village or perhaps even a small town was not too far away.

A thousand other things assaulted his senses and whispered little things in his ears.

'Good morning, Mr Samuels.'

Mr Samuels did not take the seat that was offered him, but rather strolled to the edge of the veranda, inhaled deeply and took a good long stretch, careful, though, not to rupture his dressing or rip off the piss-bag. This had the desired effect.

'I see you are feeling a little better,' she said, eyeing him over the top of her sunglasses.

'Indeed I am! Indeed I am!'

'Well, there's a blessing,' not taking her remarkable eyes off him.

It was only now that he sat. Not with the table between them, no, but beside The Woman.

'And I cannot thank you enough, dear Madam.'

'It was nothing,' she said, pushing the sunglasses down to shade her eyes again.

He pooh-poohed this.

'When I think,' he said, 'of all the trouble I have put you to I'm afraid you will have to allow me to disagree with you on that point. All the trouble you, and your colleagues, must have been put to can only make me feel the deepest gratitude.'

She did not bite at 'colleagues' but she did remove her sunglasses, the better to fix her eyes not on Mr Samuels, as might be expected, but on the table top.

'To tell the truth,' which as an opening statement Mr Samuels had long mistrusted, 'I felt responsible,' she said. 'You were there on my say-so, after all.'

'To start the mission, I understood.'

'Yes.'

'And what of the mission, dear Madam?'

'I had to pursue it by other means.'

'Successfully?'

'That remains to be seen, but signs are encouraging.'

She whisked away a fly that had momentarily settled on her arm. It careered away languidly like it could not be bothered.

'And have your colleagues helped you in this endeavour, Madam?'

Now she looked at him.

'I told you, Mr Samuels, that I worked alone.'

He felt her stare.

'Yet, and forgive me if I am mistaken, but all the business of saving me, of bringing me here and bringing me to relative health, all this surely needed some aid. If I am underestimating you, I can only apologise, but I can't imagine how I, working unaided, could have managed it all.'

'Hirelings.'

'Plural?'

'Plural.'

'Yours?'

'Mine.'

'And none others?'

'I do not ask and they do not tell. They are mine whilst they are mine.'

It was the turn of Mr Samuels to look at the table top as he tried to compute all he had been told. He was struggling, his mind still muddled by illness and sedation, no doubt.

'It is a simple affair to manage,' she said, and this might even have been an act of kindness once she had seen the gears in Mr Samuels' mind turning so fruitlessly. 'You hire a specific person for a specific job and keep them in isolation from others hired for other specific jobs. They never meet, they never converse, they are never in the same room at the same time and there are no avenues of communication between them. They only ever see me, and that rarely. As far as they are concerned, they are the sole employee and I the sole employer, as indeed I am.'

'And was I just one such hireling?'

'Oh, Mr Samuels!'

It would be a fine thing if the tone of this were free from ambiguity, but it wasn't, so there you go.

Whatever tone she had used, she shifted it to say, 'I'm afraid the other mission, *vis a vis*, finding out who assaulted you and why, remains in abeyance.'

'But why?'

'I need you back to full strength before we embark on that. I may be the root cause, or it may be you, and I a mere incidental. I need your mind, dear Mr Samuels.'

Mr Samuels' mind blanched a little at the thought.

'But,' she said, standing and offering to help Mr Samuels to his feet. He took her by the forearm, not the hand and soon they stood face to face, or thereabouts. 'You mustn't tire yourself.'

'I must admit, dear Madam, that I still feel rather weak.'

'It is only natural.'

He searched her eyes to see if this were true but came up blank. The more he looked at, and then into, those eyes the more remarkable they seemed. There were depths, undeniable depths, but these were more as if a series of flat surfaces had been layered one on top of the other. Yes, a series of deepening surfaces, each as imperturbable as the last, but their arrangement managed to draw you in, somehow, from surface to surface, seemingly without end.

'I have something for you.'

They walked around to the south-facing side of the house. The sun was fierce and Mr Samuels squinted. His unshod feet felt the heat of the stone beneath them. Telling him to wait, The Woman disappeared into small door set into the stone which, by Mr Samuels' calculation, must have been the same wall which flanked his room to the left, as he lay in bed. Did his room have such a door too? No; only the one that gave access to the house proper. If he were to attempt escape, and he was not sure yet that he wanted to escape, he would have to go through the house and out via the veranda.

She emerged.

'Here you are,' she said, handing him a quite sizeable package, done up with brown paper and string. He looked at the package and then at her.

'Just some things to make you more comfortable. Now, how about a little nap?' She patted his arm and smiled. A neat row of perfect teeth.

Mr Samuels did not immediately nap, of course. First, he dealt with the package:

One pair of shoes, brogues, brown.

Two shirts, white.

Two vests, white

One suit, brown.

One tie, brown.

Three pairs of socks, cotton, brown.

Three pairs of underpants, Y-fronts, white.

With no one to see, Mr Samuels blushed ever so slightly.

Was The Woman showing him that he was trusted, or daring him to make his escape? A good will gesture – a kindness – or a snare and a subterfuge?

Of course, all these questions aside, the clothes as clothes pleased him. He was tired of pyjamas and felt it unseemly to appear before The Woman in such a way. But of all the clothes the vests pleased him most.

'Son,' said his father, 'it is time for you to wear undershirts.'

Apparently, the Samuels' household had an allotted time when the issue of undershirts was raised, no doubt something to do with puberty, body odour, sweat and the like.

Father and son, Samuels Senior and Junior, if you will, were sat side by side at a well-scrubbed kitchen table on which sat a letter over which they poured.

'But Father,' said Son who regretted it almost at once.

'But nothing,' said Father. 'Undershirts must be worn.'

The boy was downcast, it seemed, but having looked once again at the letter, rather rallied.

'Undershirts are not on the list, Father.'

'Show.'

He did.

'It is a comprehensive list, Father.'

Indeed it was:

Shoes, black leather.

Blazer, wool, charcoal grey, with crest.

Shorts, grey, wool. (No longer than 1 inch above the knee.)

Socks, charcoal grey, with crest. (To reach within two inches of knee.)

Garters in school colours, black with yellow chevrons

White shirt, long sleeved, with crest.

School tie in school colours, black with yellow chevrons.

Cap, wool, charcoal grey with crest.

Sports shorts in black with crest.

Sports shirt in black with crest. (Reversible with broad white horizontal stripe.)

All to be acquired from Messrs Krapp and Moore, Gentleman Outfitters.

'Does it specify, you'll forgive me, undershorts?'

'No, Father.'

'And do you infer from that that undershorts should not be worn?'

'Of course not, Father.'

'Of course not Father indeed. I would be hardly likely to send you to any school that condoned the free movement of genitalia.'

It did the boy credit that he didn't snigger.

'Hardly, Father.'

'So; join the dots.' Mr Samuels Senior was always alive to the possibilities of exercising his son's faculty of reason.

'So; undershorts and undershirts are both undergarments and as undershorts are taken as read, so might undershirts,' the boy piped with precision.

'Exactly.'

The boy still looked a little downcast at the prospect of shirt, tie, and woollen blazer being underpinned by a yet further layer. He tried not to show it, but his father's eye was keen. He took to his feet the better to hold forth.

'Son,' he said, 'the undershirt, or vest as I believe some people prefer to call it – although never confuse it with what the Americans refer to as a vest because they are wrong indeed, as wrong as when they refer to trousers as pants. Never make that mistake. Take note of the discrepancy, know which is correct, but be prepared to make proper allowances for those Americans you might come across. They will be few, but they might not be wholly avoidable. There are other words to which the same applies, but we will leave those to another time. Yes, the undershirt is an item of clothing that I believe has fallen out of fashion, a situation, I might add, that further recommends it to me. Worn beneath the shirt it is of course visible in outline, unless one is wearing the thickest of material, such as wool. I believe that this might well be the grounds for which it has suffered a decline in popularity. Consider those grounds, though, and you will see that they are nothing but vanity and vanity, as we know, is a dangerous condition for anyone in general and for those engaged in our line of work in particular. Beware of vanity, my son, as I have impressed upon you on more than one occasion. So, we can dismiss the grounds based on what might be termed aesthetics; simple vanity. I have heard another objection, and perhaps this is the one that exercises you now. That it is too hot to wear a further layer of clothing, i.e. the undershirt. Do we hear the same of the undershorts, or pants, if you prefer? No. There are considerations that make the undershort – an extra layer of clothing, mind — a necessity within polite society. Chaffing, for one. I shall not dwell. Now, as your own logic so well demonstrated not a moment ago, undershorts and undershirts are both undergarments and so what might be true for one should be true for the other. So, if undershorts provide a level of comfort, might we not expect the undershirt to do the same? Now, follow me carefully, I do not claim that the comfort benefits of the two items are the same. That would be ridiculous because the undershort and undershirt are deployed on different parts of the body and so entail different conditions and considerations. But the principle — the *principle* — holds true. The particular comfort of the undershirt lies in the realm of temperature. Obviously, an extra layer of clothing, especially one which traps air close to the body, is a natural boon in cold weather. Hot weather, such as we now endure, does not negate the comforts, but reveals a further property of the undershirt; it soaks up the sweat. This in itself is desirable, as I am sure you will agree that no one wants to see sweat marks all across someone's torso. Yet, there is a further benefit. As the undershirt traps the sweat close to the body, so the evaporation of the sweat is also kept close to the body, and, as this evaporation of sweat is the body's natural cooling system, one actually is kept cooler with an undershirt than without.'

Mr Samuels had worn a vest ever since, come rain or shine. In turn, he had tried to impress the benefits of the vest on his own boy, but had failed. If the school couldn't even muster a proper shirt, what hope was there for the vest? None.

Where was the boy? Perhaps Mr Samuels should have asked but something told him that now was not yet the time.

fifteen

I had a pleasant morning in the garden. That'll teach me.

It was early, so the sun had not had time to become the bastard it invariably is, day on day. Light glanced off the water and algae of the pool as dragon flies flitted about. Very nice. Birds chirruped, as they are wont to do. A pigeon flew down to drink the rancid water, spied me, then took flight, its wings making a high creaking noise. I put this down to a pigeon with a dodgy wing, but then a second flew down to slake its thirst and again the same creaks could be heard. More like squeaks, perhaps, but definitely coming from the act of flight, for when it settled and I could admire its pretty collar and subtle colours the noise stopped, and when it took flight inevitably the sound returned. Now, I am no expert on pigeons, but not being an expert on something is no barrier to banging on about it, so bang on I did, in my head. Actually, the more expert someone is, the less likely it seems to me that they are to bang on about it. If I were an expert in pigeon anatomy – and surely such people exist, like the pigeon fanciers of years gone by, to mention only them, or some dedicated ornithological specialist who has spent years in lab and in the field studying pigeons to the betterment of pigeons and mankind alike – I would just say 'the noise of pigeon wings is because of X', where X would be a precise formulation that would brook no argument and around which a consensus of pigeon specialists would gather. Unless of course, some maverick pigeon specialist were to pipe up and say 'that man and his X is talking pure nonsense; the reason is definitely Y' and then a battle would ensue between the X camp and the Y camp, and some loony would no doubt say 'but M is the answer' and then the X and Y camps would band together to utterly destroy the M heresy before turning their attentions once again upon each other until X was proved or Y was proved and simplicity could reign once more. So, a burst of banging on every now and again but with a tendency towards saying little or nothing, preferably.

I, on the other hand, have no expertise whatsoever so am free to say anything I like, if only to myself. My first thought was to wonder whether the sound of a pigeon in flight was a new thing. I'm quite sure that there have been pigeons in my past, but, until that moment in the garden, I hadn't been aware of the creaks. Yes, yes, this probably says more about me than it does about pigeons, but the possibility occurred to me that perhaps this was some new mutation designed to give a pigeon an edge over silent ones. Take parrots, for instance. They don't go chattering in broken English in the wild, but learn to do so when some dotty old maid dangles a peanut and says 'Pretty Polly, Pretty Polly' often enough through the bars of its decorative cage. Yet I couldn't imagine what advantage was gained. Is a creaking pigeon in flight advertising itself, perhaps? 'Look at me, here I come with my fine creaking wings; a sure sign of health and vitality if ever there was one.' Procreation raises its head. It would have to be something of that order, I suppose. But then I thought, perhaps it is just a mistake, that pigeons are made badly in some way, that their joints are so poorly designed that a creak is just the sign of a thoroughly botched job on someone's part, nature's, no doubt. Doesn't seem to do pigeons any harm, mind you, as they seem to be everywhere, if memory serves or if my garden is anything to go by.

About pigeons cooing, I have no opinion.

So, that passed the time.

I then worried about the flies that bothered me as I contemplated the pigeons. Now, flies are a given. Where one is, there are flies, on the arm, the leg, the mouth, or, if they are really lucky, the eye. If pigeons are everywhere, then flies are much more so. I tolerate them as best I can, letting them settle on me for as long as I can bear, unless they settle on the eye or thereabouts. I am sensitive about my eyes, it seems, but couldn't give a damn about my legs unless the fly is a biting type and action has to be taken. But, I wondered, why do I attract them at all? I might not emit the perfumes of Araby, but I don't smell like shit or a rotting corpse. At least I don't think I do. No doubt bits of me are rotting, I thought, for example the oddly dry and yet also damp skin between my toes which seems to be in a constant state of corruption. Yes, I thought, perhaps I am rotting from the bottom up and the head will be the last to go. Yet the flies were not overly drawn to that area – I was barefooted – and that wouldn't account for the love of the eye and mouth, unless those areas somehow exuded the scent of decay. This I could readily believe. So maybe the flies that alighted on my limbs and torso – for I was also bare-chested – were the less fortunate ones. They had to settle for settling on the body when the eyes and mouth were the prime locations, as it were. I further wondered what they thought they were about when they alighted. Was I food, or a place to lay eggs? If I allowed a fly to linger long enough, would I find in time a batch of maggots crawling out of me? Somehow, I doubted it, and if they fly was hoping to lay eggs in me, I pitied them, for all their efforts would have been in vain. In the end, though, I decided it was more likely to be food, which begged the question of why they mistook me for carrion or shit, if mistook me they did. Was it not rather I that mistook them? I thought flies ate carrion and shit but, not being an expert, was I sure that this was the case, or invariably the case? Would they not, perhaps, be drawn by salt, for example, which no doubt covered my body given the actions of sweat and its evaporation in this intolerable climate? I was a walking salt-pan, or lick, open to all the flies to plunder as they liked.

So, that also passed the time.

If there had been lilies I probably would have considered them too, but there weren't, so there you go.

By this stage, the sun had defeated me and I beat a hasty retreat. The garden had been pleasant, and then it became unpleasant. So it goes.

Would a goat help with the fly problem or make it worse? Would the goat and the shit of the goat be so alluring that I would be left alone, or would it just mean all the more flies to go around? Perhaps I should add a swarm of Praying Mantis or a host of Chameleons to my imaginary menagerie and nurture a Venus fly trap and perhaps a few of those bucket-type plants into which flies and the like are lured, trapped and juiced.

Instead, I was offered a dog.

George must have slipped in whilst I had been out in the garden, for on returning to the kitchen, there he was, as large as life.

'My friend!' he said. I let this go. 'Letter for you' as he dropped this to the counter, 'and a little surprise.'

'I don't like surprises.'

'Everyone likes surprises.' This was immediately refuted to my mind as George seemed surprised by my not liking surprises and hurt by the thought. I might have raised an eyebrow, but didn't push the point. 'You'll love it.'

He went into the body of the house and I stood expecting my surprise. To be fair to him, I was surprised, but to be fair to me I still didn't like it, for when he remerged he held what can only be described as a puppy in his arms. Don't ask me what breed. I have no idea. It was a dog, and that was enough for me. It wriggled in George's arms and made to lick his face or bite it, perhaps. To bite, I understood; to lick, I did not. George made some sort of high-pitched exclamations based around the idea that the dog was a little man, and a little guy, rubbed its head, then placed it on the floor. It went snuffling off at speed, cramming its nose into every corner of the kitchen as rapidly as possible as if rapt by an orgy of smells.

I suppose I should describe the thing, but it would only amount in the end to the fact that this was a dog or, if one were to be nice about it, a young dog. It was not a goat.

I was speechless. This gave George his chance.

'Now, I know what you're thinking,' which he patently did not for at that moment I was cursing our ancient ancestors for letting a bunch of wolves snuggle by the fire.

'Martha, mate! She's so worried about you, I can't tell you!' which always seems to mean that one is about to be told, regardless. 'She said to me, she said "he sees no one? All on his own in that great big house? Just you to look in on him from time to time? No wonder he wants a goat! But what he wants is a dog; it'll keep him company, get him out walking," and stuff, you know? Good for you. "No one wants a goat, not really," she said, just saying what she said, you know? "I mean what can you do with a goat," she said. "The poor man," she said. She was beside herself, I can tell you. Up half the night worrying about you, rattling about in this place and never going out.

'Call me a softy,' he said – the thought hadn't crossed my mind – 'but I can't stand to see her worrying like that and, you know what, it got me thinking, "She might have something there, 'cause who actually wants a goat, I mean! Dog might be the thing, and who doesn't love a dog about the place?" Eh?'

By this stage the hound was making its way towards me, nose first.

'Now, you won't believe this. There I was thinking that a dog might be the thing and I get a call – straight out of the blue – and it's Mike; cousin Mike, well Martha's second cousin Mike and he says to me, he says "hear you're in the market for a dog. I've got a beauty, yours for nothing, just need it taking off my hands." Now, you can't ignore a chance like that, can you? It's like the Universe or summat telling you to get a dog, in't it? Like Karma. So I said to Mike, "Mike mate, let me take it round and see what he says," so here we are.'

It was snuffling at my foot, oblivious to the rest of me. Perhaps I had a look of disdain, because George then applied the real pressure.

'Thing is, Mike says to me if you don't want it he'll have to…, you know.'

I didn't.

'Get rid of it.'

I thought that had been the plan all along. Perhaps I shrugged.

'As in…' said George

'As in?'

'Take it to a farm,' with a skewing of the eyes.

'That sounds nice,' I said.

'No. A farm,' and he flapped two sets of fingers in the air for reasons that were beyond me.

The animal had moved on to the other foot, which was just as engrossing.

'As in…' and here George drew his thumb across his neck and made a rather odd, guttural creak.

'Oh,' I said.

'Yep,' he said.

The animal was now licking my foot, trying to shove its tongue between my toes.

'But it's up to you,' and here George flapped his arms up and down. He was full of gestures, it seemed. 'If it was up to me…' He was no less full of an inability to finish a sentence, it seemed.

'But it is not,' I said.

'No,' he said. 'Martha's allergic.'

'So it is me or death?'

'That's about the size of it.'

I looked down at the mutt and, for the first time, it looked up at me with its great brown eyes, as if to melt my heart. I did not feel it melting in any way. Nor hardening, to be fair. Just beating away as normal. Me or death did not then and does not now seem like much of a choice, but then why should a dog be blessed with options when I, for one, was not? Me or death is precisely the situation I find myself in everyday, after all. The dog seemed to have had enough of me and took itself off to piss against the fridge. Copious amounts. George watched it, and I watched it as great streams of the stuff began to yellow the floor.

'Well, he needs training,' said George, 'but what's a little piss, eh? Least it's not carpet.'

Thoroughly relieved, the dog shot off out of the kitchen and in to the innards of the house. We gave chase, of sorts, and found ourselves in the living room, which was indeed carpeted. George looked alarmed and ran around the place trying to get hold of the pup, and I thought he was alarmed at the thought of the carpet. Perhaps not, though, because I began to notice that there was something not quite right about the room. The great portrait of Paul still hung above the disused fireplace and maybe that demanded my attention for a while, but I soon could not ignore the sense that the room was somehow emptier. True, it had been a while since I'd been in it, and my memory is not what it was, but I was sure that it had once had more furniture. It's not like I'd ever done an itinerary of the place but the feeling I had was a strong one.

'Is there something missing?' I asked George as he chased after the dog, breathing heavily.

'What?'

'Is there something missing from the room?'

'Like what?' as he lunged for the beast.

It was a good question and one I couldn't answer. Like something; something that had been there that was no longer there.

'You little rascal,' said George holding up the dog triumphantly. He slid open the French doors, chucked it into the garden, and slid the door shut again. It scratched at the glass before getting distracted by a fly which it snapped at unsuccessfully. So no hope of help from that front.

'Shit! The piss!'

George shot off in the reverse direction that the dog had shot off at not moments before, leaving me standing in the room that looked as it had always done but did not feel as it had always done, well, when Paul and Cass had been in residence at least. Maybe the difference I felt was just their mark fading away; their aura diminishing or somesuch. Or, as I suspected, that some furniture was quite simply missing.

George was mopping and cursing. He stopped the cursing when he became aware of me. 'Just a little mop, and it's just like new. No bother at all.' Nonchalantly he enquired, 'Go into that room much?'

'Never,' I said.

This seemed to lighten his load.

'Probably best,' he said. 'That white carpet won't stand a chance with a pup. Then there's the sofa. He'll be nibbling at that in no time.'

The carpet and sofa meant nothing to me.

'Has it been done?'

'Has what been done?'

'The dog.'

'Done?'

'You know.'

'No.'

'Neutered.'

'What?'

'Snipped.'

'Snipped?'

I would have to call a spade a spade.

'Castrated,' I said.

'Castrated!' And he fell against his mop for support, overwhelmed, I assume, by the thought. 'You want to cut his balls off?'

'Isn't that what one does with a puppy, in the end?'

'Oh my god! You can't cut his bits off! It'll ruin him. Won't be a proper dog at all. He'll get fat. He'll lose his instincts. He'd just be useless. Jesus. It's just cruel, that's what it is; just cruel.'

I kept my counsel for a fair while.

'I'll keep him,' I said, but I will get him done, I thought. Castrated but alive seemed fair enough to me.

I don't know why I said I would keep him, but once something is said it cannot be unsaid.

sixteen

'Don't be shy now. Whip out the little man and I'll whip out the little bugger.'

Mr Samuels was disconcerted by this on a number of levels. Firstly, he feared that 'little man' was a reference to his genitalia in general and his penis in particular. Secondly, he feared that the 'little bugger' referred to the catheter tube and that 'whip out' implied quite a sharp, and no doubt painful, extraction of said tube. But most of all, Mr Samuels was disconcerted by this utter stranger who had appeared beside his bed, roused him from sleep with a shake, and declared an imminent procedure.

The man was large. To Mr Samuels' well-trained eye, he was over 6 feet and 15 stone. Mr Samuels had never got used to the metric system when it came to a person's height and weight. When it came to things, he thought metrically and was happy to do so. He never bought a pound of apples, but always a half kilo. He checked his speed in km/h and never mph. He looked at a garden wall to be scaled, as sometimes they had to be scaled in his line of work, and thought to himself, 1 metre 20. But he could never look at man and think to himself, 175cm and 80 kilograms. His brain could not do it and would not accept it and another part of his brain railed against the fact that this was so.

How nice to have numbers rather than words for a change!

Whilst the man was large, his voice was not. It was loud, but oddly high, as if an operatic diva had been inserted into his bulky frame.

Having parsed what the man had said, he deduced that he must be a doctor. He soon downgraded this to a mere hope as the man was not dressed in a manner to induce confidence. He wore what I believe is termed an Hawaiian shirt, full of palm fronds and gaudy parrots and at least one bikini-clad maiden. He further wore shorts with a profusion of bulging pockets and a camouflage motif. Sunglasses were propped up on his head, which was shaved and apparently polished to a high sheen. His nose was red with sunburn, as were his cheeks, or perhaps it was not so much sunburn as alcohol.

'You have me at an advantage,' said Mr Samuels, which seemed to be becoming quite a favourite opening gambit.

'Yeah, but I won't take advantage of you. Scout's honour.'

The man's laugh was a wheezing cackle that gave way to a coughing fit that doubled him up for a moment or two. He banged his chest, made an alarming noise in his throat, swallowed, then declared that 'That got it.'

In Mr Samuels' experience, male doctors came in two varieties: the obese and the funereal. They either looked as if they were about to explode or expire. He had never known a healthy looking one. He wasn't foolish enough to think that this meant all doctors fell into these two groups, but nor was he foolish enough to dismiss empirical evidence. This man fell into the obese category and his apparent ill-health Mr Samuels soon put down to high living. It's understandable. You spend your entire working life dealing with those little, middling and massive signs of mortality on a daily basis, so you think sod it, might as well go out with a bang, and so indulge in every unhealthy practice known to medical science, and even some that are not. Mr Samuels understood this, but he did not condone it, not for a moment.

'Look mate,' said the man as he sat himself down on the bed beside the prone Samuels, 'no point beating around the bush. Let's just unplug you then I'll give you a quick once over and that'll be that.'

'I trust you won't mind my asking,' said Mr Samuels, 'but are you a medical professional?'

The man cackled again but stopped short of a fit.

'Depends, don't it.'

Mr Samuels rather thought that it didn't.

'Depends on your definition.'

'Are you actually a doctor?'

'Ah, mate,' said the man, 'thereby hangs a tale and no mistake.' The man looked wistfully off into the middle distance. What he saw there, Mr Samuels could only imagine.

'But don't you worry. Might not be up to heart surgery these days, but I still know how to whip a tube outta dick.'

Mr Samuels was not comforted by this, and was further discomforted when the man produced a syringe, as if out of nowhere.

'Come on, get those jammies off and we'll crack on.'

Mr Samuels demurred.

'Look, mate, I've seen it all, me. Dicks in all states of disrepair. Flaky dicks, wonky dicks, dicks with sores running pus all over the place. Bollocks the size of balloons, too. Nope; there's not a dodgy dick known to man that I haven't seen. Severed dick, once, as it happens. Poor bugger.'

Mr Samuels was in something of a quandary. He wanted the catheter to be removed, for obvious reasons, but also because he still thought that escape, if necessary, would be easier without it. Yet he was not enthusiastic about this man being the agent of his liberation. The more the man talked, the more concerned Mr Samuels became on this point. Yes, he was on the horns of a dilemma, or thereabouts.

The man waggled the syringe and leered.

Mr Samuels eyed the needle and wished he knew exactly the role it was to play.

'Over in a jiffy,' said the man

Mr Samuels did not move.

'Fucks' sake man, get a grip!'

Was it this appeal to his masculinity that moved Mr Samuels? Perhaps. He cautiously lowered his pyjama bottoms and raised his eyes to the ceiling. He felt some pressure as the syringe was inserted but he was pleased it was not inserted into him. Into what it had been inserted he couldn't say. He felt a little queer; the sensations in his nether regions were not ones he could identify, not having felt them before, but relief, yes, relief was among them.

'The bag you can do yourself.'

'Is that it?'

'Yep.?

It didn't amount to much in the end, in truth.

'How does it look?' asked Mr Samuels?

'Penis Intacta, mate; penis bloody intacta.'

The man then examined the knife wound, in a rather perfunctory way thought Mr Samuels.

'Yep; that's all coming along nicely. Nice job that. Gotta blow your own trumpet, eh? No bugger else will.'

'So you have ministered to me all this time?'

'Ministered might be pushing it,' said the man. 'Patched you up and plugged you in is about the size of it.'

'And kept me sedated?'

'All part of the service. Oh yeah, about that; you might feel a bit itchy but that'll go soon enough.'

Mr Samuels had suspected as much.

'And who am I to thank for all this? I really would like to thank you properly, if I may.'

The man looked at him narrowly for a moment, then his eyes widened, as did his mouth into a grin as he offered his hand. 'Reggie,' he said.

'Reggie…?'

'Reggie's all your getting.'

'Reginald, thank you.'

'Reggie,' said Reggie. 'No one calls me that other thing. Not since,' and here again he stared off into the middle distance.

'I'm off,' as he came back from his reverie and headed for the door.

'Know what,' as he stood at the threshold, 'thanks for the thanks. No thanks any more in this business. You'd think they'd be grateful, but no. Well, not since… It's just here's your money, now fuck off. Not like when I was on the wards. Then it was all like "Doctor, it's a miracle, how can I ever thank you!" Then when I suggested a couple of possibilities, they struck me off. Fuckers. Do people even know what gratitude is these days? Fucked if I know.'

He turned to the door again, but threw a last comment over his hefty shoulder.

'Look out for that one, if I were you, and look after number one.'

The removal of piss-bag proper was the work of a moment.

Dressed as was his custom, Mr Samuels considered that there was a distinct lack of peril. Lurking apprehension, which in a lesser man might have been an intimation of impending doom, was about as intense a feeling as Mr Samuels could detect in his situation, at least as it presented itself to him. Yes, he had been stabbed and poisoned – but by whom was still unclear. Yes, he had been sedated and catheterised – but whether for ill or good was still uncertain.

Yes, his son was being kept in an unknown location – but to what end was still undetermined.

He steeled himself to bring things to a head, and so buttoned up his jacket accordingly.

Mr Samuels did not care for confrontation, considering it to be a failure of more subtle means. But when push came to shove, and options crumbled left and right, it was a path he was willing to tread.

'Madam,' he would say, 'do not think I am ungrateful for all that you have done for me and my son during what must have been precarious times that needed all due delicacy and tact, and not a little planning. I realise that, without your intervention, my situation would have been considerably worse and that of my son possibly no less so. Yet, Madam,' he would say, 'and I hope you will forgive my being so direct in the matter, but as one professional to another, as one skilled practitioner, shall we say, to another, there are a number of issues on which I feel I must insist on a few crucial clarifications. I see you are a little surprised,' he was going to say this whether she was surprised or not and he rather suspected she would not be given the admirable control she had over her face, 'and I surprise myself, I might add. Yet, needs must and I do not use the word insist lightly, but I do use the word, Madam; I most certainly do.

'Now, if you could clarify the following, I would be much obliged:

'One. Am I free to leave?

'Two. Where is my son?

'Three. Is he in any danger? Am I in any danger? Two points, I know, but intimately connected, I am sure you will allow.

'Four. If he or I are in any danger, from whom and for what reason? A hypothetical question, I realise, but I lay out all the points from the beginning in order best to understand each other.

'I await your replies, which again, please forgive me Madam, I must insist upon.'

Unfortunately, this never happened. He went to the veranda; The Woman was not there. He went into the kitchen; again empty and with no sign of recent use. He systematically went from room to room, scoured the garden and inspected the driveway; nobody and nothing.

Mr Samuels scratched himself as he pondered in the shade of the veranda with the birds scuttering over the sky and the thrum of a thousand insects filling the air.

It is now that the journey of Mr Samuels begins. About bloody time.

seventeen

The letter had not slipped from my mind. Well, it had slipped from my mind, but then it had slipped back in. It had slipped from my mind because of the shock of the dog and the unease I felt about the living room. It had slipped back in when I saw it once more on the counter where George had placed it.

First the dog demanded my attention. He was scratching at the door and whining to be let in. Mad dogs and Englishmen, apparently, so at least this dog wasn't insane. A gust of hot air accompanied him into the kitchen. I found a bowl, filled it with water from the tap, and set it before him. He launched at it before lapping at it desperately. Such a noise.

The handwriting on the envelope alone told me it was from Cass. That, and the fact that it was a letter. Whereas the post-card had been in purple ink, the letter was in green.

The dog stopped lapping and started pawing at the water, for reasons best known to himself.

After a preamble that I failed to understand, she wrote:

'I am stuck. Ensnared and engrossed within the sublunary world. Shackled to the false real when I could be wandering happy amidst the true forms. I have tried so hard to move through the veil but something is holding me back. All that Gaia nonsense only helped to set me back further, my Guide tells me. It made me even more chained to the earth when it is the earth that I need to be unchained from. Thank God I got away from that charlatan before the damage was too great. A lucky escape. But that was just a symptom, a sign of how deeply I need to de-gross myself, to move through the veil and to realign myself with the right.'

Admittedly, I also failed to understand this, but at least it was in an English of sorts.

'My Guide tells me I must resolve things on this plane before I can hope to ascend to the next level. He was holding my foot at the time and found a lump on the ball. A tight, hard, lump. A sign, he said, of a lasting tension and a lasting connection to the false real of this world. The feet, you see, are the true windows of the soul. Not the eyes as so many wrongly believe. It is the feet that anchor us to this world and where the battle to free ourselves is most keenly felt. That is why my Guide spends at least 3 hours a day standing on his head. Oh, I wish you could see him! Like a column of pure spirit! Reversing the polarity, he calls it. I can't stand on my head yet, but I will one day, dear, if only I can shake off these shackles. It is not a question of strength or balance he says. It's not a question of the body at all. It is a matter of the mind. Free your mind, he says, and the feet will follow and will point you to the sphere of forms. All I can manage at the moment is a half hour or so on my back with my legs above my head. It is so frustrating! But frustration, he says, is a pointless attachment to the false real. It's just a trick to tie me down, to keep my feet on the ground, when my energy could be flipping me over and showing me the way. I feel the energy within me and it has a colour. It is green. A bright green, like a new leaf. He says that this is a good sign and that makes me happy, but then he tells me off for being happy like that because it is a false happiness. It is not coming only from within. It is connected to another body, you see, and that is error upon error. I mean, he says I'm happy because he approves of my energy colour and I shouldn't care if he likes my energy colour at all. It is my energy colour, and that is all I should care about.

'He says I have been doing really well. I was really good at the two week toe-wriggle retreat and I can even splay my toes apart now and, if I feel the energy properly and focus on the green, I can wriggle each toe in turn. You see, we have to master feet before we can redirect them. Step by step, he says, and then we laugh. For half an hour, making sure we laugh not only from the diaphragm but all the way down to the soles of our feet. So freeing. I'm good at that too, he tells me. It took me a while to get used to the toe-sucking. It is natural, he said, at first to be put off by the idea but that is only because of our false perception, our false separation. By bringing mouth and toe together, we complete the circle. I can't suck my own toes yet, so for the time being I suck his toes and he sucks mine at the same time and that way I get to unity through him. He is so selfless!

'But if I am to suck my own toes and stand on my head, I must be prepared to let go totally. That's my problem, he says, and that's why I'm stuck at this engrossed level.

'So, this letter is my saying that I shan't be back. I cannot worry about you either, and you mustn't worry about me or think about me at all. You worrying keeps me ensnared, he says, and so does my worrying about you. To kick myself free of this world, he says, I must kick myself free of all the ties in my life. This letter will not be enough, I know, but it is a start I have to make, he says. Just because I won't be worrying about you or thinking about you doesn't mean I don't care about you. In fact, it means I care all the more because I am giving you the gift of breaking those emotional shackles that bind you to the false real too. So, not caring is true caring and the end of loving is the beginning of true loving.

'Trust your feet and step into truth.

'Cassandra-Podia.'

I had managed to concentrate on the letter despite the fact that the dog had been licking his arse throughout. Not that the concentration did me any good. Well, it perhaps did me some good, because I was left with the impression that Cass would not return. That she might return was possible, but, for the moment, she was determined not to return. That was about the size of it. What I was meant to do with this information I was unsure, but it was nice to be told.

The other thing I was left with was the laughing. I pulled myself up to my full height and ha-ha-ed. This had no discernible effect, other than to stop the dog licking. I ha-ha-ed again; nothing. I took a deep breath and let out a string of ha-has. This left me dizzy. Was that the point? I rallied, and ha-ha-ed for a good minute or so, and the only effect of this was that the dog started to howl. He howled and I ha-ha-ed.

In fairness, I have spent worse minutes. I'm not sure I can say the same for the dog, for he returned to his arse-licking at his earliest convenience. Or maybe it was his balls, such as they were. Or his penis, such as it was. I don't know. Arse, balls, penis; what does it matter? He seemed happy enough.

It was not a Friday. I am quite sure it was not a Friday, which doesn't mean it wasn't a Friday, of course, only that I was quite sure it wasn't a Friday. It was being sure that made the sudden appearance of Marina a surprise. What a day of surprises; first the dog, and now the woman. She came bursting in to the kitchen in a flap, it is fair to say, all breathless and flushed. She rushed to a drawer, took out a tea-towel, dragged a stool into the corner of the room and started to climb on top. This did not go unnoticed by the dog. He leapt up, leaving balls, arse and penis be for the time being, and leapt around yapping in a most excited manner. On top of the stool, she draped the tea-towel over something or another which was wedged between wall and ceiling. She leapt down, grabbed another tea-towel from the drawer, dragged the stool to an opposite corner and repeated the operation.

A word about the drawers. They have no handles. Why they have no handles, I cannot say, but they don't. This had given me no little trouble in the early days, for back then not only could I not find the fridge I could not see any drawers. I reasoned that there must be drawers and cupboards and the like, what with it being a kitchen and everything, but I couldn't see any. It was only when I happened to lean against a counter before pushing myself back upright with my lower back that a drawer appeared. It hissed open as if of its own volition. It took me sometime to realise what had happened and to make sure I wasn't mistaken I went around the kitchen gently pushing at the blank surfaces beneath the counters to see if they too would open. I had mixed success, but what success there was revealed that the kitchen did indeed have quite a number of drawers and cupboards, as indeed a kitchen should. So, no banging or the like accompanied Marina as drawers were opened and shut; only a slight exhalation, of sorts.

From her vantage point on top of her stool in the corner, she scanned the room with frankly frantic eyes.

'Morning,' I said.

'Sssh,' she hissed.

The dog was jumping around the foot of her stool, barking and snuffling turn and turnabout. She didn't shush the dog.

'Can I …?'

'Sssh,' she said. She put a finger to her lips and then used the same finger to tap her ear. She stood atop the stool in rapt attention.

'Is there…?'

She held out her palm towards me and froze. I froze too, not knowing what else to do. The dog did not freeze; he had started to chew the leg of the stool. It wobbled, but Marina remained a statue, albeit a statue on a dodgy plinth. Remarkable balance. She stood stock still for some time before descending, grabbing me by the arm, and dragging me out into the heat of the garden.

'It's safe here,' she whispered. 'Least I think it is!'

She dragged me further away from the house, thankfully to the shade of a large tree, of god knows what type.

'What on earth...?' I said. She stopped me short by placing her finger to my lips.

'Not so loud! I don't know if he can hear us out here too.' Again she cast about wildly, looking for I didn't know what.

Panic suited her, in a way. It brought a flash to her eyes and a colour to her cheeks. She pulled me further into the garden and only felt safe when a bush hid us from the house. Bees swarmed about its pretty, multi-coloured flowers, giving a nice drone beneath Marina's whispers.

'He sees everything and hears everything, you know.'

I asked the obvious.

'George.'

'George George?'

'Everything. Cameras all over the house, watching you all the time.'

I was about to ask her how she knew, but she saved me the bother, which was nice of her.

'He told me. Threatened me with the sack. Said he'd got you and me on film talking and that that was a sackable offense. Said he should sack me there and then, that he would sack me there and then if I didn't do what he wanted.

'I can't lose this job, I can't! How would I live? I can barely pay the rent as it is!'

'Now, now,' I said, patting her on the arm. Least I could do.

There was a hiatus whilst she wept a little. The dog urinated against a tree, then chased after a fly. The bees flitted from flower to flower. A pigeon creaked overhead.

'Look,' she said, but I rather think she meant 'listen' because she sucked up her tears, lowered her head and lowered her voice still further. 'He wants me to tell on you. Tell him everything you get up to when I'm around. Ask you stuff about him. "Get the low-down on him." That's what he said. But I don't know anything, do I? That's what I told him. I come, I clean, we've chatted twice, and that's it. Nothing to know. So then he asks me about what goes on in your bedroom-office, room thingy. "Nothing," I said, because all I do is pick up your dirty clothes and give the bathroom the once over. I don't go rooting around the place, I swear. Anyway, he wants to know what you get up to in there, what you write, he says. Do you write anything?'

'A little,' I said. 'Nonsense, mainly.'

'So there's nothing to know, and that's what I told him. Thing is, he hasn't got cameras in there I don't think. Else why would he be asking me, see?'

Impeccable logic, I thought. Swift of mind and small of frame.

'So, I didn't say no, not exactly anyway, and I defo didn't say yes. I don't know what else I could have done and keep my job. But then he says there might be other ways I can help him if I wanted to keep my job, and then he gave me such a look! I can't tell you!'

Indeed, she couldn't for the tears came again, but thicker and faster now. I feared for her breathing. I patted her arm again, but this did nothing. I may have stroked her hair. It's unlikely, but I've seen it done and might have thought it would have helped. If I did stroke her hair, that would have been the full repertoire of consolatory gestures. Obviously, these were not enough as she threw her arms around me and buried her head in my chest. She sobbed.

What was a man to do? The dog was equally bewildered.

eighteen

If Mr Samuels were a crow, he would have immediately headed north east. Roughly. Perhaps north north east, or north east east. But, not being a crow, Mr Samuels thought better of this. If he had headed that way, earth-bound as he was, it would have meant enduring the mountains and valleys of the interior; an interior that was blessed with few people and fewer settlements of any size. In fairness to Mr Samuels, the thought never crossed his mind as his mind was crossed by more pressing, more practical considerations.

In truth, I envy Mr Samuels his mind.

These considerations were as follows:

A) How most quickly to find his way home,

B) How to do so without detection,

C) Given A+B, how best to plot a course that would allow him to make best progress and to access the resources he would no doubt need whilst not exposing himself too much.

This amounted to an issue of people and places, which makes a change, does it not? And things, a little bit. There they are again.

Of course, Mr Samuels being Mr Samuels and his mind being his mind, he immediately seized all this without actually needing to think it through. Indeed, all this had been settled by the time he unbolted the front gate and gained the road beyond. It had been shaded by trees until lately, as the stumps along the verge attested. Disease, perhaps, or a tenuous grip in the shallow earth had meant they had had to be cut down and any wayfarer would have to make do without the welcome respite from the sun. Low scrubland stretched away beyond the strip of tarmac. It seemed to gently undulate, but Mr Samuels was not fooled for a moment. What looks like an easy enough trek at a distance turns out to be a bastard in the execution. As far as he could see, there was no house or farm or hovel or shack. That didn't mean they weren't there; just that he couldn't see them. Yes, Mr Samuels trusted his senses, but he tempered them with experience and reason. The sea, for example. He couldn't see it, but he knew it was there, somewhere across that scrubland. True, walk far enough in any direction in these parts and you hit the sea, which is also true of Australia now I come to think of it, but that isn't likely to come as any relief to someone abandoned in the midst of the continent with only arid, orange desert as far as the eye can see. Luckily, the sea was not so distant. It was there within reach. A half day's walk, perhaps more, depending on the terrain.

Christ, man; get him on his way!

It shall be recalled that Mr Samuels had heard the sound of bells one previous morning. Church bells, to be precise. They were not tolling now, but Mr Samuels headed towards where he had triangulated they were likely to be, through a process of calculation too tedious to mention. Why I am all of a sudden concerned about tedium, I don't know. He was not so foolish as to approach the direction head on, but took a roundabout route across the scrub and rocks and soft, dry earth of what was a plateau of sorts. After an hour or so, he regretted his jacket, although not his vest nor his brogues, the latter especially as the going was as tough as he had feared. His way was crossed by a white, dirt track which he thought remote enough to be able to take in safety. What a relief to be on solid, packed earth. It was on this track that Mr Samuels had his first piece of luck. Looking over his shoulder, a cloud of dust seemed to be approaching. A car or truck no doubt. He weighed this up, took cover behind a low tree, all gnarled and aged, and watched as a flat-bed truck bumped its way slowly past. Slowly enough for him to see the driver who seemed far to be old to be in charge of anything, let alone a vehicle. And far too small too, for that matter, for his head barely showed over the steering wheel. Mr Samuels' experience of little old men had, on the whole, been positive over the years. They had a habit of cackling for no apparent reason, or of harrumphing under their breath, or of breaking wind without fear of favour, but he had known little or no malice about them. Apart from that one time, of course, when one little old man had hired him to get the dirt on another little old man because of an ancient enmity between them arising from a shared passion for the same girl when they themselves had been just striplings filled with lust and honour. Yes, all those youthful juices had turned to bitter bile and no mistake. It didn't matter that the girl in question had been long dead. But that, reasoned Mr Samuels, had been the exception that proved the rule where little old men were concerned. He watched the truck pass, the dust rise and fall, and then followed.

He soon came across the old man by the side of the road wrangling an enormous goat. Neither man nor goat seemed in the best humour. The little old man and the enormous goat might not have been getting on, but they did see eye-to-eye in terms of height. His horns rose from above his long, dangling ears, and arched in an impressive display of which any goat would have been proud. The issue seemed to be that the little old man wanted the enormous goat to go somewhere that the enormous goat did not want to go. The man was pulling a rope attached to the goat's neck, and the goat was pulling in the opposite direction. A stand-off, with neither man nor goat giving an inch. The sun glared down on them both.

Mr Samuels seized his chance by leaping into action and grabbing the goat by the horns, shouting, lest the little old man were deaf, which he probably was, 'allow me, sir.' The goat quickly apprised the new situation and tried to butt his new foe with all his might, but, in a move that would make a toreador proud, Mr Samuels swung his body out of harm's way whilst keeping a firm grip on the horns. He and the goat were now facing the same direction and

Mr Samuels was in a position to urge the beast forward whilst the little old man pulled the rope. Pulling and shoving, they edged the goat towards the truck. Hooves were dug into the earth and rock to no avail.

'Hold him,' shouted the old man, lest his new friend were deaf, which, as we know, he was not. He lowered the back door of the truck and leapt up onto the bed before pushing out a plank to act as a ramp. He really should have lowered that door and deployed the ramp before he had tried anything with the goat, when you come to think of it, but there you go, he hadn't, and perhaps this was a sign that his faculties were beginning to fail him just a little because he would have been in a right old pickle if he had managed to get the goat to the truck without any way of getting the goat into the truck. He was a lucky man, it seems.

Mr Samuels held the goat by the horns until all was ready and then the pulling and shoving began again as the goat was man-handled up the ramp. The old man tied the rope to the truck, and all was done. He leapt over the side of the bed. He was a spritely little old man. They exist. Mr Samuels rather more sedately lowered himself from the back of the truck.

'He, he, he, he,' said the old man when Mr Samuels joined him. 'He, he, he, he.' Yes, he was indeed a cackler. 'He'll be the death of me! The death of me!' The gravity of the words were belied by the cackling glee with which they were delivered. Perhaps the little old man was very much looking forward to shuffling off this mortal coil sometime soon, and at the hooves and horns of a goat no less.

'He's after the ladies,' he said. 'He can smell them a mile off and no mistake. A little whiff, that's all he needs and then there is just one thing on his mind. Doesn't matter what you say to him, sex – he, he, he -, a bit of rutting, all he cares about. One track mind, that ram. Food? Couldn't care less once he's got a bit of the ladies up his nostrils, let me tell you.'

Mr Samuels looked about for a sign of the said ladies, but he could see no she-goats, nor any other goats at all for that matter, save for the one eyeing him from the back of the truck. Basilisk eyes with letter-box pupils, out-staring him, discomforting him, in truth.

'Oh, let me tell you,' said the little old man, 'I've chased the randy bugger all over,' and here he broke wind; he was ticking all the boxes, 'up and down, miles and miles sometimes. I build a new pen, what does he do? Kicks it to pieces, that's what he does, when he has the urge. Know what I mean? The urge. Kicks it to smithereens. So I catch him, build a new one, and he smashes that one to smithereens. So I catch him again, build a new one again and then he gets the urge again, and he smashes that one to smithereens so then I go and catch him again, build a...'

'Sir, said Mr Samuels, 'would you happen to have drop of water with you that I might have?' He wanted water, it was true, but more urgently he wanted the little old man to stop banging on about the sexual history of his goat.

The little old man reached into the cab of the truck, took a large bottle of water, and handed it over.

'Thing is,' he said, 'I don't mind. Not really. He's only doing what comes natural, at the end of the day, and he's only a goat, to be fair, just a big randy goat with an itch he's got to scratch. In his prime, he is. Yes, he'll bury me yet. But what'll happen then?' Here the little old man grasped Mr Samuels by the arm and tried to look him square in the face, tilting his head back to do so, necessarily, for he was, as has been said, a little old man when push came to shove. 'Who'll look after him then? Who'll come out and catch him and take him home? Who? He'll go wandering off, his blood all up, and who'll care when I'm six feet under, lying next to my Maggie, god rest her soul?'

Mr Samuels thought he saw a tear creep into the old man's eye as he gazed with love at this goat that would outlive him.

'It'd be better just to kill him now, really. Slit his throat and be done with it.'

Mr Samuels looked at the beast, placid now, resigned to the interruption in his amorous wanderings.

'But then I think it'd be better just to let him go. Not chase him all over the place but let him run after the ladies all he likes until he drops down dead. He'd find food enough for long enough I reckon to let him have a few flings. Yeah; there's a few flings left in him yet, a few years of rutting away. I tell you, you should see him at it!'

The thought of a long drawn out description of the goat at it, spurred Mr Samuels to ask, 'I know this is an awful imposition, but could you possibly give me a lift to the nearest town? If it is not out of your way, of course?'

'Don't do towns,' said the old man, grumpily perhaps because he had been cut short just as he was about to launch into the details of the goat at it. 'Not since the boy buggered off. Broke my Maggie's heart.'

'A village, then, perhaps?'

'I do my village. Let the goat gallivant about; I stay put. Now, anyway. Let me tell you, though, I did a fair bit of gallivanting too, in my day, before Maggie, mind. Oh yes. He, he, he! Little terror, I was. No girl safe for miles around! Called me the terrier they did, always yapping around the girls, and quick up a hole, if you know what I mean! Wush! Rat up a drainpipe, me. Had half the dads of the district wanting to string me up, just like Boris here,' and he jerked his head towards the goat. 'Two of a kind, aren't we Boris? Before my Maggie, mind. Not so much as put a foot off the straight and narrow since I first clapped eyes on her, seems like yesterday. Mousey little thing she was – well, that suited me just fine; not like I'm a six footer! He, he, he! No, she was just the size for me and I was just the size for her. Two peas in a pod; that's what we were;

two peas in a pod. I said to myself, "no more mucking about lad; she's the one for you!" And you know what? I was right. Couldn't be more right. I was as right as a man can be. Never met a righter man in all my days.'

'So, your village? Could you take me there, perhaps?'

'Nothing easier. I owe you one anyway, what with Boris and all. Besides, not really dressed for being out here, roaming about, are you?'

Indeed, he was not.

'That's town clobber, that is. No use up here at all. Right, hop in then.'

The old truck, its suspension shot, trundled along the white track.

'Married yourself, then?' Shouted the little old man over the din of the engine.

'I fear not,' said Mr Samuels.

'Young lad like you? Sharp dresser, too! Get yourself a Maggie, man! That's my advice. Not that there are any more Maggies, mind. Unless,' he glanced sidewise at Mr Samuels whilst letting go a high-pitched fart, 'unless you like playing the field, eh? He, he, he! Footloose and fancy free! Girl in every port, is it?'

Mr Samuels gave a thin smile.

The village, thankfully, crept into view and, in time, the truck pulled alongside a low, shack-like homestead on the outskirts.

I miss my old hovel. This one was like that, I fancy, but out in the country rather than snug in the town.

'Come in, son, come in,' said the little old man.

Mr Samuels demurred.

'For a moment.'

Further demurral.

'Take a breather.'

Mr Samuels declined.

'Have a beer to set you up!'

Mr Samuels regretted that he could not.

'Wash the dust and goat off yourself, at least!'

Mr Samuels reassured the little old man that that would not be necessary.

'Put your feet up for a mo. Give yourself a break. Have a nap. Rest your eyes. Take a load off. Gird your loins. Have a bite to eat. Do yourself a favour. Gather yourself together. Refresh yourself. Take it easy. Have a natter. Have a chinwag. Cup of tea? Shot of coffee? Something stronger? No good rushing off. No point going off half cock.'

Mr Samuels remained politely resolute.

'Cunt,' said the little old man.

'Oh, yes,' he said, 'I know your type, with your suit and your shoes and your city ways, looking down on the likes of me and my goat, looking down on an honest home with some honest beer and some honest grub. Not good enough for you, is it? You know why you haven't got a Maggie? I'll tell you why you haven't got a Maggie! Poncing around in your fancy shoes, never doing a day's work in your whole life, that's why. Never up at the crack of dawn, scratching at the soil, following the herd, roasting in the sun 'til you flop down like a dead man at the end of the day. Look, look at these hands, ya bastard. Look at this face! Nah, nah. You with your central heating and your air-conditioning and your cars bigger than this house and your fancy restaurants and your flighty whores, riding you for your money. That's the truth of it, innit? My goat, my

Boris, least he's honest. Knows what he wants, and they want it too. You lot? All about the money! Now fuck off. Fuck off out of here, you posh city git.'

There are some comments that do not brook discussion.

nineteen

Marina thought it best, once the sobs had subsided, to quit the scene. It was not a Friday and given it was not a Friday her presence would have been suspicious. So she reasoned. She would be back in the morning as usual, but not for the usual. So, it was a Thursday. She slipped out by the back gate leaving me and the dog to weigh our options as best we could. He was better at this than me, because he quickly decided to apply himself to his balls once again.

No, the usual would no longer be the usual. A new usual would have to ensue, when I had only just got used to the newest usual. There had been too much action for my liking, too much change, too many events. Putting aside all those events that led to me fetching up in this mausoleum of a mansion, since that time, Cass had gone, George appeared, Marina popped up, a dog arrived, Cass sent a card and a letter, bookshelves had been rearranged and then abandoned being rearranged, and now there was domestic blackmail to be added to the list. That is a lot of stuff.

I've grown to like the word 'stuff'. The word 'event' still fills me with something like horror.

So, I took myself off to my bedroom-cum-office to ponder the situation. Oh, don't worry, I had a good old root around to make sure there were no cameras tucked away. Mind you, the cameras in the kitchen didn't look like cameras anyway, so maybe there was a camera disguised as a book or a nic-nac or a snow-globe or a metronome or a pen or a paper-weight or a picture-hook. The fact that were no snow-globes or metronomes or pens or paper-weights or picture-hooks in the room was only established after no little time. That left just nic-nacs and books. Nic-nacs were few and far between as Paul had not been a nic-nac man and I had brought none with me. When I say few and far between, I mean there was one. This was a series of metal balls suspended from a small cradle-like structure. After messing about with it and setting the balls clacking back and forth I satisfied myself that they had no hidden depths. This just left the books. In for a penny, I must have thought, or might as well be hung for a sheep as a lamb, and so I went about examining the books with as much system as I could muster, until I discovered a pamphlet, if the word is not too slight, which slipped out of one of the meatier tomes.

'The Iniquity and Corruption of the Soul, the Abuse of Morals, the Enticements to Lust, Perfidy, Calumny and Self-Abuse caused by the Late Plague of Fictioneers, Theatricals and Other Vagabonds.'

Which was followed by a rather nice wood-cut print of a man with a devilish grin hunched over a desk brandishing a quill. The title went on:

'In which, for the betterment of Child, Man, King, Kingdom and the General Commonweal; for the Instruction of Husbands in the Maintenance of Domestic Rectitude, Free from Corruption of Foreign Influence and Licentiousness; for the Sober and Sombre Reflection and Subsequent Condemnation of the Secular and Spiritual Custodians of the Realm; for the Public and Private Dissemination of Right Thinking, Chastity and Godliness, the Author Exposes, Lays Bare and Brings Light upon the Most Fiendish, Depraved, Pagan and Godless Machinations of that Cult, Sect and Scion of Beelzebub that is the Lying Profession of Untruths Masquerading in the Form of Tales to Distract and Entertain.'

The foot of the page read:

'Honoured Sir, read with discretion lest you too fall foul of these evil machinations. Peruse these words, which needs must detail the most heinous abuses of common decency, morality, chastity and decorum only to expose that abuse, with all due caution. These words are not for those prone to the promptings of lust, but only for those pure in spirit who wish to see the Devil for who he is in the printed word and upon the common stage, and to contend, confront and constrain the excesses of those vessels weaker than themselves, be it child or woman or lunatic or unlettered member of the laity for whom Paganism and depravity are as bread and ale.'

I slipped it back in the sheaves of the book from whence it came and then took to my bed, for safety.

The morning was heralded by an unfamiliar smell. Now, my sense of smell has never been the keenest, I admit, so the fact that there was a smell to smell at all was remarkable in itself, as evidenced by the fact that I am remarking upon it. The smell was at once sweet and putrid, like a corpse, not that I have ever smelt a corpse, a human one anyway. I have smelt a fair few dead cats in my time and a rat on at least one occasion and a mouse that rotted away in a kitchen cupboard back in the old house for many a day until I finally found it, maggoty and mushy amongst the canned goods. So, I was not entirely ignorant, on this point at least.

This smell was so strong as to leave a tang in the back of the throat, and no doubt my gorge rose at it a little as a gorge is wont to do. I had no idea what it was or where it came from. It seemed stronger by the door and yet I could see nothing. Now, don't get the wrong idea. It was not so strong a smell that I clamped my hand across my face, but it was strong enough.

I would have tracked the stench down then and there if the dog had not at that moment bounded up to me, mouth agape and tongue lolling. I'd forgotten about it in the night and yet there it was as large as life. It jumped up, wagging its tail and thrusting its paws in inappropriate places. I kneed it to the floor, shut my door, and dressed. My habit of padding about the place in just my pants, at least for a little bit of the morning, would have to be put aside, and who knows if the dog was not doing me a favour for, as I put one leg into my trousers and then the other, I remembered the cameras that Marina had warned me were practically everywhere. Had George all along been watching me in near nudity, with only a pair of old pants hiding my modesty, such as it is? Poor man.

The dog was still there when I re-emerged in shirt and trousers. He jumped up again, but I just kept on walking, not knowing what else to do, frankly. He leapt around, dodging in front of me, and then behind and then from side to side as I made my way to the kitchen. He didn't yap, which was a relief. Bad enough to have a mutt; worse a mutt that yaps. What had I been thinking? What on earth possessed me to take this canine into the house at all? Why had I not just said, 'Sorry, but I cannot and if that means the dog will die then the dog will die.' But presented with the ultimatum, I had buckled and now here the bloody thing was, under my feet and tripping me up on what used to have been the simplest of walks from A to B.

I refreshed his water bowl. He lapped noisily.

The dog business made little sense at all anyway. Aside from my agreeing to take the beast, there was the inexplicable matter of George offering it to me in the first place. If Marina was right, and George had some sort of agenda which he was pursuing through blackmail and surveillance and who knew what else, where did the dog come into his nefarious plan? I couldn't imagine. Perhaps even the most Machiavellian of men has a soft spot. Perhaps Machiavelli himself had a pet duck called Prince, or Lucretia Borgia a set of love-birds she doted on, or Attila the Hun a marmot from the steppe he had raised from a pup that he cuddled up to at night before a little light pillaging in the morning. Just look at Caligula and that horse. Christ, I know a lot of nonsense.

So, the dog made no sense to me at all, on a number of levels. He added to these levels by once again pawing at his bowl, and then overturning it with his nose before chasing it around the room. Much clanging.

I resolved to ignore the dog as best I could.

Given the revelations of the previous day I thought it best to get a clearer sense of whatever shenanigans were afoot. I left that well-trodden path between office and kitchen and launched myself into the other areas of the house. I started up-stairs. Paul's room seemed to be as I had remembered it. I was wrong; the large mirror was gone. The oval bed was there, dominating the place as I had remembered, but now it stood alone, marooned. Now, the fact that I thought there had been a large mirror facing the bed does not necessarily mean there had been a large mirror facing the bed at all. I thought I remembered such a thing, I could even see it in my mind's eye if I pushed myself, but that proved nothing. Well, it proved I thought I remembered, I suppose, but that is not the same as proving I remembered and much less that the thing had ever existed. Had it ever existed? Had there ever been a large mirror facing Paul's large oval bed? I could see no way of establishing the truth of it.

So, I went along to Cass's room, reasoning that maybe there would be something to confirm the absence of the mirror. Quite how going into a room in which a thing never existed would confirm or deny whether a thing had ever existed in a quite different room is open to question, I admit. But, there you go, it was the solution to which I rallied.

Her room was as I remembered it – here we go again – less all the dresses and such that had been scattered all over the place when last I had been there. This didn't bother me, because I knew that Cass had been sorting them out at the time with a view to getting rid of them. So, no cause for alarm. The multitude of pictures still hung on every wall. So far so good. But there was something off. It was only when I sat on the bed to take things in a little more leisurely that I realised the mattress was gone. I remembered the mattress because I remembered memory foam and further remembered not knowing what it was. Now, I thought, now we are getting somewhere: if the mattress is gone, then perhaps the mirror had existed and I had rightly remembered it and it too was now missing. I felt even more sure when I noticed the screen behind which Cass had been known to dress – there really must be a word for that – was also no longer present.

Yes, things which had been present were no longer so.

There were a host of other rooms on this level but I had never been in them so it was pointless checking on them now. You can't remember a room you have never been in and judge what is missing or not. At least, I don't think you can. So, I headed downstairs to the living room, thinking that maybe now my slight sense of unease of the other day might change to a definite sense of something missing.

George, out of breath and panting, appeared from out of nowhere and cut me off at the foot of the stairs.

'Ooof,' he said.

He leant against the wall, doubling up as he tried to regain his breath. I let him.

'Not fit,' he said, clutching a hand to his breast. 'Ooof,' he said again. This was followed by quite an alarming rattle from the depths of his throat. The sweat coursed from his hairline, such as it was.

'Thought,' he said. Whatever he thought would have to wait, for his breath was leading him a merry dance in his attempts to catch it. His eyes protruded and his tongue lolled amidst his dentures. He jabbed a finger at his open mouth, flapped his hand at me and headed to the kitchen. He made a staggering bee-line for the fridge, took a bottle of water from it and downed it in one go, dribbling profusely on to his chest hair and shirt.

Now, I had resolved to ignore the dog but this was proving difficult as the dog found it impossible to ignore George. As soon as he entered the kitchen, the pup was upon him, jumping up at him, getting under his feet, nipping at his heels. His motives were unclear. George tried to push him away with his foot even while downing the water. He could be quite a co-ordinated man when he needed to be.

'Can you get the bloody thing?' By which he meant the dog. What he meant by 'get' I was unsure, so I did nothing.

Still breathing heavily, he grabbed the dog by the scruff, hauled it across the floor, the paws scrabbling, and shoved it out into the garden. He managed to slam the door in its face.

'Ha, ha, ha,' he said. 'He's a feisty thing, in't he? Right little terror! There's a good boy!' he cooed through the closed door. The dog scratched at the glass with both front paws, eager to get in or to get at him.

'Thank God it's only you,' he said, a smile breaking his face. 'Just in the front door and I heard a noise upstairs, so I thought "Hello! That's not right! Who's up there? He never goes up there! Burglars!" I thought. "Thieves," I said to myself and so I dash to catch 'em in the act. Can't have people wandering in and ripping you off. Some bad types around, believe me. But turns out it was just you. Phew!'

I let him relax onto a stool. He seemed shaken by the experience, to be fair. I went so far as to get him another bottle of water from the fridge, which I placed in front of him on the counter. He eyed me sideways as he drank. I don't know what he saw.

'I know what you're thinking,' he said. 'How unfit is he? It's only a hop, skip and jump from the front door to the foot of the stairs and he's about to croak it! Ha, ha.'

I hadn't been thinking this at all, but it now occurred to me to be a fair point.

'Thing is — and you're not going to believe this — but Martha's got me on a health kick thing. "George, my love," she said to me, "we're not getting any younger. Need to take care of you a little bit, get fit a little bit." I tell you,' he said, 'I feared the worst: salad and no booze 'til the end of my days! Ha, ha, ha. That's what I thought, anyway. But, turns out she just wants me to do fast walking — steps she calls it — whenever I can. So that's what I was doing — my steps — on the way over here. Tell you,' he said, 'sounds easy enough, but I'm knackered.'

He was right. I didn't believe it.

'You poor man,' I said.

'Tell me about it.'

'I just did.'

'Yeah, so you did. Ha, ha, ha.' He really needed to vary his laugh a little. Throw in a good guffaw or break it up with a titter every now and again.

'Anyway,' and he slapped his thighs with both hands, 'reason I'm here.'

'Yes?'

He eyed me sideways again.

'What?'

'Yes?'

'Oh, right! Yes! Reason why I'm here…'

'Is?'

'Is what?'

'The reason why you're here.'

'Yep,' and he seem to cast about himself a moment, 'is the dog.'

'The dog?'

'Well, the dog and my Martha. "George, you can't just dump a puppy on the man like that." Always thinking of others that woman. Saint, she is.'

'Was it not her idea?'

'It was! I know! That's what I said to her. "Martha," I said, "it was your idea in the first place!" So she says, "Yes, but I didn't mean for you to just to land him with the poor puppy without warning. But that's you all over George: rushing in where angels fear to tread." It's true. Always going off half cock, me. Anyway, long story short, I've sorted out some dog food for you – good quality stuff, don't worry – and a trainer.'

'A trainer?' I thought he might have meant a shoe for the dog to chew, but sadly not.

'Yeah, Mick. Cousin of mine. Brilliant with a dog. You'll have him rolling over and playing dead in no time.'

'Not Mike?'

'Who's Mike?'

'I thought Mike was the dog man?'

'Right! No. Mike is the dog man, I mean he was the one that had the dog, but Mick is the one that'll help you train it. He'll come round twice a week and you'll have the best trained dog in no time at all. Promise.'

I look at the dog pawing away at the pane and whimpering.

'No,' I said.

'No what?'

'No trainer.'

'No trainer?'

'No Mick.'

'But he's the best!'

'I'm sure.'

'So?'

'We'll manage.'

'Really?'

'Or we won't.'

He looked at me for some time.

'Right you are,' she said, slapping his thighs again before getting to his feet, 'you're making a mistake if you ask me. If you don't mind him shitting and pissing all over the place and ripping things to shreds, well, that's up to you. Me, I'd get Mick in, but it's up to you. Your house; your dog.'

He may have left in a huff. He certainly left. And I was left believing not a word of it.

twenty

Mr Samuels walked long into the night. The half-moon was bright and picked out the light grey of the tarmac of the road that led from the village to the coast. Wary of the road yet wary too of going astray, he followed its path but at some distance, reasoning that he could always find cover in the brush and scrub if need be. He needn't have worried. The road saw no traffic that night. A blessing or a curse.

Eventually, tiredness grew upon him and just as that tiredness threatened to become too great, Mr Samuels saw in the half-light a set of ruined walls. How convenient! What a well-ordered world this is. No sooner does Mr Samuels need rest than a sort of shelter looms up out of the gloom. True, the world could be still better ordered. He could have happened across an abandoned, but fully functioning car, for example, with the keys in the ignition and a full tank of petrol. But he did not. He could have happened across a rural holiday home with a pool and a multitude of rooms that the owners had inexplicably left unlocked. He would not have been so fussy as some and gone from room to room to choose a perfect bed, no. He would have taken his ease in or on the first comfortable bit of furniture and dozed until dawn. But that did not happen. Instead, as he picked his way towards them, the ruined walls seemed to offer some shelter and not a little discomfort. Nor did they offer any way of returning home. A car would have been ideal, when all said and done, but Mr Samuels allowed himself the thought that anything with an engine would do, or even, failing that, a bicycle, though he had not ridden a bicycle in many a year, many, many a year indeed. A lifetime. Strange, then, that the thought of a bicycle had cropped up, once again.

So, limited shelter was offered and accepted. The ruins were extensive. There was no roof at all, nor even the remains of one on the ground which was covered with the same scrub and brush Mr Samuels had been trudging through all day, or near enough. Walls crumbled into piles of rubble here and there, but Mr Samuels found one good corner. He trampled down the weeds as best he could, like a dog wheeling about to make a bed but with more method, it should be said. Carefully, he took off his jacket, folded it neatly and arranged it as a pillow tucked into the lee of the walls. This would have to do. His throat ached with thirst. His skin was sticky with sweat and dirt. He lay himself down and looked up to the impassive stars.

Mr Samuels was woken by a poke in his chest. On opening his eyes he saw that he had been poked in the chest by the muzzle of a shot-gun, at the further end of which was a little old woman. Well, we've had a little old man, so why not a little old lady? Is there no strapping young thing in these parts, bursting with vitality and joie de vivre? No, there is not.

'Watch it!' said the old lady.

Mr Samuels was very much inclined to watch it.

'Don't you move.'

Moving couldn't have been further from the mind of Mr Samuels.

'What do you think you're doing?' said the old lady, already hoarse, apparently, as if she hadn't strung so many words together in fair while. Hoarse or not, she repeated the question, which was an odd one, really. Were what Mr Samuels doing and what he thought he was doing so likely to be greatly at odds with each other? He was quite obviously waking at the point of a gun, but perhaps he thought, if only for a moment, that he was waking at home in his bed, surrounded by his few, but precious things, or that he thought he was waking on a luxurious divan of Eastern design surrounded by the soft coo-ings and gentle glances of ministering maidens.

The old lady had a long nose that curled downwards. She also had a long chin that curved upwards. Her mouth could barely be seen, all but encircled by these features from which stiff, black bristles sprouted. Mr Samuels assumed eyes. What eyes there may once have been were lost amidst a mass of deep wrinkles engraved in her leathery skin. Her bosom and knees were in close proximity to each other and all were swathed in a dirty, black dress topped by a no less dirty and no less black cardigan.

Unpromising as all this no doubt was, Mr Samuels had little choice; he threw himself at the mercy of the woman. He spared her nothing, detailing all that had occurred from the stabbing onwards, but stressing in particular his anxiety concerning his son, who was who knows where and no doubt pining and worrying for his dear father as his father was pining and worrying for his son. All this was delivered without moving an inch and with a measured tone which waivered only when the son was mentioned. Mr Samuels was pleased with this manipulation of his tone and with his self-control to remain utterly still, even as he became aware of a sharp thistle or some such thrusting into his buttocks.

If Mr Samuels could have seen this woman's eyes, would he have seen a softening?

If Mr Samuels could have had a better view of this woman's mouth, would he have seen a slight quivering at the mention of a lost son?

What he could see was the muzzle of the gun waiver, droop and finally withdraw. The old woman broke it over her arm, turned on the heel of her left black boot, and began to walk away.

'Come on, you,' she said over her shoulder.

Shaking the earth from his jacket, he followed her over the scrub and through what was now a maze of ruins. The broken walls in which he had slept was but a tittle of the scattering of ruined and abandoned buildings that could now be seen jutting out of the scrub and parched, low bushes. There was no sign of disaster, no charred beams or scorched walls to show what had happened. There had been houses, lives lived, and then, for reasons unknown, those lives were no longer lived, or lived elsewhere, and the houses were slowly succumbing to time and neglect. Save for one. The old woman had led Mr Samuels to the one house that still had a roof and a door. It's neighbour, a ruin, had been adapted into a goat shed-cum-pen. Decidedly, this was goat country. Had the old man's randy goat ever strayed so far? Had Boris pillaged the pen?

Sheep? Why are there not sheep? There are not, that is all. Perhaps sheep and goats had been separated long ago.

The old woman kicked open the door of rotten wood and battered corrugated iron and beckoned Mr Samuels in with a wag of her devil's finger. Luckily, Mr Samuels had not been blessed with a nightly fairy-tale at his mother's knee. Nor his father's, for that matter. Nor anyone else's, for that matter. Luckily, for he felt no thrill of fear nor any lurking doom as he followed the old woman into the gloom of her hovel.

'You'll be wanting some water,' and Mr Samuels soon heard the screech of a rusty tap, the gurgling of dodgy plumbing and the splash of water in a glass. Yes, it took some time for Mr Samuels to grow accustomed to the lack of light but when he did he saw just the single room. A bed poked out from niche in the corner. A large, rustic range occupied one wall. An array of battered pans stood on its top. Save for the bed, there was nowhere to sit except for two wooden chairs drawn up to a warped wooden table. It was on this that the old woman placed the water, but in a ceramic mug rather than in the glass Mr Samuels had assumed.

'There you go, sit yourself down,' and then she applied herself to some dark corner of the room before emerging with a slab of bread and a hunk of pale white cheese. 'This'll tide you over.'

'Madam,' said Mr Samuels as he took his place at the table, 'I cannot express how grateful I am.'

She shuffled over and took the seat opposite. If he could have seen her eyes, Mr Samuels would have seen they were fixed upon him with rheumy attention as he applied himself first to the water, then to the cheese and then to the bread, which was stale but welcome nonetheless.

'Never turn away a stranger. They might be an angel in disguise. That's what my Nanna used to say.'

Quite how this squared with approaching a stranger with a shotgun was not a question Mr Samuels wished to raise.

'I fear, Madam, that I am no angel. I am though a man much put upon of late and who was greatly in need of a little of the milk of human kindness that you have supplied and for which, never fear, I will return in kind if it takes me a lifetime. And if not in kind, then at least some recompense worthy of the name. I can only swear this as I now have nothing with me, not a jot or tittle, which I can offer in return.'

'Jot or tittle?'

'Neither, Madam.'

'What on earth do you mean, jot or tittle?'

'I have nothing, Madam, but the clothes I stand up in.'

'No money?'

'No.'

'Oh dear. You won't get far with no money.'

'True, my dear lady. Very true.'

'Can't get a bus nor anything like that.'

'No.'

'Not that there is a bus, mind.'

'I see.'

'Not since my boy was a boy. He'd take it to school, see, but then he didn't need the bus anymore, and no one else needed the bus anymore, I suppose, so the bus stopped and that was that. I suppose you'll be wanting to get away to the city as soon as you can, eh?'

'If at all possible, Madam. My son, you see.'

'Oh, yes. You've got to watch after that son of yours, mark my words. Take your eye off him too long and who knows what he'll get up to, what he'll fall foul of. I know, you know. Could see it coming when his Dad,' and she hurriedly crossed herself, 'couldn't take him in hand anymore.'

Mr Samuels was now very much torn. On the one hand, refreshed by his meagre meal, he was keen to get back on the road; on the other he owed the old woman at least something of his time. She had helped him, and, momentarily poor as he was, time was all he had to give. He also knew a preamble to a life story when he heard one.

'Your husband passed away, I take it?'

'Not then, no. Not long after. Never a well man. The runt of the litter. Barely the strength to get out of that bed near the end. But he'd drag himself out and give the boy a good talking to with the back of his hand when needed. But then the boy got strong enough to give him a slap back.' She wiped her eye with her besmeared sleeve. 'That was the end of him, that day. Oh, he kept going but he was on the downward slope and the slope wasn't too long. But my son, well, he kept pushing at him to make him slip down even quicker. Up to all sorts. Gallivanting around with the floozies from up there' and he she jerked her head in the vague direction of the village, 'getting into scraps with the other boys. He'd come home black and blue but his head held high. "Mum," he'd say to me, "if they punch hard, I punch harder; if they give me a kick, I crack them over the head with a stick; if they come after me with a stick, I bash them with a rock." Then he'd turn to his dad and shout that he'd like to see him try and bash him now. He was as weak as a lamb by this time. Could barely raise his head, but the boy kept worrying at him.'

'It must have been a trying time, dear lady.'

'Trying. That's what it was.'

'I'm sorry to hear it, indeed.'

'And I thank you for your sorrow, son. My boy had grown up into a right little hooligan and I could not do a thing with him. I begged him, right here in this room, on bended knee, to mend his ways, to treat me and his dad with a bit of respect, a bit of love. I mean, we did our best. Might not have been much, but we did our best, tried our best. I was just here,' she pointed over to the ground before the stove, 'down on my knees, pleading for him to turn over a new leaf, to be a good boy, a proper man. That's when it happened.'

If Mr Samuels could have seen the woman's eyes he would have seen them moisten.

'What happened?'

'He kicked me.'

'Your son?'

'My son,' a brush of the sleeve across her eyes once more. 'Kicked me so hard that I fell back against the stove and cracked my head clean open. Blacked out. When I came to, he was gone. He'd taken all the money we kept in a jug, just over there, and smashed the jug for good measure, and cleared out.'

'And your husband?'

'Stone dead.'

'Had your son...?'

'I don't know. What does it matter? He'd killed him just as sure as he'd plunged a knife into his heart.'

Mr Samuels remained silent for a while, as the old woman lowered her head and crossed herself repeatedly, for the sake of her dead husband or for the sake of her errant son, Mr Samuels could not say. For both, perhaps, and for herself too, no doubt.

Well, that took rather a dark turn, and no mistake.

What made Mr Samuels linger? Do not think for a minute that thoughts of his son were any less urgent than before. The son was the prime mover still. Yet he lingered with the old woman in her hovel, moved perhaps by her misery. Sorrow shared, and all that. Moved too perhaps by her telling him her woes at all. True, Mr Samuels had known many who had unburdened themselves over the years. More often than not, though, they had unburdened themselves only when brought to a certain level of intensity through some catastrophe, often at the hands of Mr Samuels in some way. That makes him sound like some skilled torturer. That is not it at all. Sent on a mission – which invariably involved duplicity and deceit and some form of ruin or another – it was only a matter of time in Mr Samuels' experience that the truth would out and the whole story pour forth. Mr Samuels only listened to these speeches to confirm his suspicions and to ascertain whether or not his mission had been truly brought to a close.

But the old woman's tale was different. Neither circumstance nor Mr Samuels had brought her to any sort of pitch at all. Nothing had been brought to a head. Her woes had just oozed out of her; a chronic, weeping sore. Mr Samuels was not such a man as to believe that the sight of him and him alone could have prompted her. No. Anyone would have done. Any man, perhaps. Was it memory of the son or of the husband that were reignited? Or was the male form enough to bring them both before her, as real as if they were there once again in the room.

He lingered because it would be rude not to.

Did he linger because the little old woman reminded Mr Samuels of his own dear old Mum?

No.

Did Mr Samuels have a dear old Mum?

Practically once, yes, obviously.

Emotionally now?

No.

He lingered too because she offered to rustle up some form of stew to set him on his way. The goats bleated in their pen. Crows cawed from time to time. A shutter was rattled by a sudden warm gust. Otherwise, all was quiet in this dark shack amidst the ruins of a long-abandoned village.

'Stew'll be ready in a jiffy.'

'Thank you Madam.'

'You rest yourself, dear.'

twenty-one

Friday.

If everything keeps happening on a Friday, as it seems to be doing more often than not, then eventually we will hit a Friday 13th. That will set the cat among the pigeons, to those of a certain cast of mind. But that would entail my doing dates as well as days. Not going to happen.

Anyway. Marina came in as usual and, surprisingly, for the usual. Not even the pretence of the usual, but the actual usual usual. There is no pretence as good as the real. I was a little disappointed, I have to say. I had spent the hours between dawn and her arrival gearing up for a bit of skulduggery, a bit of espionage or subterfuge. I admit that my gearing up had only gone so far as to come up with these three words, but the effort was there, even if the knowledge was not. No, even given my involvement in the Paul and Violet affair, I was still hopelessly hazy when it came to the business of the surreptitious investigation.

Luckily, Marina had a somewhat clearer idea.

She came in from the garden as I was sitting in the kitchen, the dog momentarily passed out at the foot of my stool. He soon sprang to life at the sound, or perhaps the whiff, of her and went bounding off to investigate. His method was not surreptitious at all but it seemed to gather whatever information he needed and he bounded back to the foot of my stool once again and flopped to the floor.

I felt the cameras upon me. Should I make a bolt for it? Run off so it seemed like Marina and I had not met at all?

'Morning,' she said, in a neutral tone.

She disappeared into a walk-in cupboard that I had not even known was there – again that slight breath as she pushed at a surface that revealed itself to be door as it opened – only to emerge a moment later with a mop and bucket and a second bucket filled with what I assumed were cleaning products. There were a lot of them. Now, back in the day, I had made do with a single detergent and some hot water and I had not been entirely convinced about the detergent element at all. It seemed to me that the water did the heavy lifting and the detergent was just a frothy ornamentation; all effervescence and no substance. Now, back in this day, I realised that perhaps I had it all wrong and it was not less I needed but more, much more. A product for the floor, for the counter, for the stove, for the oven, for the windows, for wood, for metal, and for glass. She attacked the counter in front of me with one such product, firing it liberally from a plastic bottle with a trigger on top. It made my eyes water and my throat catch, so God knows what it did to the grime of the surface and all the microbes happily breeding away, if that is what they do – breed. Perhaps they just divide and separate, I don't know. Whatever they had been doing, though, I had no doubt was being brought to an abrupt end as Marina sprayed and swabbed with a cloth. As she swabbed near to me, I saw that a piece of paper was hidden beneath the rag. She glanced at me and urged me with her eyes. I took the hint and as she let the piece of paper slide from beneath the cloth I slid my hand over it.

Quite remarkable how capable I was proving to be. Not only had I looked her in the eye and seen the urging glance, I had then interpreted the glance, connected it with the paper, and acted promptly and not without a little guile. At this rate I will be writing an opera or discovering a vaccine for the benefit of all humanity before you know it. But then I rather ran out of this capable streak. There I was, my hand over the illicit piece of paper, but how was I to read it – as surely there was something written on it to be read, I mean you just don't go around passing pieces of paper to one another unless there is some message being sent, or unless it is cash, obviously, a nice crisp note adorned by some dead worthy – given that the cameras were no doubt running and all would be seen and the jig would be up. Or is it gig? Luckily, Marina's capability was still functioning. She held my gaze again and then flicked her eyes to the garden door. It took me a while to process this in truth, but eventually the dog and I gained the outside.

Blisteringly hot.

He gambolled about a bit, realised it was blisteringly hot, and headed for the shade of a tree. I did the same, but without the gambolling.

Safe from the prying eyes of the house, or at least I hoped so, I unfolded the paper.

'ACT NORMAL'

Do children still pass messages back and forth in class? The teacher's back is turned, the chalk scratches on the blackboard, and a flurry of missives fly back and forth, declaring love, loathing, fancying, sharing gossip and obscenities. Aspersions are cast on someone's paternity. Someone else has the fair reputation of their mother besmirched. An assignation behind the bike sheds is arranged. A pornographic suggestion is made, yet all is quiet and still when the teacher turns to face them once again.

Now, the words were simple enough but their meaning was much less so. Once again I regretted my ability to decipher the written word. Never does anyone any good. 'Normal' is a word that I have struggled with on occasion, it is true, but I was doubly unsure now. Did she mean behave as I usually behave, or did she mean try to behave as others behave? Was it my normal, or a generally accepted standard of normality? If the latter, what the hell was it? My greatest encounter with the normal lately had been Mr Samuels, but he was only probably normal to me and to someone else might seem positively eccentric. Yes, what I considered normal and what might be normal might not coincide at all. Was George normal? He had a job, and a wife, and a host of relations, and that must count for something. Maybe Cass was the most normal, standing on her head in some far off land trying to align herself with the true forms. Or Paul, renouncing all worldly goods, or nearly all, and living up in the mountains with his first love whose mind, and even I knew this, was not as secure as might be hoped.

If 'normal' meant my normal, as in behave as you usually behave, then I was on better ground; just do the stuff I had always done. Pootle in the garden. Marvel at the algae in the pool. Sweat. Sleep. Write nonsense. Pass the time. But now Marina was asking me to act these things rather than do these things, and that gave me pause. Was I meant to be acting normal, but really doing something else, and if so, what? I was very used to doing my normal, but if I was to act normal then I needed a much clearer sense of what that normal looked like. Doing something is not the same as knowing what you are doing, to my mind. To perform something, surely some sort of script is needed, or at least the outline of a scenario that one is meant to stick to.

My shade was shrinking and the heat was rising. At least that was normal. The dog had found a patch of bare ground and was digging a hole, dust flying about the place. When it was happy with the hole dug, he flopped down into it, his head on his paws, and harrumphed. Dust scattered on his breath.

Not knowing what to do, because not knowing what the right normal might be, I went to bed. If in doubt, and all that.

In time, Marina joined me there. Not in bed; just in the same room. There would be no room in my narrow cot anyway, even for someone as petite as her.

The room was in its usual midday gloom; the blinds drawn all the way against the glare of the outside. She shut the door behind her and the gloom deepened.

'Safe?' She whispered.

'Safe.'

Her small frame became still smaller as she sagged in relief. I stood and she took the opportunity to sit on the edge of my cot. Not even a hint of disgust at the state of the sheets and their sweat and other stains. Other things on her mind, I supposed.

'Well done,' she said.

'For what?'

'Acting normally.' Well that was a turn up for the books and I felt a surge of something like pride. When push came to shove I had acted normally, whatever that meant.

She put her palms together as if in prayer and frowned as if in concentration.

'He has to think nothing has changed, you see. Like I didn't talk to you yesterday. Didn't tell you everything. So, we have to go on seeing each other in the kitchen and stuff, you know, like we do. Anyway, I'm meant to be spying on you or whatever, aren't I? He'd know something was up if we were never in the same room ever again, wouldn't he, and then I'd definitely get chucked out, unless I did that other thing, and I won't, I won't.'

'Quite right,' I said, not having any clear idea what this other thing might be.

'But,' I said.

'I know, I know,' and this got her to her feet, 'we can't just keep acting normal for ever.' Not the way I would have put it, but it was fair enough. 'But we need to buy us some time. Find out what he's up to.'

'He's stealing,' I said.

I told her about the mirror and mattress and the screen thing that really should have a name but apparently doesn't.

'I don't go up there.'

'Nor me, normally. Do you go into the living room ever? To clean, dust?'

'No. Strict instructions: only those bits of the house that you use. That was said that from the off. Said he wasn't going to pay me for stuff that didn't need doing.'

I mused. Some people might have calculated, but I mused. I considered the areas I used: this room, necessary house and shower room adjacent, the corridor, kitchen and garden. This left rather a lot of the house free from my presence, even if the house was all I could see from the outside or surmised from what I knew of the inside. If there was a basement or an attic tucked away somewhere, then there was even more. Plus the outhouse where Paul had kept his numerous cars, and what happened to those I wondered. So, there was quite a lot of house, known and unknown, when I came to think of it.

'Do you read these?' The books, of course.

'No.'

She moved over to the desk and cast an eye over its mess of papers. I just stood where I happened to be, which was in the corner.

'And this?' Gesturing to the desk.

'Nothing.'

'It's a lot of nothing.'

This was undeniable.

'Why don't you leave?' I asked.

'I'm sorry,' and she moved away from the desk, 'just curious. Oh God!' She put her hand to her mouth. 'I'm not spying! Not like he wants me to. I'm just, you know.'

I didn't.

'Interested.'

'In what?'

'You know,' I didn't, 'you, what you get up to, why you're here all by yourself, why George hangs about. I mean, what does he actually do?'

'I don't know. He appeared one day. After Cass had left.'

'And you never asked?'

'No.'

'Never wondered?'

'No.'

'Never?'

'Never.'

'Never asked him anything?'

'I asked him for a goat.'

'What happened?'

'He gave me a dog.'

'What's it called?'

'What?'

'The dog?'

'Dog.'

'It doesn't have a name?'

'No.'

'You should give it a name. Boy or girl?'

'Boy, I think.'

'We had a dog when I was growing up.' She sat back on the cot. 'Hunting dog, not that it did any hunting. Dad kept him in the shed, but I let him in when Dad wasn't around. He'd sleep on my bed. Then one day, he just wasn't there. No idea what happened to him. Ned; that was his name. Ned.'

'Why don't you leave the job? That's what I meant.'

'I can't. The money, you see, and well, you know.' She looked at me. 'Christ. I'd better get out of here. I usually just pop in, grab your dirty clothes and get out.' She hurried about the room picking up a shirt and, I'm afraid, two pairs of underpants.

'Whilst I'm asleep.'

'Yeah, but I like it better now you're awake. Best go.' She turned at the door. 'Look. See what you can find out, and maybe there's some way out of all this.'

She smiled, and was gone.

Well that was all very pleasant, was it not?

twenty-two

In the old woman's hovel, seated at her warped table, Mr Samuels felt distinctly drowsy. Usually, the morning hours saw Mr Samuels as bright as a button, all his senses at attention, even if the night had been spent out in the field in a ruin. Not that he had ever spent a night quite like that. Plenty out in the field over the years, though, on a stake out or on the hunt or merely in the performance of his duties that required they be carried out from dusk to dawn. Not now. His head crawled through a fog of blurred impressions, none of which settled into any clarity. He could not even be sure if he had indeed thanked the old woman at all. The phrase had sounded in his head but whether it had been formed by his lips was unsure. He thought he heard urgent whispers from the woman and thought he saw her shove something into those folds between bosom and knee, but maybe he just saw and heard the confused swirlings of his own mind.

Given how he slipped into sleep – let us not be overdramatic – it makes sense that rousing from same took not a little time. His senses came to him one-by-one.

First, was his sense of touch. The table beneath his open palms was still no doubt made of wood, but now he was keenly aware of a grittiness to it and of a pulse of something throbbing through his fingertips.

Second, was his sense of smell. His nose was expecting the scent of the stew, perhaps, but what it slowly discerned was the scent of a scent. It was musky, but with a touch of sweetness and, somewhere in its undertones, a hint of magnolia.

Third, taste. His own mouth dominated for a good while. There was something lurking in the back of it that he could not identify; a taste that stuck to his throat but refused to be named.

Fourth, his hearing. The goats still bleated and the crows still cawed but now there was something new. Beneath his own rattling breath – and for a man who prided himself on his even respiration this in itself gave Mr Samuels a momentary cause for concern – he began to find two further tones of quiet breath being taken into the air.

Sight was the laggard, not least because his eye-lids fought against opening and even when they had his sight was obscured by a watery haziness which he tried to blink away. Inchoate forms swam in the darkness of the room. How long it took to see what was there to be seen, Mr Samuels would never know.

'There you are. So glad to have found you.'

The Woman.

She sat across the table from him, as collected and pristine as when last she had been seen and her voice as calm and even as ever.

The old woman hovered in the corner by the bed. If Mr Samuels could have seen her mouth, he would have seen a grim smile.

'You!' said Mr Samuels.

'Me.'

'But how?'

Poor Mr Samuels may have recovered his senses but his faculties were far from fully functioning.

'Magda and I have an arrangement, don't we Magda?'

The old woman nodded vigorously and wheezed out a laugh.

'So,' The Woman pressed her long fingers on the table and raised herself up, 'shall we make a move?'

'Where?'

'I've a surprise for you. Come along now.'

The Woman took Mr Samuels by the shoulders and raised him from the chair.

'Magda? The door please.'

Magda obliged and Mr Samuels was blinded by the sudden glare of the sun at its zenith, or thereabouts. Meekly, he slowly moved out into the light with the hands of The Woman still grasping his shoulders, pushing, supporting and guiding him in equal measure.

Insects flew up from Mr Samuels' shuffling feet as the two of them picked their way through the scrub and ruins to where a large, black car awaited them on the road.

All that effort, and for what?

Nothing gained. Not even a sniff of an insight. A ramble across some rough country, some dodgy encounters with a couple of octogenarians, a night under the stars with a thistle up the arse, and Mr Samuels is back with The Woman. All that wrangling to escape her clutches and still it is not sure if they were clutches at all! Is it even certain that The Woman is up to no good? Might those clutches be caring caresses, of a sort; little acts of kindness – no; large acts of kindness, when all considered – given through nothing more than a feeling of obligation or even, heaven knows, humanity, of a sort? Haven't even got a name out of her yet. And if no name yet, what hopes for getting the lowdown on motivation, let alone intention?

Nice woman does nice things to a man in need because she is nice.

See? That would be lovely. Nothing could be clearer.

He should have stayed where he was, catheter and all. At least the bed was comfy. At least his needs were cared for; the physical ones, such as they were. It was a pleasant enough spot, after all. Just the sort of spot to retire to after a lifetime of doing the right thing; of going to work and paying the bills and paying the taxes; of raising the kids, schooling the kids, sending them out into the world, of feigning interest in grandchildren; of saving and investing and getting by, just to finally pack it all in, when it is not indecent to do so, and to have a comfy bed and a nice veranda with shade in the morning and a sunset at death of day, all brushed by a gentle breeze from the north, while you wait for some illness to put an end to it all, or to usher in those final years in the care of hired strangers who you confuse for the very children who never visit. A place of momentary respite before the rigours of the end.

But no. He had to go a-wandering. Urged by the thoughts of his boy, Mr Samuels had no choice, perhaps, but to give it a go. The time for a bit of respite is not yet truly upon him. Still some thrashing around to be done.

As sluggish as he was in the back of the car – The Woman had taken care to secure his seatbelt – Mr Samuels knew he was in an odd position. Oh, he had been bundled into the backs of cars before, and they had nearly all been large and black. He had been bundled into the boots of cars too on at least two occasions. So finding himself in the back of a black car was not odd. What was odd was his state of not knowing.

This was what Mr Samuels did not know:

Had he been bundled into the back of a black car? Had he not rather been carefully guided and gently placed in the back of a black car?

Had Magda slipped him a sedative, or was this still the effects of the stabbing and subsequent treatment, kindly administered?

Was the old crone's name actually Magda?

Had he been right to make a bid for freedom?

Had it been a bid for freedom at all? Had he perhaps been free all along but in need of care and recuperation which The Woman and Reggie had provided, the former out of the goodness of her heart, the latter for financial gain?

Where was the boy, and in what state?

Oh, there were many more things he did not know, but that's enough to be going on with. It wasn't so much the fact that these things were not known, but that Mr Samuels had acted without him knowing so many of them that bothered Mr Samuels as his head sagged and bobbed in time with the motions of the car. It was against all his training, all his instincts.

'Son,' his father had said once they had gained the summit of a not inconsiderable mountain after a trek of some time.

'Yes, Father,' Mr Samuels had said, aching to drink from the bottle that still hung from his father's khaki backpack.

'Do you know why we are here,' and he made a sweeping gesture to encompass the scattering of pines and cedars, scrub and rocks that spread below them.

'For the view, Father?'

'For the view!' said Samuels Senior, with a derisive snort.

'For the exercise?'

'The exercise!'

'To reconnoitre?'

'Reconnoitre!'

Mr Samuels had stared at the ground beneath his feet, but the earth remained silent.

'Then I don't know.'

'You don't know why you are here, and yet you are here.'

'Because you said we would go for a hike, Father.'

'And so you came and here you are.'

'Yes, Father.'

'But you are here for no other reason than blind obedience?'

Mr Samuels stared at the ground once more.

'I'm sure you have a good reason, Father.'

'Aha!'

'Father?'

'Now we have it! You are here because you trust me. I say we go for a hike and so you follow me all the way up here, in the glaring sun, because you reason that I must have a reason. Ours is not to reason why! So, Son,' he took a long draught from the bottle, took a handkerchief from his pocket and wiped his mouth, 'you have acted with reason in this matter?'

'I hope so, Father.'

'Hope!'

'I think so, Father.'

'Think! Do you know so, Son?'

Mr Samuels had scanned the cloudless sky but it was silent.

'Sit,' and Samuels Senior indicated the rock on which he wanted his son to perch. Dutifully, he did so, and gazed up at the figure of his father in dark silhouette against the sky.

'Reason from an insecure premise is as bad, worse perhaps, than not applying reason at all. You reason that you are here for a reason because you trust. You trust me and so you trust I have a reason. But that is where you fall down. At the first hurdle. You have built your house on sand, my boy. Trusting is not knowing.'

'But you have never given me any reason to doubt you, Father.'

His father had admonished him with a single raised finger.

'One day, Son, the sun will not rise.'

Mr Samuels, crouched on his rock, had felt none the wiser.

'Is that why you have brought me here, Father?'

'Elucidate.'

'Well,' and he had gulped, partly through trepidation but also through extreme thirst, 'you have just explained to me that trusting is not knowing.'

'Correct.'

'And that when I trusted you I was perhaps wrong to do so.'

'Ah!' The finger was raised again. 'Careful now!'

'That I was wrong, rather, to reason that you had a reason based on my trust of you.'

'Better.'

'But,' another gulp, 'was not your reason to bring me here to tell me about trust and knowledge, so I was right to trust that you had a reason because you did have a reason.'

There had been a pause of some moments as Samuels Senior scanned the horizon. Then, without a word, he marched off.

Mr Samuels had called out, 'Father, may I have some water please?'

'Should have brought your own,' had come the reply. 'Never go anywhere without knowing what you are doing, why you are doing it, and what you will need.'

Perhaps that had been the reason. Mr Samuels Junior, hot, confused and thirsty, followed after the form of his father as it descended the slope.

The driver of the car had an immense neck poking out above his stiff, white shirt collar. His attention remained fixed on the road throughout as it wound its way beside ravines and through desiccated fields. Before long, the shimmer of the sea could be seen in the hazy distance. Mr Samuels' head slumped against the blackened window and The Woman, beside him in the back seat, remained silent.

'You will see, Son,' said Samuels Senior, 'that I have brought you to the same exact spot.'

'Yes, Father,' Mr Samuels had said.

'Have I consulted a map?'

'No, Father.'

'A compass?'

'No, Father.'

'No, indeed. All stored and accessed in here,' and he had tapped his forehead. He took out his watch from the breast pocket of his shirt. 'It is now 12:45. Can you confirm?'

Mr Samuels took out his own watch from his own breast pocket.

'Now 12:46, Father.'

'True,' his father had said. 'At precisely 12:50 I will descend the mountain the way we ascended. At precisely 13.30, you will descend the mountain.'

'12:50, you descend. 13:30 I descend. Yes, Father.'

'Do you have a map?'

'No, Father.'

'Good. Do you have a compass?'

'No, Father.'

'You recall where we left the car?'

'I think so, Father.'

'Think!'

'I know so, Father.' Mr Samuels had tightened his little fist in determination.

'Be at the car by 15:30, or I shall be gone. If I am gone, you will proceed to home as best you can. Clear?'

'Clear, Father.'

'Questions?'

'None, Father.'

'It is customary on such occasions,' his father had said, 'to wish someone luck. I do not wish you luck. Luck is not to be trusted. It is a chimera. If it is anything, luck is merely preparation meeting circumstance; nothing more. Look to yourself, my boy, and yourself alone.'

He had stared at Mr Samuels a moment, up there on the high reaches of the mountains, nodded to himself, and began his descent.

Once again, Mr Samuels had watched the form of his father recede.

A murder of crows sprang up the tree tops and took flight.

A murder of crows sprang up from a field and took flight.

The sky was filled with their cries.

twenty-three

The time had come, I realised, to become better acquainted with this house which was meant to be my home. But I was alive to the dangers inherent within this plan, if that's what it was, and it wasn't really. It was just a sense that it was something to be done, and had not Marina urged me to do something? Indeed, she had. Plan or not, the dangers were still there. If not dangers for me, then for her.

Night would be my friend. Yes, now the time for skulduggery was upon me, dark would be essential. I rallied to this conclusion after entertaining others, prime amongst them was the thought that if this was my house – which I felt it might be in some obscure way – then I had every right to explore it at will. Nothing could be more normal than a man taking a stroll around his property, taking an itinerary, perhaps, or to see what repairs might be necessary, or just because he felt like it. An Englishman's home is his castle, so why should not my home be too? But I felt it to be a house in which I just happened to live rather than a home upon which I had some claim, and which had some claim on me. It is true, I have never felt the same about this house as my old ruin. It doesn't suit me, nor I it.

Of course, if I were to start to wander, the cameras would pick up my every move. This, I did not want. What had Marina said? Act normal. Nothing would be less normal for me than a sudden interest in what lay beyond my usual run. George would be sure to notice.

So, I waited for night.

Our nights are not nice. The sun sets, luring one into a false sense of security. A breeze might pick up for a moment, but that too is just a trick, for soon the hot, damp air descends. Where the moisture comes from I haven't the slightest idea, but it lies doggo all day and then creeps in under cover of dark and swathes everything in a thick, breathless blanket. This makes the sweats of the night different to the sweats of the day. In the day, the sweat springs to the surface of the skin and is quickly burnt off, to be replaced by a fresh wave. At night, layer upon layer builds on every limb, on every inch of flesh until a one is awash in one's own rancid, viscous muck. Like I said; not nice. Unless you don't sweat. I've heard a shock, a trauma, can stop one's ability to perspire. It might be worth looking into, although I must say the notion has the whiff of bollocks about it.

I did not just wait for night, oh no. I waited for the depths of the night. A large, bright moon hung in the sky. Stars flashed their colours against the black. The dog had come with me into the garden to see what I was up to, I suppose. I looked at the sky and he looked at me looking at the sky. Long, pleasant moments. I even went as far as patting him on the head before making a dash for the kitchen and shutting him out. The last thing I needed was a dog trailing me on my midnight ramblings. It was a betrayal, I know, giving him a nice little pat on the head and then legging it. But even a puppy needs to learn the ways of the world.

I turned off the kitchen lights and made as if to go to bed. I even waited beside my cot in the dark for a few minutes to give the right impression. I might even have flushed the toilet and run the tap in the bathroom sink for a moment. Yes, I was warming to this acting malarkey.

As I gained the corridor, I realised the flaw in my plan: I couldn't see a thing. The bright beams of the moon didn't penetrate this far. I stood in the utter dark until it was no longer utterly dark, my eyes becoming accustomed, I suppose. Still, making my way down the corridor in an unfamiliar direction was not easy. I kept my left hand on the wall as I took tentative steps.

My left hand came across the big double doors to the living room. No point going in there, I thought. I'd had a shufty at it not that long ago. I knew something was off with it. I kept going. The corridor seemed immensely long. All my hand felt was wall and more wall for not a little time. Then, a door. I patted it for some time before I found the handle. Thank God it was only the kitchen that had the no handles policy. Without seeing it clearly, I knew it was a splendid handle, actually more of a nob. My hand cupped it most naturally and, although metal, there was a certain softness to it in the palm of my hand that I cannot account for. I would have gladly stayed there, nob in hand, for a couple of hours, in truth, but I was mindful of my mission. I pushed on and in.

Large, floor to ceiling windows let in the moonlight. Long oblongs of light reached into the room, askance. It was large. I know my experience of rooms tends to have been with the smaller variety but I felt reasonably sure that this was large by any normal standards. There's that word again. Is normal becoming more normal, to me? Perhaps it seemed large because it was empty except for a piano; one of those curvy, horizontal ones. The moonlight glanced of its dark wood and by its reflected shafts I noticed that one side of the room was curtained. Inch by inch, lest the noise alert someone, I slid the curtain aside to reveal a mirror. Now, this mirror was definitely large. It took up the whole wall. I pulled back the curtain all the way to make sure. This necessarily increased the light in the room because of physics, or optics or something like that. It was this that allowed me to notice the floor. Padding along in my bare feet, I had sensed that it was a different surface – there was even a coolness to it – but now it showed itself to be made up of small bricks of highly sheened wood. My sweaty feet had left a guilty trail across it.

The room left me immensely sad. I have no idea why.

The next room, also rather conveniently overlooking the garden and hence illumined by the moon, did not have the same effect. For a start, it was thickly carpeted, as my room had once been before I got rid. This just made my feet feel even hotter than they actually were. I ploughed through it. Again, not much there at all, save for a large bracket on one wall. That was it. Whatever it had once held was now gone. The moon was strong enough for me to make out a dirt or dust mark in the shape of an oblong surrounding the bracket. With my back to this, I then noticed, picked out by the moonlight, four dents in the carpet directly in front of it.

I didn't know what to make of either room. Who is to say what goes on in the innards of other people's houses?

Next was the torture room. So I surmised from what remained within. Again a large mirror along one wall, but not curtained this time. The floor was of some sort of rubber-like substance so my footprints left a mark once more. Not to worry, I thought, when the day's heat kicks in that will soon disappear. I stubbed my foot on a strut protruding from the floor and then noticed a small forest of same; thick screws or bolts or some such, as if planted and destined never to grow. In the middle of all this was a large contraption, a mess of bars and wires and metal, bigger than a man, bigger than me anyway and, when all said and done, I am a man, of sorts. It was this that brought torture to my mind. Oh, not as much as a rack, or an Iron Maiden, or a Judas Cradle, but I could well imagine some unfortunate splayed across it being urged to recant, or confess, or just suffer. That's what it is all about in the end, after all; suffering.

As I picked my way back along the corridor I realised what an immense waste of time this little expedition had been. Yes, I had discovered rooms I had never known, but I was left none the wiser as to whether they had been looted or not. Never having seen them before, I had nothing to measure them by. Oh, I know there were tell-tale signs, but this could have easily been signs of legitimate removal rather than illegitimate theft. Hand on heart, or thereabouts, I could not say that a whole host of removal men had not been in, contract in hand, or instructions in head, and done what they had been instructed or contracted to do. True, I didn't remember a slew of hefty blokes dragging no less hefty items to a fleet of waiting lorries or vans, but just because I didn't remember something didn't mean it had not happened. Getting born, for one, is proof enough of that.

Why this mania for irrefutable proof, all of a sudden? Live in the haze; if I had ever had a motto, that might have been it, or something like it.

My hand – the right this time as I headed back to my cot – had just traversed the expanse of the front door when it came across an unknown handle. Unknown to me, at any rate. I assume the architects, builders and carpenters had a fair idea about it, and then Cass and Paul and the army of cleaners they no doubt had, but whom I never saw. I tried it – the handle I mean. This was a proper handle and not a nob. I pulled it towards me; nothing doing. I tried again, but this time pushed away from me, which even in the dark seemed on the narrow side, and again nothing. I stood before it flummoxed for some time. Something told me the door was not locked and yet push and pull had achieved nothing. Perhaps the lateness of the hour meant my logical faculties were not what they might be – but when are they? – but it took not a little time for me to realise that a door can go in, or out, or along, by which I mean slide. This met with success. Why this was a sliding door and all the others not, I couldn't say. My old dread of the threshold stirred. This was no surprise. What was a surprise was that this dread stirred in what I can only term as my nether regions. Oh, I could find other terms, but decorum and all that prevents me.

I crossed the threshold. I fell. Then, blank. All dark in the darkness.

twenty-four

Mr Samuels was at sea. Not all at sea, but on it. He came to realise this when the sensation he thought was only in his head revealed itself to be of the real world. The gentle swirling and pitching were no doubt going on inside too – how many mollys had he been slipped, he wondered – but he soon felt sure that it was not his inner life alone that was unsteady.

Can't I just leave him there being rocked gently to and fro on a calm and calming ocean? No. No, I can't. Things to be done.

Light played on the ceiling most prettily. Light reflected on water and then refracted by the glass of the portholes made for a nice shimmering display.

Can't I just leave him there admiring the sight? No. No, I can't.

He lay on a bunk, not knowing how he had got there but knowing that his shoes had been removed. Mr Samuels had had little or no experience of boats, luckily for me, but he did know that normal shoes were not to be worn upon them. Quite why, he was not sure. The wood of the deck or something like that demanded it, hence deck-shoes. Yes, that made sense.

Wriggling his toes as if feeling them anew, Mr Samuels slowly got a sense of where he was and where he had been. At least, where he could last remember being. It was a good job, no doubt, that the chauffeur had been on hand to lug him out of the car and onto the boat, for surely The Woman couldn't have managed it herself. Or there might have been a whole host of deck-hands to help her. Perhaps the driver had a clear sense of his responsibilities, his rights and privileges and how these did not extend beyond the confines of the land, or perhaps his terms of hire were more fluid and he was at The Woman's beck and call on sea as on land and, who knows, in the air too, if necessary.

All this is just so much dither and delay.

Mr Samuels regretted that his socks left little sweat marks on the wood as he padded his way to the ladder and up into the light of the deck. The glare was horrendous. It is enough most of the time to suffer the harsh light of our skies but to then have this bounced back at you from below – well, it really is not very pleasant. Oh, I know, people love the dappled light of the ocean under a blue sky and I am not saying it cannot be pleasant. Did I not just wax lyrical about the kaleidoscope on the ceiling of the cabin? I did. Actually, I am saying it cannot be pleasant. Relentless brightness from all angles. Damn it, the sun has a lot to answer for, when you come to think of it, what with burning this and desiccating that and irradiating god knows what. One day, the sun will have had its day; a great explosion and then a great black hole consuming all.

But not today.

Assaulted by the light, Mr Samuels took some time to adjust. He shielded his eyes with his palm but that still left the glare bouncing of the water. He'd need a pair of sunglasses to be quite comfortable. But the eye is a wonderful thing, is it not? For soon he was able to see well enough to catch sight of land in the offing, as I believe the phrase might be, to starboard, if that is the word. The sea stopped and a white cliff began some five-hundred metres away and on top of the white cliff the beige and brown scrub of the land and on top of that the relentless blue of the sky. So, blue-white-brownish-blue, give or take. Roughly the same to port and aft but beyond the prow the sea stretched away into a haze of the horizon.

The reason why Mr Samuels had little or no experience of boats is that he didn't like them, and the reason why he didn't like them is that he could not swim.

'Terra firma,' his father had said, 'is all that you need.'

'But Father,' the boy Samuels had asked, 'what if your target takes to the water?'

'Wait him out, my boy; just wait him out. A man at sea will come back to shore, no matter what.'

Mr Samuels Senior had not mentioned that he was a profound hydrophobe.

'Mr Samuels! Won't you join me?'

The unseen Woman hailed him from above and so Mr Samuels padded up another flight of stairs to gain an upper deck. Quite a big boat, really. But not a ship. No, more of a yacht, but a yacht without sails, so I don't know what. How am I supposed to know? When have I ever been on a yacht, with or without sails? Never. And I never will, I fancy. Now, a raft! That might happen. Or a rowing boat, at a push. But a yacht? No, I have never been on one and know I never will.

The Woman did not suffer the sun; she embraced it. Mr Samuels came cross her lying on a luxuriant lounger angled to maximise the exposure to the rays. Her clothing, such as it was, seemed to have a similar goal. Surely now would be the time that Mr Samuels could make a more accurate estimation of her age. Now, with her wearing only a two-piece swimsuit that barely deserved the name, Mr Samuels could take everything, or almost everything, into account and do his computations. He declined.

'There's a G and T there for you,' and she waved her fingers at a table set next to second, no less luxurious lounger beside her. 'That's your tipple, isn't it?'

This was something of an exaggeration. Mr Samuels was not one for alcoholic stimulants, as a rule. A glass of champagne at New Year, perhaps, or a nice red with the Christmas turkey were not unknown but whole swathes of the year would pass without a drop passing his lips. He never drank on duty and as he was always on duty, or thereabouts, he never drank. However, it had been a habit of some standing that when a mission had been completed he would allow himself to celebrate with a small gin and tonic, with ice and a slice, in a comfy chair in the garden in the relative cool of the evening.

He had always thought that he'd been alone on these occasions, drinking in the dying day and the G 'n' T, but perhaps all along he had been under the watchful eye of The Woman diligently noting his habits, knowing that one day this little snippet would come in handy. If she had kept this little bit of knowledge to one day put Mr Samuel at his unease, she had succeeded.

Now, it is one thing to be uneasy, and another to let it be shown. Mr Samuels was not about to let that happen.

'How kind,' he said, 'but I try not to drink during the day.'

'Oh, but Mr Samuels, surely we can bend the rule a little. It will perk you up, I'm sure.'

Perhaps it would, for The Woman was herself nursing a gin and tonic and seemed much more perky than she had ever seemed before. Her breasts appeared to be her own and free from augmentation. Her voice had a new softness to it; the cold edge that lurked beneath the surface had been replaced by a warmer tone and was there even a hint of a tinkle to it? There was.

'Lie back, have a drink and relax a little, you poor man.'

Well, put like that, it was hard to refuse. Mr Samuels did not like reclining during the day but that rule too was soon bent.

So, there they are, side by side on their luxuriant loungers under the full force of sun, sipping their drinks while the yacht moves to and fro, to and fro, beneath them.

'I can tell you now,' she said, gazing out to sea, Mr Samuels assumed, from behind her sunglasses.

'Please do,' as he squinted towards the horizon.

'I am Mia.'

This information would have left Mr Samuels cold if he had not been uncomfortably hot. His vest was doing a fine job, to be sure, but its cooling capacity was being sorely tested. It would have left him cold, because he did not believe a word of it.

'Mia?'

'That's right.'

Either Mia had not inferred from the rising, hanging tone that Mr Samuels wanted a surname to boot, or she had inferred it and ignored it. Either way, thank God she now has a name, and a short one, rather than that The Woman nonsense.

But is it Mee-a or My-a?

If Mia was going to withhold her surname, then Mr Samuels was going to withhold his first name. She probably knew it anyway.

'Lovely, isn't it? The sea, the sun, the gentle swell of the ocean.'

'Are we at anchor?'

'Oh, yes. No cruise this time, I'm afraid, Mr Samuels. We're expecting visitors, you see.'

He did not.

'In a little while. Which gives us,' as she swung her long legs off the lounger to sit facing him, her glass dangling between thumb and forefinger, 'a little while to get to know each other better.'

He kept his eyes fixed on the horizon, mainly.

'Madam, I am sure you know all there is to know about me.'

'Oh, I don't know about that! Still waters run deep and can one really know another person, in the end? You can keep a dossier for years and not really know what makes a person tick, in the heart,' and she lay her manicured fingers on her breastbone just where a bead of sweat was making its way down.

'So you have kept a dossier on me, Madam?'

'Of sorts. Over the years. Not just me, of course.'

'But you said you worked alone.'

'Do you think I could pay for all this, just on my own?' She rose, the better to gesture to the yacht on which they sat, which was really a very fine yacht indeed and no doubt worth a few bob. 'I do alright for myself, Mr Samuels, but even I cannot quite stretch to all this.'

She took herself off towards the prow, if that is the pointy bit, and leant against the low rail, Mr Samuels directly behind her. This was a ploy, just as a hand to the chest had been a ploy.

'No, Mr Samuels, gone are the days when I worked alone and barely made ends meet.'

These words found a resonance within Mr Samuels' depths. She shifted her weight from one leg to the other, then back again.

'When you're at bottom, it's hard to see any way up the greasy pole, but you have to grasp it and pull yourself up, just the same. You might slip down, back to the bottom, but that just means you've got to get a good grip and give it another go.'

'But if there is no pole,' and her she turned back to face him, throwing her hair back as she did so, 'then you get nowhere at all. I found a pole, and I grabbed hold, Mr Samuels. I took a good strong hold.'

'This pole of which you speak, Madam, is a metaphor, or perhaps even an analogy, for an organisation of some sort?'

Was Mia deflated? To her credit, she was not. Resourceful woman that she was.

'Oh, Mr Samuels! Always straight to the point; to the issue at hand!'

'I try.'

'You try, and you succeed!' Her laugh was light, lighter than one would have thought, given the timbre of her voice.

'But,' she playfully placed a finger to her lips for an instant, 'of them I cannot speak.' She twisted her fingers as if to lock her mouth. 'Of me, though, I can say what I like!'

'But would it be the truth, Madam?'

'Would you like it to be the truth, Mr Samuels?'

'I find it preferable.'

'But how will you know?

'I have my ways, Madam.'

'And I mine.'

'To dissemble, if I am not being too harsh, Madam?'

'Oh, Mr Samuels! We are not children!'

'No, indeed.'

'Indeed, no.'

She swooped back to her lounger.

'You dissemble, Mr Samuels. Or shall we just call it lie?'

He was at a disadvantage. She could read his eyes but hers were shielded by the darkest of lenses.

'I have recourse to subterfuge,' he said.

That steely edge was back when she broke out into a laugh.

'As do we all, Mr Samuels. As do we all.

'Now,' she reached over and patted his arm, 'time to dress for lunch. Our guests are on their way. Drink up.'

She sprang up and slinked off with admirable skill.

Mr Samuels sat on, having nothing to change into for lunch, as far as he knew. He also knew himself immune to flirtation and had enough respect for Mia's professionalism to know that she knew he was immune to flirtation, which left the rather troubling question as to why she had been applying flirtatious methods. Of this last point, he was sure. Immune as he was, he had been able to study both male and female variants of glances and smiles and wiggles and giggles that people sometimes indulged in. At first, back in the old days, he had been fascinated and a little confused by it all, if truth be told. A little later, he had found the whole thing exasperating and fondly wished that the species had devised another way to oil the wheels of procreation and desire. Something along the lines of a peacock tail or the colourful arse of a baboon. With greater age came greater tolerance of these little dances and the ability to catalogue their techniques.

Had Mr Samuels ever deployed these techniques professionally?

No.

Had he ever employed them in a more personal capacity?

No.

Yet, he had often seen them in the field, and had even been the target of them, on occasion, so he knew flirtation when flirtation occurred.

What bothered him, as he sat sweating under the sun on a calm sea, was why Mia was using these techniques now. Offering up her name seemed to have had the air of finality about it, as if an end had been reached, so defences could be let down and confidences shared. A wistful look back at all the trials and tribulations overcome, with a wry smile and a few self-deprecating remarks, might have even been in the offing. Such a thing had happened sometimes when Mr Samuels had rubbed up against his fellow professionals at the close of a case. If he had read this mood aright, then the sudden appearance of flirtation made little or no sense, unless it was just to tease him, glory over him in her relative youth and definite beauty. But he rather thought, on reflection, that perhaps he had not read the mood aright at all. Perhaps the flirtation had been to suggest that mood so he would indeed let down his defences and let slip a few confidences.

It was a professional flirtation deployed for professional ends, which Mr Samuels could not yet grasp.

And his father had been wrong. If your target died at sea he, or she, might never return to terra firma, but sink into the ooze of the sea bed to be picked clean by fish and crustaceans, cephalopods and worms, or just be ripped about by sharks at the surface.

Lunch, thought Mr Samuels, and especially the guests for lunch, might shed a little light.

twenty-five

Slowly the darkness lifted. Well, my own darkness lifted. By which I mean, I came to. How long I had been unconscious, I could not say. Can one ever say? I mean, one does not check the clock just before losing consciousness, and then check it again once consciousness is recovered and so come to an accurate understanding. Oh, sure, one might slowly get a sense of time lost by, I don't know, looking at the state of the day, the sinking or rising of the sun, the passage of the moon or some such, but what if one had been out for days? Or weeks? Whole months, even, comatose with not the slightest notion of time nor anything else, for that matter. So, on recovery, the eyes slowly flickering open, one might find it is winter when last thing it had been spring, but which winter and of which year? One might look to one's body, I suppose, and have a stab at duration based on emaciation, or bed-sores, or general decay, but what if one had been diligently cared for? Emaciation kept at bay with a feeding tube rammed down the gullet, for example, or just pumped straight into the gut, if such a thing happens, and I'm not sure it does.

One is so awful. You would have been better. Never mind. No matter.

Anyway, quite how long I had been out was left uncertain. I knew it had been night when I slid open that door but the room in which I now found myself was pitch black so I had no way of knowing if the day had dawned or if the moon had made its way across the heavens. No light was available at all, as far as I could tell.

There was an odd sensation in my head and on my head. Odd as in unusual. Actually, in all honesty – all! – the sensation in my head was not all that odd. It hurt. It throbbed, in fact, but the throb had a keen edge to it. No, what was truly odd was the sensation on my head. There was a wet stickiness somewhere above my right eyebrow. I am not saying this sprang to my attention as soon as my senses came back to me, but sooner or later I became aware of it. I wiped at it with a finger, brought the finger to my eye, but could see nothing; not only could I not see what was on my finger but I could not see the finger itself. Remarkably dark. The darkest dark I have ever known. I thought I might have been blind, but no such luck. So, seeing buggered through want of light, I rallied to taste. I touched the tip of my finger on the tip of my tongue. Not nothing, but not enough, so I gave it a good old suck, just to be sure. Sticky, yes, but slightly sweet, with a hint of something metallic in it. Not unpleasant, in truth.

Yes, my head was bleeding. Lucky, because now I had been blessed with the knowledge of at least two things:

One, I had not been out for days.

Two, I had not been accosted.

One, because if I had been out for days, or just a few hours, the blood would have dried. Of that, I was reasonably certain. Whether my blood is dangerously thin or dangerously thick, or just run of the mill consistency, I have no idea. Well, I have some little idea that it is not dangerously thin to the point of being haemophiliac. And as to dangerously thick, well I have yet to have had a heart attack or stroke or aneurism, but who knows if one is not just lurking around the corner. I might not even get to the end of this thing, whatever it is; this, relation.

Two, because the wound was at the front and not at the back of the head. I have tripped, I must have thought, or just fallen, head first, down some steps perhaps, and hit my head on the way down. That is what I had thought, at the time. In the clearer light of day, today that is, I see that this is faulty. You are not always accosted from the rear, after all. Perhaps I had surprised someone and they had charged up the stairs with a sharp or blunt implement in hand

and given me a good old dint to the skull and I had not fallen down the stairs and hit my head, but my head had been hit and then I had fallen down the stairs.

So, one was reasonably secure. Two was a little dodgy. That's not a bad ratio, really.

There was another thing I was sure of. I was completely in the dark. It was such a dark that it made me think again about my sometime preference for darkness. I had just been playing, flirting with darkness. Many had been the time when I welcomed night and the gathering gloom. Many had been the time when I sat in what I flattered myself was the dark, thinking to myself 'Ah, this is the life'. Not proper dark at all. A mere lessening of the light rather than its absence.

Too often I must have thought, 'Ah, this is the real thing!' when it was not.

Being utterly in the dark, then, was something new. I was surprised, to be frank. I was surprised by how little I liked it. Normally, if you like a thing then you like a bit more of it, and if it a bit more of it pleases, then you want a bit more of it, and so on, until you have got all of it and contentment descends. Or so I imagine. Yes, I'm sure things are meant to work out that way. A delusion, perhaps, and certainly so with the dark, because now that I was in true darkness I was not content at all. I was not scared or if I was it was a new kind of scared. The darkness had a weight to it. I felt it pressing on all sides, on each limb, on each inch of my body. Yet, at the same time, my body seemed to be drifting off from me. I could feel all of it. Feel it more, in truth, than normal, as if the dark hemmed me in and gave me added form. Yet, I felt scattered too. That is not the word. Disconnected. I wiggled my fingers, for example, but I wasn't sure that they did wiggle, or that they wiggled but far, far away from me, as if in Patagonia. So, I felt both more dense and more diffuse than I had ever felt before.

I can't say I recommend it.

So my life in the dark began.

It seemed impossible, I soon realised. Or realised after quite a while. Time was not present. But, whether quickly or eventually, I came to question all I had surmised and I did so due to one small fact that I had not considered before: the utter darkness of the darkness. Had I not slid open the door? Did not the door lead to the corridor? The corridor had not been bright, true. I had had to pick my way along it with care and a groping hand, but it had not been pitch black. Surely, then, some light must be available? And yet there was none. I sat, waiting and thinking 'give it time, your eyes will become accustomed to even this dark' trusting I suppose in the physical properties of light, of which I was clueless. But nothing happened. The dark remained dark. So, I thought, the door must be closed. Sealed, like a tomb, with not the slightest chink of light creeping in. But how was the door closed? I was reasonably sure I had not closed it. Well, I had no recollection of doing so, which, yes, I know, I know, but Christ on a bike, sometimes you have to let these things go. If only I could let more of these things just go. That would be nice. Regardless, I was sure as sure be damned that I had not slid the door to. Someone else must have done it. And if someone else might have slid the door to, who is to say that that someone had also not shoved me down the stairs? Well, I had no recollection of being shoved, but given the sorry of state of my memory in general, and at this point in particular, it was not an impossibility. At this point in particular due to concussion, perhaps, or general, and I would like to think understandable, discombobulation.

Now, this threw my Point Two bit of knowledge into not a little doubt. Perhaps I had indeed been accosted, but subtly. Rather than a crowbar to the head, just a teeny-tiny tap at the right moment had sent be plummeting into the dark and my head had split as I fell. It was worth thinking about, so I thought about it. Up, down and sideways; with scepticism, with credulity; with reason, with intuition; with system, and at random.

That got me nowhere.

I resolved to become better acquainted with my surroundings. I had started out wanting to get better acquainted with the house, and now I wanted to get better acquainted with just a small bit of it, which sounds rather like the law of diminishing returns. Of course, my ability to do this was also diminished. Of my five senses, one was useless, so I had to turn to the other four. Taste would not be much use, unless I went about licking each and every surface and that was something I was not prepared to do. I needed to be a snake or lizard, flicking out my tongue and tasting the air, but I was just a man. So, I was down to three of the five. Smell didn't prove much of a help either, in truth. Oh, I could detect a certain mustiness but this seemed all-pervasive and told me nothing more than the room was beneath ground and not ventilated. Worth knowing, and yet useless at the same time, like so much. So, that just left two out of five.

Extraordinary thing, by the way; I can never remember the five senses without going through a little rigmarole of touching the relevant bits of my body. You would have thought that I would have got the hang of them by now but, there you go, I have not.

Hearing at first seemed promising. I could hear my breath, and when I tapped the floor I could hear the harsh report of concrete or something very like it. I concentrated to hear beyond these immediate sounds – to hear some distant hum, or gurgling, or rattling – but nothing came and the more I tried the more I could only hear my own breath and then, disturbingly, my own heartbeat. I had pointed my sense outward only for it to return with a vengeance. 'Take that, you bastard,' my hearing had said to me, 'listen to that din I have to put up with second upon second; in-out, in-out, de-dum, de-dum, de-dum, without let up from the moment you were born until the moment you will die.' Yes, my hearing was in a vindictive mood.

So, that left touch.

I got down on my hands and knees. Both, or all four I suppose, confirmed the floor was of a rough concrete. My hands further confirmed that dust or grit layered the surface. Not knowing which direction I was facing, or what I was facing, I just resolved to move forward until I could no longer move forward due to a wall or some such. I did not fear a ditch or sink-hole or crevice. For no good reason, I was sure that the room was free from such. Oh, my naivety! Not that I did fall into a ditch or sink-hole or crevice, for I didn't, but when would I learn that just because I felt something to be the case for no good reason that this didn't mean it was true. You would have thought that all that had occurred to me would have made me a little more, what is the word?, circumspect. No matter. I sallied forth on hand and knee until my head butted against a vertical. A wince of pain. Now taking to my feet, I followed the vertical with outstretched arms and palms until I met another vertical abutting it. This, I told myself, was a corner. Nothing had yet fallen across my path for me to fall over. So, I followed this new vertical which proved to be as uninteresting as the first. But the third vertical, now, that is where things took a turn. I was making my way, palm stroking the wall, which was also concrete – perhaps it was a bunker of sorts – and feeling nothing but concrete when the vertical suddenly disappeared and my left hand slipped into a void. My palm retraced its steps and reconfirmed the sudden nothingness. Wall to void; that seemed about the size of it. I had no idea what this void might entail so I got back on to my hands and knees the better to explore. With my right palm approximating where the wall should have been, I crept along, hoping that before too long wall would again be in reach. I wasn't disappointed. A wall, exactly the same as the one so recently left, at least in terms of touch, presented itself. I paused. Either I could go on tracing this new bit of wall, or I could backtrack and tackle the void, so called. I nailed my courage to the sticking point, or whatever, and backtracked, turned and faced the space, but back on my knees, just in case. Fingers first, I inched my way into I knew not what. I fancy my fingers fluttered as if antennae or the whiskers of a blind mole. If I stayed down there long enough, would my own sense of touch take on new powers? Or would generations of me have to elapse before a leap in sensory acuity was achieved? Obviously, both thoughts left me cold; I'd be dead of dehydration and starvation, surely, before the former kicked in, and for the latter, I would need a mate with whom to sire the future generations and there was no mate to be had, and even if there had been mate, what good would have it been to me that a great-great-great-great-great-great grandchild had a slightly better developed sense of touch? No good at all. Inching forward, as said, it took I don't know how long before my hand met a new vertical. This vertical, however, did not remain a vertical for long. No. Soon, it was joined by a horizontal and this horizontal soon gave way to another vertical. Hello, I might have said to myself, what's all this then? I'm not sure at what point, or how many small verticals and small horizontals it took for me to realise, but realise I did, that what was front of me was a set of steps. From this, it was but a leap of reason to suppose that these were the same steps I had fallen down and that, if that were so, the door would be found at their top. So, again on hands and knees, which wasn't easy I can tell you, I made my ascent, only pausing when my right hand felt something sticky beneath it. Don't get distracted, I might have told myself; push on, push on. I pushed on until my head struck a vertical, but my head told me this vertical was made of wood. It even wobbled a little as I struck it. Another wince of pain. My hands confirmed my head. It was the door.

Saved, I must have thought, and I was, in a sense.

This had the makings of a key moment. Would the door slide open and my life in the light resume? Or would the door be locked and my life in the dark continue? Much hinged on this, in truth.

It would be nice if someone could make a decision on this point.

Not that a lot cannot be made of me in the dark at the top of some stairs before a door that might or might not open.

Shall we say that the door slid open? Yes, let's say that. It might be best.

The door slid open and I was bathed in a pallid, grey light. Bathed might be overdoing it, but, after the excessive dark, even this early dawn interior light seemed to overwhelm, or at least whelm.

I broke the habit of long years and looked into a mirror, to check on the wound. I re-hung the mirror in the bathroom beside the office for this very purpose; the mirror I had taken down and turned to the wall. The blood had stopped seeping from the cut on the edge of my hair-line and had encrusted itself on my forehead. A bit of my hair had been ripped away and I found it later stuck to the side of the wall beside the stairs to the basement, or whatever it was; more of that in due time, I suppose, if all goes well. I shouldn't have mentioned it here at all, really, but not everything can be mentioned at the proper time or in the proper place.

Anyway, it was not the blood nor the raw scalp that drew my attention so much as the overall reflection in the mirror. When had I looked on myself last? Ten years, give or take, and excepting the odd fleeting and incomplete sight of myself in a window every now and again in which my features were obscured by the vistas beyond or by some reflected glare or another.

I shall not detail what I saw. Safe to say, it was not an experience I rushed to repeat.

So, I suffered my own gaze long enough to wipe the blood from my face.

twenty-six

Not wanting to let the side down, whilst not being sure which side he was on or whether there were indeed two sides, Mr Samuels thought it best to freshen up a little before lunch. Waiting for him was a pristine white linen suit, shirt, cravat, panama hat and white canvas deck-shoes. Mr Samuels had always been suspicious of such garb, thinking it overly smart and having not a little whiff of the plantation about it, but he was glad of it on that day as he recalled that he was still wearing the clothes in which he had slept in the open.

But there was a further reason: camouflage, of sorts. If he had appeared once again in his habitual brown suit and tie and about him were people dressed in a variety of white, summer fabrics, he would stick out like a sore thumb. Such a thing was always to be avoided. Perhaps it had always been Mr Samuels' wish, in the recesses of his heart, to go unnoticed. I thought it a learnt skill to aid in his work, but perhaps it was the other way around; he was drawn to the job because of the possibility of going unnoticed. Why then, I hear you cry, did he not just take on a faceless desk job, or go into the civil service? Fair point. And the answer to that is this: I have no idea.

Mia had also taken the opportunity to freshen up a little and Mr Samuels found her on deck in a long, white flowing linen shirt, long, white linen trousers and long, white linen scarf; the sort that chokes you to death when caught in the wheel of a speeding sports car.

What does it matter? She wore stuff; he wore stuff. Now, off we go.

'Mr Samuels! You look splendid! All fits well, I hope?'

'Perfectly, Madam.'

'Mia, please.'

Mr Samuels was not prepared to go there yet, and maybe never would be. Truth to tell, he was even a little distracted by his feet, so powerful was his dread of fungus and mistrust of canvas.

'They've just left the dock' and as she raised her arm to point to the shore her finely turned wrist was exposed and Mr Samuels was so much more moved by this than all the flesh on display earlier in the day. I'm not saying he was greatly moved, but there was movement of sorts.

A lot of white, I fancy, so the white speedboat split the blue waters as it hastened to them, casting a tumult of white waves in its wake. The nearer it came, the clearer one could see three people on board. One at the helm, and two – male and female – reclining on a banquette to the rear. Sunlight on water plays havoc on perception, so it was not until the boat was almost alongside that Mr Samuels could identify his boy among them.

Mia kept a close eye on Mr Samuels. What she saw must have pleased her a little as her mouth flickered into a slight smile.

What did Mr Samuels feel as boy and boat hoved into view? He identified a quickening of breath and then a long exhalation of air. He recognised an increase in heart-rate. He suspected a small widening of the pupils. He discerned a fresh burst of perspiration from beneath the panama hat. There was a minuscule urge to forward motion, followed by a no less miniscule rocking back on to the heels. There was a sudden itchiness in his right palm. There was a slight parting of the mouth but not enough to break the seal of lip upon lip. There was a small heave in the stomach.

The speedboat pulled to at the rear of the yacht and the driver leapt on to the platform-cum-deck designed for the purpose. He tied a rope to a spigot, if that is the word, before offering his hand to help his passengers aboard. Mia and Mr Samuels saw it all from the upper deck. Really, quite a sizeable vessel, the more I think about it.

'Hello there!' hailed Mia, waving and once more exposing that wrist.

The female down below waved back, and the boy looked up and smiled. Mr Samuels was not sure he was the one being smiled at.

Mr Samuels had to admit, if only to himself and if only for a moment, that his usual ability to size up a situation was somewhat impaired. The boy was uncanny. It was his boy, undoubtedly, but changed. His clothes, for one, were not what the boy would have normally worn. Linen was again much in evidence, with blue shorts and white shirt, neatly pressed, or as pressed as linen can be. His hair had been cut and a centre parting effected so that strands fell on either side of this face. His skin seemed healthy and clear. His posture had certainly improved and he seemed to have learnt to close his mouth whilst breathing. All this, Mr Samuels saw from a distance; he could read the signs but he could not make them mean anything, as yet.

'Come on up, my dears!'

'Madam,' said Mr Samuels, 'how long was I under your care at the house?'

She flapped away his concern with her hand, 'Oh, long enough to get you better, my dear man.'

The boy seemed to have grown and become thinner, or so Mr Samuels estimated as the boy extended his hand to him. They looked each other straight in the eye, before Mr Samuels broke the gaze in something like confusion, if such a thing can be imagined.

'How are you?' asked the boy.

'I am well, or getting well.' The boy still grasped his hand. 'And you?'

'Never better!' He gave Mr Samuels' hand a further shake.

'The longed for reunion!' chimed in Mia, brightly. 'So touching, isn't it?'

'Lovely,' said the girl at Mia's side.

'Where are my manners!' said the boy in mock alarm, 'this is Melissa'. He let go of Mr Samuels' hand and gestured him towards the girl who slinked forward, smiling and stretching out her hand to him.

'I've heard so much about you!'

'I wish I could say the same, but I am pleased to meet you.' Her hand felt cool and small in his.

Mr Samuels was not sure what mode of address to use for this girl. 'Melissa' was obviously a non-starter, and 'Miss' struck him as somehow inappropriate. He considered 'my dear' for a moment, but she wasn't dear and she wasn't his, so he just thought it best to use no mode of address whatsoever. Moreover, he wasn't sure that thinking of her as a girl was quite right; young woman might be nearer the mark. She seemed a little older than the boy, a year or two perhaps, but the most striking thing about her was her resemblance to Mia. She was tall and willowy, like Mia, but there the physical resemblance ended. Her face was pleasantly oval and framed by luxuriant black hair. Her skin was dark, and her eyes a deep brown; so deep as to seem to merge with her pupils to make it look as if they were all depth and no surface. True, she wore almost the same outfit as Mia and this might have increased the sense of similarity but it was more a case of a shared bearing. From posture, to how she tilted her head, to how she raised her eyebrows a hairsbreadth were all Mia.

'And are you feeling quite well, Mr Samuels?' Her smile was a brilliant array of bright, white, perfect teeth. 'We have been so worried, haven't we?' She turned to the boy.

'Of course,' he said.

Melissa took her hand from Mr Samuels and offered it to the boy, who accepted it without hesitation, without even a hint of embarrassment and perhaps even with a look of amused defiance, whatever that looks like, at Mr Samuels. They held hands with ease, their fingers interlocking.

'I am feeling much better, thank you.' Although at that moment he felt more uneasy than well.

'And looking so much better too, Mr Samuels, in that suit, if you don't mind my saying,' said Mia. 'Most handsome.'

He gave a little bow in thanks.

'Of course,' said Melissa, 'Sam has worried most of all, poor boy.' She stroked back the boy's hair with her free hand. 'But Mia kept us up-to-date on how you were doing and made sure Sam had everything he needed.'

'Mia has been amazing,' he said, 'but so have you,' gazing at Melissa fondly, before casting his eyes back to Mr Samuels. 'She really has been amazing.'

'I'm sure, and I'm grateful.'

'No need! I wouldn't have had it any other way. Else, I'd never have got to know Sam, would I?' She giggled in an oddly adult way.

So, The Woman was Mia to the boy, and he and Melissa a couple in some sense that Mr Samuels did not feel strong enough to contemplate. Perhaps he was not as well as he assured everyone he was.

'Oh,' gasped Melissa, suddenly, 'not that I'm glad, Mr Samuels, that you were, you know.'

'Stabbed and poisoned,' said Mr Samuels.

'Now, now, Mr Samuels, no gloomy thoughts,' Mia took him by the arm, 'not on such a happy day.'

Perhaps it was her close proximity that made Mr Samuels acquiesce.

'Of course, Madam.'

'Now, you two have time for a swim before lunch, if you like. You'll find swimming suits for you below.'

'Come on, Sam.' Melissa skipped off dragging Sam in her wake.

Mia and Mr Samuels, side by side, watched them go and listened to their light laughter.

Mia lingered on the arm of Mr Samuels.

'He is a credit to you. He has borne it all so well.'

'No doubt Miranda aided in that, Madam?'

'Miranda?'

'Melissa. But no less admirable.'

'Oh, Mr Samuels,' with a little laugh, 'You!'

She patted his arm and then detached herself.

'A protégé of yours, perhaps?'

'High time for a glass of wine, I think.'

She lifted up the seat of a banquette and produced a chilled bottle of white wine.

'Everything laid on, you see. Will you? No? Then I hope you won't mind if I do. Lovely. I find a little glass of wine on a day like today a real tonic, after all the hard work is done.'

'And is it done, Madam?'

'Mia.'

'Of course.'

'I rather think so, Mr Samuels.' She gazed out toward the horizon, the sea moving from blue to turquoise to green and back again, the horizon itself a hazy line of sea and sky, each merging into the other. 'But you and I have been in this business long enough to know that what seems like the end is not always the end.'

'Indeed.'

'Indeed, indeed, Mr Samuels. Indeed, indeed.'

'The boy looks well.'

'Doesn't he!'

'Unrecognisable, almost.'

'He's certainly blossomed.'

'Under Miranda's care?'

'Melissa.' She took leave to lie upon the luxuriant lounger. 'She was certainly a great help, and you see how close they are.'

'Indeed.'

'Makes one yearn for one's youth, doesn't it?'

'I couldn't say.'

She took to her feet.

'Oh, Mr Samuels, please forgive me! That was cruel! Thoughtless and cruel.'

'No matter, Madam, no matter.'

'But still...'

'No. No matter.'

'Least said soonest mended?'

'Of that order.'

They pondered the ocean together, but apart; she looking to starboard, he to port.

Their parallel reveries were broken by squeals and splashes as the boy and young woman took to the sea. Mr Samuels and Mia found themselves together again at a rail watching youth being youth in the midst of the ocean.

'To look at him now, Mr Samuels,' said Mia, 'you couldn't imagine the anguished adolescent he was when I broke the news of your incident.'

'You broke the news?'

'I felt it only right.'

'And you took him in hand?'

'Of course. With help.'

Melissa and the boy floated, spread-eagled.

Mr Samuels broke away from The Woman. Even now, he thought of her as such.

'Madam,' then he considered, 'I will have a glass of wine, if you'd be so kind.'

'That's the ticket,' she said, and handed him a freshly poured glass. He held his by the bowl; she by the stem.

'Madam,' he said.

'Mia.'

'Of course. Mia, Questions arise.'

'Naturally, I think.'

'Yes, I think naturally. But when I phrase them – to myself, you understand.'

'Perfectly.'

'Thank you. When I phrase them they seem ungrateful, or ungenerous and, I am sure you won't mind me saying this…'

'I'm sure I won't.'

'Thank you. A little suspicious of your role in,' and here Mr Samuels racked his brains before landing on 'events.'

They stood face to face, or near enough. She was a little taller, it has to be said. A proper distance was maintained between them throughout. Now is not the time for bridging that divide, even though the sun shines and the sea sways and the light glances prettily and the cries and laughs of youth play across the water.

She let that hang. He watched her letting it hang.

'Words, Madam'

'Mia.'

'Of course. Words, Mia, so often say more than one would have them, and so often stray from their mark.'

'You prefer to listen and watch.'

'As do you, and, if you don't mind my saying, staying silent on certain issues when it suits?'

'Of course! Please don't say another word.' Mr Samuels was much relieved. 'Sit with me.' She took her place once again on her luxurious lounger and patted same for Mr Samuels to join her. He thought it best to sit on his own, bringing them not only face to face but practically knee to knee.

'Whatever I have done,' she said, looking him straight in the eye, 'I assure you I have done for the best: for you, the boy, for everyone. I had to step in, Mr Samuels, knowing that the event, as you called it, was down to me. I had asked you to meet me there, after all. So, I took care of you first…'

'With help?'

'A modicum. But then my thoughts turned to dear Samuel. It is no small thing to be suddenly alone, not knowing where to turn, not knowing even how to boil an egg.'

'I've tried to teach him.'

'I'm sure you have, Mr Samuels, I am sure you have. I told him you were safe. I told him that your dearest wish would be to have him safe too.'

'As it was.'

'I'm sure. But not knowing why the event occurred, nor who arranged it, I thought it best for you to get better alone, whilst Samuel was taken care of.'

'You thought him in danger?'

'I did. Call me over cautious, perhaps, but I did. Did I do wrong, Mr Samuels, did I?' Her arm stretched across the gulf between them and she grasped his linen-clad knee.

'No, Mia. No, indeed.'

twenty-seven

Did I wait for the full dawning of day to return to the sliding-door and plumb its depths? No, I did not. I did not return at all. Curiosity only gets me so far and no further. Why would I want to go back there, in any case? I had been pootling along quite happily not knowing there was a pitch black room in the bowels of the house and as soon as I had become aware of it injury and incarceration had ensued. A better man than I might well have gone straight back, determined to see things in the cold light of day. Good luck to him.

I went to bed, resolving never to think of it again, unless forced.

'Man in Bed'; what a lovely story that would be to tell! Nice, languid lines of prose not once wrinkled by anything that could be mistaken for action or event. One day, perhaps.

As I slipped into sleep, it occurred to me that much could be deleted of all this nonsense without anyone much minding, least of all myself.

Screaming headache on waking. Nothing like a good old headache to make you feel alive and to blot out all of life's incidents.

'Man with Headache'; that'd be good as well.

But headaches never last. You think they will last forever, that you will never be free of the vice-like clutches, but they, like all else, soon pass leaving you dishevelled, exhausted and sunken-eyed but otherwise very much as you were.

I lay on my cot for quite some time, just to make sure.

There would be no visit from Marina. A thousand things told me it was not a Friday. That left only George as a possibility.

George burst in but without his usual bonhomie. No, indeed. He burst in with fists and kicks flying as he set about me.

It was in these early moments of this assault that I realised my mistake. It was not George at all. In my defence, my head had been turned away when the person had entered and as it was turning to see who it was when the fist was applied. So, I assumed George without actually seeing George. How wrong I was. After the fist, came a stamp on the chest, right on the breastbone. It winded me but not so much as to not recognise that this person lacked method as a pugilist. Surely, it would be better to focus on one bit of the body, and then the other? Having already got the nose under attack, aiming a few more blows in that direction would be a much better course of action than to open up another field of operations entirely, or so it seems to me, but perhaps this person was less a schooled fighter than an enraged piece of irrational viciousness.

How did I know it was not George? Hair. Lots of it flying about as the blows rained down upon me. And a skirt. I got a glance of the latter as the person left off for a moment to grab a heavy volume from the bookshelf. It was this same volume that then liberally and repeatedly battered my head. I did not see anything for quite a time after that.

The fact that I had not been bludgeoned to death by a book was only confirmed later. I suppose confirmation could have come sooner if I had actually been bludgeoned to death by a book. Perhaps a bright light beckoning me onwards, a flash of my lifelong struggles, or, who knows, flights of angels singing me to my rest. If nothing, then nothing; confirmation or otherwise.

Life, or what passed for it, slowly returned. The book seemed to have beaten the last of the headache out of me, contrary to all expectations and, contrary to all expectations, I came to with what can only be described as a sense of urgency. I did not sham dead to gain advantage. No. I snapped to, bolt upright on my cot the better to face my assailant. What I imagined I would do after facing my assailant I am not sure. I took up neither a defensive nor offensive posture. I grabbed neither weapon nor shield. Even now, I am not sure what would have made a serviceable weapon. She, whoever she was, had made good use of a book but the shelves were some metres from me and I didn't fancy making a dash for them, which was a shame, because a book could have been both weapon and shield, I mean a good size one; a dictionary or encyclopaedia or some such. Little damage to be done by, say, a psalter or a single volume of verse. I say psalter without ever having laid eyes on one, so maybe they come in all sorts of sizes, I don't know, but I fancy a full-blown Bible would top a psalter any day when it came to battle.

At bottom, I did not want to do battle.

She sat in my chair, behind my desk. She was undeniably a woman. It had crossed my mind on the third or fourth occasion that the book was applied to my head that rather than being an actual woman it might have been a man in disguise. I reasoned that the force and intent shown might be more in-line with the male than the female half of humanity. How wrong I was. In my defence, the possibility of it being a man in drag – for reasons best known to himself – was made more likely in my mind, as it was being pulped into unconsciousness, by the inability to think just who the woman might be. It was obviously not Marina because of the build and the force, but also because I fondly thought that she would look more kindly upon me than this woman appeared to. It was not Cass, again because of build, but also because she was in foreign climes attuning herself to the sky or something or other. It was not Pauline (build again), nor Violet (build once more) and I couldn't imagine either of them wanting to assault me in such a way, although given a fair wind and a good reason, or a flash of insanity, maybe they could have mustered something along these lines, but on the whole I thought not. That brought me to the end of women I knew which led, as night follows day, to the women I did not know or to it not being a woman at all.

The latter possibility I can further defend because the build of this woman had a passing resemblance to the build of George. Imagine George with a full head of hair, padding in appropriate places, and a full-ish body-wax treatment. All this was very plausible but no less wrong for all that. It was a woman.

The question remained: what woman?

The further question of why could be left until later. One question at a time, please, if you don't mind.

'Don't you move,' she said, and heaved herself up from the chair.

I'm quite sure I didn't move, but my head was beginning to swim a little.

She took a leisurely stroll over to the bookcase, her broad back turned towards me. Now would be my chance, many might have thought. Her back is turned, now would be the time to set about her as best I could. But the breadth of her back deterred me. Her blouse barely contained it. Ditto her skirt which stretched between powerful thighs.

Anyway, she had told me not to move.

She took a small, thick volume from the shelf and gauged its heft. It was bound in yellow leather, if memory serves.

'Knew it'd be up to me, in the end,' still weighing the book. 'It's just the way, isn't it?' I took this to be rhetorical. 'All this fannying about. I should have just grasped the nettle from the start.' She looked over her shoulder at me. This would have been a good time to fix her face, but my vision was not all that one might have hoped. 'But no. "Softly, softly catchy monkey," that idiot said.' Her voice was a gruff whisper. 'And I was an idiot to listen to him.'

'Now,' she said, moving towards me with the book raised, 'I don't like being made to look an idiot. Who does?'

I took this to be rhetorical too. I was wrong.

'Who does?' she repeated but tapping my head with the book to emphasise each word. This didn't have the desired effect, so she tried again but with a longer sentence. 'I said, who does?" Four raps on my skull.

'No one?'

'Right' and she slapped the book across my left ear. 'No one. Not me, that's for sure.' She spun away from me the better to let my head ring and to give herself a bit of a breather, perhaps.

'"Don't worry,' that daft bastard told me, "he's away with the fairies half the time. Won't know a thing." But oh no, you had to go poking around just because that cleaner bitch flashes her eyes at you. Seriously,' she said, 'what is it with men? Dozy gits most of the time but a little, teeny-tiny bit of attention from a little-ickle woman and they go all doolally.' She approached again with the book raised. 'Go poking their nose,' at which point she rather predictably wacked my nose, 'into things they should stay well out of.'

It took a little while for my nose to start bleeding but once it did it flowed with abandon, snot and blood dropping into my lap. They go quite well together, aesthetically speaking.

'So, here I am, sorting it all out like I always knew I would.'

Perhaps she was suddenly struck by the asymmetry of her assault because she then slapped the book across my right ear. She had an impressive backhand, it has to be said. A bit of blood from my nose flew across my sheets making quite a pleasing splatter pattern and a lovely contrast of deep red against off-white.

She got down on her haunches in front of me and raised my chin with the edge of the book. If anything, she was even more blurred at close range than at long and her eyes seemed to merge into the semblance of a Cyclops's gaze. She banged the book into my forehead, the better to get my attention I suppose. In truth, I was very much aware of her. Oh, I'm not saying that I was not aware of the ringing in my ears, the throbbing of my nose and the renewed pulsating pain in my head. I was very much aware of these indeed, but not so much aware that I didn't have enough awareness spare to focus a little on her, albeit a blurred focus admittedly. A hint of a moustache which gathered at the corner of her lips. There, that proves it.

'Listen,' she said, and I tried. 'Gloves are off now. Know what I mean?'

I didn't dare take this to be rhetorical.

'Yes.'

'Good. So no more nonsense. Right?'

I nodded and it felt like something surged across my skull.

'What I say, goes.'

Nod again.

'Good. If you take one step out of this room… You listening? One step! You're fucked. What are you?'

'Fucked,' I said, not seeing any other option.

'You do what I say when I say or you're fucked. What are you?'

'Fucked.'

'You look at me wrong, you give me any lip, and what are you?'

'Fucked.'

'Fucked.'

She got to her feet and looked me over before giving me a parting crack to the skull and throwing the book to the floor. There was a little blood on its binding but otherwise it was unharmed.

Well that was all nice and clear. Nice to know where one stands, for a change.

Twenty-eight

Lunch was an all-round lovely affair. The sea rippled as did the laughter and light banter on the boat.

I don't do banter. I'm not even entirely sure what it is.

Lovely it may well have been, but it left Mr Samuels, who exempted himself from the laughter, with much to mull over and the focus of his mulling was naturally enough the boy. He didn't have much to go on, in truth. The physical differences in the lad had already been noted but not yet brought to book. His demeanour, but not the reason for it, became a little clearer as salad and fish were consumed. For a start, the boy had now not only mastered chewing with his mouth closed but also the proper use of cutlery. Could this have been achieved in so short a time? But then Mr Samuels was still unsure about how much time had elapsed, so that was moot. He seemed relaxed, polite, more at ease in his skin, and countless other unfathomable alterations from the surly boy he had last seen slouching off to school on the day of the assault. But he had little to go on, in truth, because the boy rarely directed his attention towards him. He smiled at Mr Samuels pleasantly from time to time. He politely answered when asked a direct question, which Mr Samuels was careful to keep in neutral territory at all times, not even daring to ask 'but what about your schooling?' although the question was much on his mind. Nor did he ask about the nature of the relation between the boy and the young woman, which, if anything, was even more on his mind. Not once did the boy address himself to Mr Samuels unbidden. The boy's eyes strayed to Melissa and Mia whenever they could. This left Mr Samuels somewhat lost as to what to make of it all.

Mulling on the boy necessarily meant mulling on the girl, Melissa, too. She gave off the same air of confident ease that the boy had somehow acquired. Really, a very personable and no doubt accomplished young lady. She was attentive on the boy whilst neither condescending nor overly effusive. She had a frank openness about her that hinted at naiveté without actually being such. She stroked the back of the boy's hand from time to time and was much given to gazing and smiling at him, which was nice.

What do I know of the ways of young women? I haven't seen one in years. She seemed nice and she seemed to like the boy, Samuel. That is all. That is more than enough.

Mr Samuels was well aware, amidst the smiles and repartee, that The Woman was keeping a close eye on it all.

Mia had arranged for a car to take them home. Home, at last. It would have been better if Mr Samuels had never left. As the speedboat sped away from the yacht, the boy waved at Mia and Melissa on the upper-most deck. Driver and car awaited them on the shore. Not a word was shared between Mr Samuels and the boy. Not a word was shared on the journey back to the city but this might have been because Mr Samuels soon succumbed to sleep, sedated by nothing more sinister than the smooth ride, plush upholstery and the wine consumed at lunch.

Mr Samuels and the boy, for reasons perhaps even unknown to themselves, felt the need to linger side-by-side at the garden gate, sizing up the house and what it might mean. The grass could have done with a trim, and some flowers needed dead-heading.

'Come on,' said the boy after some little time, 'let's get you in and settled. Mia said you still need to recover your strength.'

'Yes. Yes, you are probably right.'

The boy was all polite efficiency. He even smiled as he took Mr Samuels by the arm and led him into the house. It was pristine. The Woman, no doubt, had seen to a deep clean whilst Mr Samuels and the boy had been away.

'In our out?'

'Out, I think.'

So the boy led Mr Samuels to the back garden and placed him in a comfy chair to enjoy the evening as it drew in.

As the sun gave up the ghost somewhere in the west, the temperature dropped a tad and the sky began to darken. A bat might have flitted about. The insects of the night began to stir.

Was Mr Samuels lulled by this general easing? No. No he was not. Oh, he felt a general sense of greater calm; he was home after all. But greater calm is not calmness.

'I have made you a gin and tonic,' as the boy took another comfy chair and placed the glass on the table between them. So, now he knew how to make a gin and tonic. Admittedly, it is not a difficult drink to master, but the fact that he had thought of it and done it was unlike him, or so Mr Samuels could not help feeling.

'Can I get you anything else?'

'No, thank you.' Mr Samuels even gave a little smile in the gathering gloom.

The sky was becoming a deepening green. Boy and man watched it change.

'Glad to be home?' asked the boy.

'I am.'

'Good.'

'And you? Are you glad to be home?'

'Mia gave me a list of instructions.'

'Instructions?'

'About getting you better, and stuff to watch out for.'

So, he still said 'stuff'; that was something.

'I mean, signs of deterioration or complications,' said the boy.

'Such as?'

The boy took a small notebook, leather-bound, from the pocket of his shorts, consulted it, and then put it back in his pocket.

'Fever, dizziness, difficulty urinating, blood in urine, general confusion.'

'I see. Nothing like that as far as I can ascertain.'

'Good, but you know what they say: forewarned is forearmed.'

They might say it, but Mr Samuels never had.

The high-pitched whine of an insect broke the silence.

'How is the wound?'

'Healing well, I think. Although it itches from time to time.'

'Don't worry. I have instructions on how to change the dressing.'

'From Mia?'

'Yes.'

The Woman had thought of everything it seemed.

They sky moved towards purple and stars began to prick the night.

'The girl, Melissa? She seems a very nice young lady.'

'She is.'

'If you don't mind my asking…'

'Well that rather depends on what you will ask. Ha, ha, ha.'

The boy tittered and the man smiled.

'Where did you meet?'

'At the retreat. Up in the mountains.'

'And Mia took you there did she?'

'No, she arranged it, though. It was the day you were stabbed.'

Mr Samuels could not detect any trace of emotion in the boy on this point.

'I'm sorry to have worried you,' said Mr Samuels.

'I wasn't worried,' said the boy, despite what Melissa had said on the boat.

Mr Samuels was saddened.

'You see, as soon as I arrived at the retreat, there was Melissa. She told me all was in hand and so I mustn't worry. So I didn't worry.'

'Quite a persuasive young lady.'

'She's great.' A flash of emotion and a glimpse of the adolescent he still was. 'Mia came up that night and told me what had happened, what state you were in but that you were being taken care of and that she was supervising your progress, so I knew there really was no reason to worry at all.'

'She visited?'

'Yes.'

'I see.'

'And sent updates via Melissa.'

'I see again.'

'She thought I might be in danger.'

'Melissa?'

'Mia. So she said it was best to stay up at the retreat until things died down.'

'Things?'

'You know.'

Mr Samuels didn't and he very much wished that he did.

'Was it a nice place, this retreat, as you call it?'

'Fantastic! Had a pool and a tennis court and table tennis and mountain bikes and all sorts. The food was amazing, too.' That youthful glee was once more in evidence.

'Was there anyone else with you and the young lady?'

'Just the staff, and Mia once in a while.'

Silence once again.

Now, how did Mr Samuels feel about all this? Firstly, he was discomforted by the thought that he should feel something about all this in the first place. Yet even Mr Samuels must recognise, if only to himself, that the emotional side of things is best taken into account. Had it not done so on almost every mission he had undertaken? Indeed he had, although not his own but those of the other parties involved. Yes, then the emotional was something to be borne in mind and entered into one's calculations, the better to plan ahead, of course. Now, though, the object of his enquiry was himself. He did not have the strength. He did not have the experience. He did not know where to start. He recognised his own discomfort and considered this enough emotional insight, for the time being.

So, Mr Samuels being Mr Samuels, he considered the facts, such as they had been presented to him. Oh, his mind was still alive enough to know that facts as they are presented are not the same as actual facts, that they are prey to selection, omission, distortion and adaptation, whether by design or by humans just being humans. He regretted this state of affairs, but, when all said and done, was it not precisely this state of affairs that had made his profession a necessity? That was certainly one way of looking at it. If facts were facts and always known as facts, there would be no need for Mr Samuels and his ilk.

The facts seemed to be these:

The boy had been taken care of at a retreat by Melissa, Mia and staff. One might suspect the hand of an organisation in all of this, no doubt the one to which The Woman had alluded, but that would be speculation.

The boy had been altered by this sojourn in the mountains, perhaps under the influence of affluence and the company he kept, that is Mia and Melissa; the former as much as the latter, perhaps, for she was an impressive woman. Mr Samuels was well aware that this was an opinion, and not a fact, but he considered it an opinion that few would not share, so as near to a fact as an opinion could be.

'Perhaps' seemed to loom large in this list of supposed facts.

The boy and Mr Samuels had been returned home, together again. No 'perhaps'.

Once facts are established, it was Mr Samuels' habit to then make a series of deductions, as he called them, or working hypotheses, as he called them at other times. These were not to be confused with mere speculations as they remained within the parameters laid down by the facts, such as they were, at all times.

These thoughts ended up in similar, but crucially different, hypotheses:

Mia, Melissa (and perhaps an organisation) have taken care of Mr Samuels and the boy for unknown reasons, but in a benevolent spirit.

Mia, Melissa (and perhaps an organisation) have taken care of Mr Samuels and the boy for unknown reasons, but with a malevolent aim.

He looked at the boy in the gloom. He was looking up at the stars, his eyes fixed somewhere in the region of Saturn or Venus, or somesuch. When he became aware of being looked upon, he turned his head and gave a relaxed smile.

It was then Mr Samuels unmistakably felt something. In fact, he felt a number of things in a confused surge as if a confluence of rivers in full flood. His stomach was doing something he did not recognise. There was a feeling of being tugged towards the boy, which Mr Samuels could not tell was mental or physical. He felt himself expand and contract in turn, or all at once. He felt his eyes crinkle and moisten.

He heard himself say, 'You are turning into a fine young man, Samuel.'

He then made himself say, 'I think I will get an early night. I am still rather fatigued.'

'Do you need any help?'

'No, thank you. It is kind of you to ask, but no.'

'Night then!'

'Good night.'

In his own bed, in his own pyjamas, Mr Samuels looked up into his own dark. It took some little time, but finally he knew what he felt. He felt glad. He felt glad to be home and glad to be back with the boy. Finally, he felt glad at what the boy had become.

Outside, Samuel watched Saturn and Venus go through their inevitable course as he waited for the house to be quite still.

twenty-nine

Instructions regarding not leaving the room had been very clear indeed. Couldn't have been clearer. Instructions on allowing people into the room had, sadly, been lacking.

'Dear oh dear, she's had a right go on you, hasn't she?'

George, inching his way in and giving me a once over with his best attempt at a concerned gaze. He sat next to me on the cot and I am afraid I might have flinched a little. It's understandable. I have been beaten often enough to know that just because one beater has left that another one might not just be waiting their turn. They might regret not being the one to draw first blood but that wouldn't stop them having a go at second, third or fourth, and perhaps in the recesses of their heart thanking their lucky stars that the victim had been softened up a bit.

'The thing about Martha, see...' he said.

My ears, still ringing, did their best to prick up at this. So, that was Martha. But was it the Martha, or just a Martha. Was it George's Martha, his wife, confidante and better angel? Surely not. For had not George described her as mousey and tender-hearted? He had. The Martha who had visited herself upon me had been many things, but mousey and tender-hearted had not been chief among them. Hulking and brutal seemed nearer the mark. But perhaps I was doing this Martha a disservice. Perhaps in George's eyes she was indeed mousey; a petite flower who needed to be sheltered from the wilds of the world. Quite how George could think this I was not sure for Martha and he were remarkably similar, physically speaking. But perhaps he had not been thinking of physical mousiness, but more a species of inner-mousiness, that beneath the undoubted bulk of the woman there was a small, fluffy, nervous core. As for tender-hearted, who was I to claim otherwise after so brief an acquaintance? True, she had done much to put the description in doubt, but perhaps faced with a gurgling infant, or mewing kitten, she was gentleness itself. Perhaps she had an ailing, frail grandmother for whom she could not do enough.

But, no matter how much I tried to square the circle of the Martha as described by George and the Martha who had pummelled me with something like glee, I could not do it.

So, a different Martha all together. The name is not uncommon.

Or a fictional Martha and the real Martha. Yes, George might have lied when he had spoken of his gentle Martha, meek and mild, for reasons of strategy or just for the hell of it or to flee the real Martha, if only in his imagination, if only for a little while.

In truth, if I was to be quite clear in my mind I would need to see two Martha's in front of me: one, mousey and tender-hearted; the other hulking and brutal.

'... is sometimes she has to take control and sometimes she goes a little far.'

This seemed to me to be a fair assessment.

'Sometimes, she asserts herself.'

One way to describe what had occurred.

'But who can blame her?'

One person sprang immediately to mind.

'I mean, she has had to put up with a lot.'

I thought this lacked a little tact.

'She's been ignored, you see.'

Hard to believe, I thought, as I tried to staunch the blood still flowing from my nose.

'Not given her due. Not given what's owing to her. So she has to stand up for herself, see?'

Seeing was still proving a tad tricky.

'Been that way since we was kids.'

Aha!

'Never scared, that one, to stand up for herself. Teachers; mum; dad; didn't matter. Thing is, not to rile her.'

This advice had come a little late, I felt.

'Don't want her riled up.'

Indeed not.

'Maths teacher – Millegan or Millership or something – he got her riled up once. Lobbed a blackboard rubber – remember them? – lobbed it right at her just because she was talking or mucking about or something. Got her right on the ear. He had a good arm, that old bastard, let me tell you. Hair like a brillo pad, but a good arm. So, Martha picks up the rubber, waits for his back to be turned, then runs up and whacks him over the head with it. He goes down, surprise more than anything I guess, and she gives him a right old kicking. Well deserved if you ask me. That got her kicked out, 'course, but worth it I reckon. And she says to me, she says "glad I did it. Can't let no one push me around." Which is fair enough, isn't it?'

I did not feel in a position to judge.

'So, nothing personal, see?' He even patted my knee at this point as I stared at the row upon row of silent books.

'Twatted me with a saucepan, once, 'cause I wouldn't let her have me Action Man. Eagle eyes, he had. Oh well. So, nothing personal. Just gotta do what she says and give her her due.'

That it was not personal I was willing to believe, mainly because I had been completely unaware of this actual Martha until she had punched me in the face. Had I slighted her by chance? In another life? I doubted it but cause and effect have never been the closest of bedfellows in my estimation. The blood in my nose was bubbling as I breathed.

'You wanna get some ice on that,' said George, flatly. 'Right,' he slapped his thighs and rose from the cot, 'now you know the ins and outs, the dos and the don'ts, eh?'

I must have looked blank.

'Do what she says. Don't get her riled up.'

I nodded.

He smirked.

'Thing is, when you think about, it should have been me giving you the kicking.' He raised his fist but thought better of it. 'Or maybe I should have been the one getting the kicking. Ha, ha, ha. Dropped me right in it, you did, with your sniffing about and poking around and whispering with that Marina. Dropped me right in it up to me neck! Just when it was all going so well, too. Oh well, better you than me, anyways.'

'Have a lie down. Have a nap, ya daft cunt, and it'll all be happy families when you wake up.'

He patted my cheek.

'Yeah?'

He slapped it.

'Course it will.'

He couldn't deny himself a little turnaround at the threshold.

'Oh, and don't worry about your Marina. We've got her in hand, Martha and me.'

It must be difficult sometimes to take the advice of a man who has some vague but undoubtedly malignant intent, but I didn't feel able to resist on this occasion. I have some remote memory of learning once that the one thing not to do after a blow to the head was to give in to sleep. I can't remember why not, but death lurks around the question somewhere. In any case, at that time, the thought didn't cross my mind, or, if it did, it quickly uncrossed it mindful as I was that I was meant to be doing what I was told. True, George had said that I should do what Martha told me to do, and it had been George who had advised me to sleep, so technically I might not have been beholden, but I had enough sense about me to realise that George was in some way an extension of Martha in such matters. At least, it was safer to assume so. Anyway, the entire thing was moot because I couldn't keep my eyes open. As I drifted, I thought that perhaps one day all would become clear; all that was vague would become certain; all that was murky would become obvious.

We can but hope.

In restless sleep I dreamt of a goat, and simpler days. I dreamt of a calming hand on my brow; pure sensation with no sight of who that hand might belong to. I dreamt of diving into an icy lake. I dreamt of a soft breeze and a setting sun. It was a busy sleep.

The dog brought me back to the land of the living, so called. I awoke to it licking my face, drawn by the blood and snot no doubt, although I am quite sure it could have done without the snot. It's breath was warm and sweet; its tongue wet and soothing, after a fashion. It even whimpered a little, in a little show of fellow-feeling, perhaps. It wasn't a Saint Bernard, but it did its best, I suppose. After cleaning my face, it fell asleep beside me in the cot and I envied it. I envied its thoughtless slumber. I envied it its youth and calm; its innocence of the kicks and beatings of the world; the raging of the mind and the howls of the flesh. I envied its lack of anything to be done. Eat, shit, sleep, lick, run about a bit. It's a full enough life. But there was I, even in the depths of concussion, or so I assumed, knowing that here was a sorry state of affairs indeed. Oh, the nuances escaped me, I admit. The reasons and motivations were blurry, but there was nothing new in that. The facts remained, and I clung to them: do not leave the room; beaten by a Martha; at the mercy of a George; Marina under threat; no hope of outside help, as far as I could see. Yes, who would come to my aid, now? The dog had done its best, but there is a limit to what a dog can do in such cases. If I had had a goat, as I had always wanted, perhaps it could have intervened. In my dreams, the goat had always been a small, white thing, with little nubbins for horns but I am not so innocent as to not know that even the smallest goat, the little, frolicking kind, can't pack a fair whack if it puts its mind to it. It could have butted George in the balls, for example, which might not have done much good but would have offered some degree of satisfaction. It could have chased Martha about the house and driven her away, but I fancied she would have returned with a shotgun or hatchet and taken back control in no uncertain terms. If the dog had been fully grown and well-trained, perhaps I could have set him on my foes, but with him sleeping next to me, I was far from certain.

There was another fact, then; I had foes. God knows how, but I had.

And there she was.

'What's the combination?' She barked from the door.

The dog couldn't even be arsed to wake up.

'The combination?' I said.

'To the room,' she said.

'Room?' I said.

'Yes, the fucking room. The safe room thing,' she said.

'What safe room thing?' I said, after some little time.

'The safe room,' she said, which did little to clarify things even if she had stretched the article to quite an extent.

'That bastard Paul's safe room thing,' she said, which added some information admittedly but not the sort of information I needed to be any clearer. It did lead me to believe that she had a dim opinion of Paul, but knowing Paul myself I thought this was reasonable enough.

My mouth opened and shut. I had nothing to add, not knowing what was required.

She came into the room, grabbed me by the collar and hauled me up. Finally, the dog took a little notice but thought it best, on the whole, just to go back to sleep.

'You are such a fucker!' She said. 'Such a fucking fucker. Are you as thick as pig-shit, or just mental?'

She dragged me along the corridor and hurled me down the stairs I had so recently ascended. Amazing strength the woman possessed, when you think of it. I might not weigh much but I still feel I have a little heft about me. I couldn't pick myself up, if I were her and she me, if you see what I mean. I certainly couldn't have picked her up and dragged her along if she were she and I were me, but she didn't even seem to struggle. Nor did I, thinking that a dead-weight approach was better than a flailing one. Neither, I must have intuited, would have done me any good anyway, in the long run.

It was as I was tumbling down the stairs that I caught sight of my missing piece of hair stuck to the wall.

Fully illuminated, the room was disappointingly small. More of an ante-room, but ante to what was not clear until I noticed a set of cables running along one wall – the wall I had not examined in the dark, of course, as luck would have it – and apparently disappearing into a further wall. Just to be clear – clear! – the room had four walls. Well, four if you think of the staircase as splitting apart one wall rather than creating two separate walls. If you think that, then it would be five. But not arranged in a pentagon. No. Squareness, or near as damned, was the overall effect. So a square room with one wall bisected by the stairs. Right. Now, I had begun my fumblings in the dark, on my hands and knees if memory serves, in the middle of the wall which faced me as I got to my feet at the foot of the stairs. So, I had covered roughly half of the room before I found the way out. Now, it so happens that the cables ran into the wall which now faced me but in that half of the wall I had not fumbled along. And it goes without saying, that the wall along which the cables ran had been utterly unknown to me in my benighted gropings.

A diagram would have been easier, but never mind.

A shove in my back reminded me I was not alone.

'Over here,' she said, grasped my collar once more and pushed me over into the corner into which the cables disappeared at about head height, well, my head height. I'm no electrician, but it occurred to even me, and no doubt had already occurred to Martha, that cables have to go from somewhere to somewhere else, and yet these seemed to connect only with the wall. I let my palm play along its surface and then, remembering having seen the same somewhere without knowing where or when, I gave the wall a rap with my knuckles. I then rapped the wall along which the cables ran. The sound was different and I deduced that the latter was solid and the former was not. Wonderful. I had never thought that the rapping-the-wall thing would ever have come in handy and the knowledge of it had lain dormant for who knows how long before it was called upon and yet when the time came the knowledge, wheresoever gained, popped into my head and told me the wall was not solid, but that a space lay beyond.

'What the fuck are you doing?'

Rather than waiting for my answer, she pinned my head against the wall.

'I don't need a fucking surveyor; I need you,' an extra bit of pressure here so my mouth slightly buckled, 'to put the bloody code in.'

I tried to say 'code?' but my lips were too pressed to be of much use. She wrenched my head to face the other way, clamped my cheek to the wall again and said 'here! Fucking well here!'

Her range of expletives was poor, it has to be said.

What was fucking well there was a pad of numbers set into the wall just beneath where the cables disappeared. It took me a while to see it, in truth, partly because it was flush to the wall but mainly because my faculties were having a hard time of it, sight included. Oddly, though, my sense of smell, if anything, seemed more acute, perhaps because of the acrid stench of body odour Martha exuded.

Now, I am no mathematician. As far as I could tell, the pad had the numbers zero to nine upon it, if zero is a number. Martha had reluctantly unclamped my head so I could see the pad a little better. If the code were to use all nine numbers then there were an awful lot of possible combinations. How many, I have no idea, but a lot. More than you would think, I suspect. But of course, there was no guarantee that all nine numbers were to be used; it could have been eight, or it could have been one, or anywhere in between; five, for example. If one, then there were ten possibilities, counting the zero of course; if eight there were an awful lot, although not as many as if there were nine, admittedly, but still a vast amount. Five, less so but still I fancied rather a few.

I want to use the phrase 'power of' but have no idea what it means.

'Come on, ya bastard!'

The numbers swam before me, gathering and scattering in turn.

'I don't know the code,' I said. 'I have no idea. I've never even seen this before.'

Listen to me, getting all chatty!

I'm afraid that Martha lost her patience at this. She took my head between her two hands, turned my face to the number pad, and banged the former against the latter repeatedly and with great force.

As a method of cracking the code it was as good as any, I supposed, blood and snot streaming from my nose once again. I'm not saying it was successful; just that it was as good as any, which is to say, no good at all.

Martha's expletives echoed about the room as she stormed up the stairs. Soon I was back in the dark.

thirty

Mr Samuels dreamt of a kid gambolling in a spring meadow.

He dreamt of almond blossom gently flying on a warm breeze.

He dreamt of a butterfly flitting from bloom to bloom.

The dreams were cut short as Mr Samuels shot up in bed with something like terror. He struggled for breath and his limbs seemed to shake uncontrollably for a second or two. He felt his eyes bulge and his chest tighten.

Mr Samuels could not imagine how kids and blossom and butterflies could inspire such a sudden, violent fear. What else he might ascribe that fear to, again he could not imagine. He had been dreaming, then the fear had ripped him awake. He could think of no intervening stimulus, but, as he tried to ease himself, he considered that one doesn't remember all one's dreams. Actually, it was rare for him to remember his dreams at all.

Once he had quietened his breath and got his limbs under control, Mr Samuels thought he heard noises about the house. The boy, of course, making himself a snack in the middle of the night, or getting himself a glass of water from the kitchen, or just mooching about, unable to sleep because of the excitement of being home, safe and sound. This eased Mr Samuels still further and he slipped back into a dreamless sleep.

Mr Samuels woke later than was his habit. The sun was already very much up and cutting through the slats of his shutters, picking out thin lines of flying dust. He lifted his pyjama top, examined the dressing over his wound and pronounced himself satisfied. He even checked on his penis. No harm seemed to have been done by the whole catheter business although it was perhaps a little swollen, understandably. He did not pronounce himself satisfied with his penis.

The kitchen was clean and quiet. If a midnight snack had been made, all trace of it had been cleared away. Mr Samuels noted this with pleasure, even though the midnight snack had been only a theory and not a reality, as far as he knew. The lip of the china teacup on his own lip was a comfort indeed, like shaking hands with an old friend, not that Mr Samuels had any old friends.

Save for some inevitable growth and no less inevitable wilting, the garden was also very much as Mr Samuels had left it, however long ago. It really was high-time that this question of duration was solved, now that he had all the resources of his house available to him, but Mr Samuels thought it could wait a little longer, that he could relax into a little bit of not knowing while he finished his tea from his china cup in the shade of his veranda in his favourite comfy chair.

The boy must have been still sleeping. A boy can change, but those teenage habits of lying in bed still remained, it seemed. Rather than being annoyed by this, as previously, Mr Samuels just greeted the thought with an indulgent smile.

After bathing and putting a fresh dressing on his wound, Mr Samuels dressed with care; not in his habitual brown suit, but in the new, white linen suit in which Mia had thought him handsome.

Finally, he felt ready to face the problem of time.

Let it not be thought that Mr Samuels had not already made some effort, during the days of his captivity, to solve this problem of duration, because he had. He consulted the moon on occasion, the angle of the sun at a given time on certain days, the rise or fall in temperature from day to day, the amount of growth on his chin, the progress of his wound, yet all were flawed. Of the moon, he could have missed a whole month and he would have been none the wiser. The sun was a better bet but, as luck would have it, Mr Samuels had never kept a detailed diary of the sun's progress throughout the year so whilst it was clear that it was doing something it was unclear what this meant in terms of time. The temperature remained intolerable. Someone shaved him in his sedated sleep. Rather like the sun, his wound had progressed but he had no yardstick by which to measure this. Yes, all he knew was that time had happened, but not how much time.

Add to this that the notebook he always kept with him had disappeared along with his original brown suit.

Not to be daunted, though, Mr Samuels knew that he had a second notebook, safe in his desk. The notebook he always carried around with him was, as it were, his daily resource whenever he was undertaking a job. The second notebook was more of a ledger in which he logged the beginning and end of each job and any expenses occurred. It was from this second notebook that he drew up his accounts. It never left the house. It would be a matter of a minute to check this and then know how long ago his stabbing had been.

He threw open the shutters and light dispelled the gloom of the small, neat office.

Mr Samuels was very fond of his desk, which was rather more of a bureau, in truth. He sat in his wood and leather chair and enjoyed the array of drawers and niches laid out before him. He ran his hand along the smooth, worn baize of the desktop and took up his favourite pen to savour the snug, familiar fit. He opened a small drawer on the upper left of the bureau and felt along the underside. There was nothing there. The key which opened the large, central drawer should have been there, was always there, taped to the underside, but now it was not. He took the drawer all the way out, turned it over, but nothing. The trace of the tape was still visible and this only made the absence of the key more certain. In a sudden rush, he yanked open the central drawer and again found nothing. His second notebook, his ledger, was gone.

'Looking for this?'

The Woman held aloft the diary from the threshold of the room. She smiled evenly and entered.

'Melissa, Samuel!' she called, 'please join us.'

In they came, fingers interlocked. Melissa sported the same smile as Mia and the boy's face was blank, his mouth shut and jaw clenched. They remained on the edge of the room, framed by the doorway.

Mia, under the never wavering gaze of Mr Samuels, sauntered towards the desk, taking her time to take in every detail of the room and every detail of Mr Samuels, sitting there, fixed in his white linen suit. She admired his professionalism, his ability to remain focused and apparently impassive. Mr Samuels struggled indeed to maintain the façade. Inside, all was a turmoil, an unprecedented tumult of racing, incoherent thoughts.

He cleared his throat.

'Madam,' he said, as she ran a manicured finger along the edge of the desk, 'if you would be so kind as to give me my diary, I would be much obliged.'

'This?' turning it one way then the other, 'This old thing? All yours.' She dropped it onto the baize in front of him. 'We've had the whole thing digitised, so you might as well have it back.' Not once did her even smile and even tone alter.

Mr Samuels tried to read her eyes and failed. He gripped the arms of his chair ever more tightly. She crossed the room, turned and leant against the window sill. The brightness outside cast her into a deep silhouette and a halo played about her head.

Mr Samuels gathered himself as best he could.

'You will forgive me, Madam…'

'Mia.'

'In light of events I think Madam might be best.'

'As you wish.'

'Perhaps you have not realised the offence this violation must inevitably cause.'

'Oh, I think I have a fair idea.'

The silhouette gave Mr Samuels nothing to go on as he glared in its direction.

'Every mission that has been entrusted to me for the past five years is detailed here,' as he placed his hand on the book.

'And your record keeping is most impressive! Very thorough. All that we hoped for.'

'We?'

'Now, now, Mr Samuels! You don't really expect me to answer that do you?'

'No. No, I don't suppose I do,' and he rocked back in his chair. He was at a loss. Was there any point asking the woman anything? If she was telling the truth, then his whole career for the past five years was known to her and whomever she worked for, or with, because he didn't put it past her to be high-up in, or indeed the head of, the organisation that had taken such an interest in him.

'Oh, Mr Samuels,' she said. 'I know it must be all a bit of a shock, especially given how we managed to get hold of the book.'

He raised his head towards her but saw nothing save a dark form surrounded by bright light. It was from this that the voice came.

'We have Samuel to thank for that, don't we Samuel?'

Mr Samuels could not bring himself to look at the boy.

'Come here, my dear.'

The boy crossed the room. Mr Samuels stared only at the green baize of his desk and at the book upon it. His peripheral vision saw the silhouettes of the boy and The Woman merge in the glare of the window.

'Such a promising young man, don't you think? He followed every instruction to the letter, didn't you Sam?'

'I hope so, Mia.'

'Hope be damned! You did!'

The silhouettes merged all the more as The Woman embraced the boy.

'Now, would you mind waiting in the car with Melissa for a few minutes? I need to speak to Mr Samuels a little.'

'Of course.'

Melissa and Samuel locked fingers once again, turned and left.

'Shall we get some air Mr Samuels? It is so stuffy in here.'

After some time, he found her in his favourite comfy chair out on the veranda, sunglasses lowered against the blaze of the day. He stood to her rear, knowing that being face-to-face with her would be futile. He looked across the garden and up into the clear blue of the empty sky.

'So it is about the boy and not the book?' He phrased it as a question but knew the answer already.

'Oh, the book will be useful, no doubt about that, but you're right. Glad to see your faculties are returning.'

'They have been hampered of late.'

'Yes. Sorry about that.'

'But you needed me out of the way.'

'We needed time with Samuel, you see, to assess him.'

'And train him.'

'A little. He has a lot to learn, but he is a willing student, very adaptable, really. He has something of your talents actually.'

Mr Samuels swallowed hard. 'Thank you.'

'But more, how shall I put? More flair, potentially, and more attuned to modern methods, modern systems.'

Mr Samuels walked past her out into the full heat of the sun. It beat down upon him.

'Come on now, Mr Samuels! You always knew this day would come.'

'But it didn't have to come as a betrayal Madam,' and his anger allowed him to turn and face her, 'that is what I cannot accept. Yes, I knew he would outgrow me one day, Madam, but the betrayal? Is that necessary?'

She rose, walked to him and removed her glasses. There was a new steeliness to her voice.

'Betrayal, Mr Samuels, breaks the ties that bind. Of course it was necessary. New allegiances cannot be compromised by old ones.'

'So you told him he is not my son?'

'Of course I told him!' She laughed in his face. 'That was the whole point! Really, Mr Samuels!'

'It was my place to tell him.'

'But you were never going to, were you?'

His shoulders sagged and he looked at the earth.

'You see,' she said, 'you know you wouldn't have. I've seen it before! Father and son, father and son like some delusional dynasty.

Your father got away with it, but you? Never.' She jabbed him in the shoulder and he rocked back on his heels.

He looked up into her unfathomable eyes.

'You really didn't know?'

Silent.

'Well, now you do.'

Mr Samuels did not notice her go.

thirty-one

If you don't mind, I think I will draw a discreet veil over the question of shitting and pissing in my confinement. It wasn't that long, when all said and done. I couldn't judge the time by the all the usual methods – the sun, the moon and such – but I fancy it was less than twenty-four hours, which, given a lifetime, is not so large a span. Yet no doubt there were many sighs and my heart was faint, from time to time.

I made no attempt to escape. I didn't even go up the stairs to try the door. I don't know why. Perhaps I knew it would be futile. Perhaps I thought that both to hope and quietly wait might be the best option, in the long run. So, rather than reflect, ponder and assess the situation I did none of these things and just sat wedged in a corner and felt my face throb until dim light broke upon me once again.

'Christ, what a stink!' said George from the top of the stairs. 'What ya been doing down there?'

The veil remained intact.

'Come up. Visitor.'

I made my way up the stairs towards the light obscured by George's bulk. Rather than move and let me pass, he stood stock still on the threshold which necessarily meant that I stopped with two or three steps to go, which further meant that I faced his paunch. This shirt was no better fitting than all the others I had seen him wear. Hair poked through the gaps between the straining buttons. For that reason, and no doubt others, I kept my head bowed.

'Now, mate,' said George, 'Martha's got a right strop on, so watch it. Just give her what she wants, alright?'

'But I don't know what she wants.'

'Her due, like I told you. Your Paul buggered off and left her with nothing, not even a golden shower.'

This was eminently worthy of comment, but I held my peace.

'Handshake, I mean. Golden handshake. After doing all his dirty work for god knows how long; zip; nothing; zilch,' at which point he ran out of synonyms.

Why then, I wondered then and wonder still, had he not turned to Martha in the whole Violet affair? Why had he turned to me when he had a Martha on hand? Perhaps Martha's skills, such as they were, were not suited to the task. No, I don't think Cass would have taken kindly to Martha's methods. Martha had many fine qualities, no doubt, but not for all occasions.

How many men, women and even children had been visited by Martha at Paul's behest, I did not care to know.

George blocked my passage still. Somewhere in the house the dog yapped, then yelped.

'I mean, it's not like she's unreasonable or nothing. Years she worked for him, years and years. Yeah, yeah, she got paid and all that but there was a, you know…'

I didn't.

'An understanding.'

If there had been, it seems as if Paul had not understood the understanding at all, which would not have been like him, or wilfully ignored it, which I fear would have been very much like him indeed. Was still like him, for all I knew.

'She went well above the call of duty, let me tell you, and it's natural, in't it, that she wants, what is it?'

I had no idea.

'Her talents to be properly recognised.'

I had found her talents difficult to ignore, I must say.

'Perhaps she should appeal to Paul,' I said. I was about to add 'to his better nature' but thought better of it.

'That's what I said to her! "Martha," I said, "Martha, I don't mind all this nicking stuff bit by bit. I don't mind fleecing that poor, daft cunt" – no offence – 'but if you want your dues why not just talk to the man? Put the squeeze on him a bit." I mean, it's the natural thing to do, far as I can see: bastard owes you, you talk to the bastard. But "nah, nah," she says, because the bastard can't be found. Up there in some shack with that weirdo, god knows where, living off berries and roots for all I know. Not a trace of the fucker. I mean, who does that, eh? Who leaves all this to become a fucking hermit or whatever he thinks he is.'

It was a fair question and one I had asked myself on more than one occasion, and the only answer I could rally to was: Paul. Paul was the sort of person who does such a thing, because he had done that exact thing, as far as I knew, but I wouldn't have put it past him to have given up on the whole new man shtick, given up on that simple life with Pauline up in the mountains somewhere. No, I wouldn't be in the least surprised to learn that he was lying on a beach with a bevy of servants waiting on him hand and foot whilst he sipped on cocktails and ogled the local beauties. Not that any of that mattered. What mattered was that Paul was unavailable. Somehow he had set things up, or maybe Cass had, so I could pootle along in this thing that passed for a life without a care in the world, and that was enough for me.

'So that leaves you, mate.'

He was still on the threshold. Really this should have happened somewhere a little more picturesque, to lend some colour to it if nothing else. But it happened with me halfway up a set of stairs and his paunch outfacing me.

'And don't give me that "I don't know what's going on" bullshit. Here you are like a pig in shite, and you think me and Martha will fall for that! You know what's what and that's what we need to know or we'll let you know what's what.'

George rather confused himself with this last sentence, understandably. To make up for it, he dragged me up the remaining stairs by the collar.

The office was in a right state. The cot had been overturned. Books had been ripped from the shelves, rifled, and flung to the floor in what I imagine had been disgust. Fair enough.

Martha sat at the desk, waving a sheaf of papers as I entered.

'What's this?'

George shoved me forward and Martha flung the papers toward me. My handwriting really is not the best; a flat line of graphite with an odd squiggle, seemingly at random, but legible, I fancy, at a push. I recognised it, though; that is I did not recognise what was written, but recognised the paper and the scrawl upon it.

'Just something I fiddle with. In my spare time,' I said.

'Spare fucking time!' said Martha. 'You don't do anything! You're one big blob of spare fucking time.'

It was hard not to concede this point.

'Look,' she said, rocking back in the chair, 'you don't know the code. Fine. But you must know summat.'

I opened my mouth and flapped my arms.

'Fuckin' hell! Like pulling teeth, talking to you.' This thought set a certain gleam in her eye and for a moment I feared for my dentistry.

'Where's your money come from?'

'My money?'

'To pay for shit.'

I knew what money was for, but I didn't know how this made it mine.

'Electricity, council tax, food, water, gas. You know – shit.'

'I don't pay.'

'It gets paid though, don't it? I mean, you not living in fucking luxury for free, are you?'

I had never thought of myself as living in luxury. True, it was a lot more luxurious than my old house, but I wasn't swanning about having caviar for breakfast. It was a meagre life within a luxurious house. It was more like squatting, but with the owner's say so, if I remember what Paul had said that fateful day when he left.

'So,' she said, 'how's it all paid for?'

'I don't know,' I said, and I didn't. All my ruminations on this point over the days since Cass left had left me blank. I never had access to money and yet stuff kept working in this semi-abandoned mansion so no doubt someone, somewhere did the necessary arrangements. I ventured what I had thought most likely.

'I thought George paid for things.'

'George? This George? I wouldn't trust him with a piggy bank.'

'But was he not hired by Paul to take care of things?'

'Nope.'

'No?'

'Fuckin' hell!' she said once again. Really, she was very limited in her vocabulary. The odd 'Christ on a bike' would have been welcome. 'We told you that, you dozy bastard, so we could get him in the house and sniff out the dough.'

'Dough?'

'Yeah, the bread.'

I was now utterly flummoxed, I'm sorry to say.

'The fuckin' pot at the end of the rainbow. The stash! 'Cause there's got to be one somewhere.'

George was lurking behind me. I could hear his breath.

'I have no idea,' I said.

'What about the cleaner, then. Monica, or whatever.'

'Marina,' I said.

'Who gives a fuck! How's she get paid, or is she doing it out of the goodness of her heart, eh?'

I was sure there was a great deal of goodness in Marina's heart but I was equally sure she got paid, somehow. Martha studied me as I mulled this.

'George,' she barked. 'Get the bitch in!'

'I thought you hired Marina?'

'Nope.'

'But…?'

'You've not got it, have you? We lie. It's what we do. We lie, we cheat, we bully, we get by. All that contract bullshit was us so we could nick what we wanted when we wanted. Stupid cow fell for it.' She seemed immensely proud at this and rocked back in the chair still further. I fancy she would have put her feet on the desk if her physique would have allowed for it. Nevertheless, little inconsistencies were slowly being brought into line, which was handy. Inconsistencies that hadn't bothered me in the slightest, it has to be said. Why this mania for everything to hang together?

Marina must have already been on the premises, perhaps it was yet another Friday or perhaps George had dragged her from her home in preparation for this moment. Their patience had worn thin – a thousand little signs told me so – and so they might well have wanted to bring the whole thing to a head. Yes, it must have been trying for George and Martha. Oh, I'm sure there was an initial thrill to it all, gulling Marina and I with such ease and then squirreling away whatever moveable goods caught their eye. That must have been fun, in some sense. But fun palls, I think, and especially when you think a much greater source of fun is to be had. Look at me talking about fun as if I had the first clue!

George shoved Marina into the room. She was as small as ever, but something of the mousiness was missing. She did her best to smile at me then set her face in determined fashion.

'Here she is!' said Martha, rising from the desk and crossing over to Marina. 'Can see why you took a shine to her. Pretty little thing. Looks like she'd break in two, mind, fall over in a stiff wind.' She brought herself close to Marina and blew in her face. Marina just glared up at her. 'No? Stronger stuff, eh?'

She went back to behind the desk, took up the chair and placed it in the centre of the room, amidst the scattered books and papers.

'But you know what? I kinda like the stronger ones – pop yourself down there, love – 'cause it gives you a bit of a challenge, not like those wimpy bastards who just fold when all you do is look at 'em funny. Comfy? Lovely. There was this one bloke – one of Paul's jobs as it happens – CEO of something or other, can't remember. Doesn't matter. Looking at him you'd think he'd be a challenge, all suited and booted and arrogant. Thought the sun shone out of his arse he did. Says to me "I'm sure we can make a deal, you and me" and I says, "I'm sure I can fuck up your kneecaps" and that's all it took! Didn't even touch him! Crumbled right there and then. Art of the deal, my arse. Depends on how highly you value your knees, I suppose. You love,' and she bent down in front of Marina to rest her hands on her bare legs, 'what do you reckon your knees are worth?'

I could see Martha dig her fingers into Marina's thighs and Marina, without even a wince, staring back at her.

'You remember that time… ,' said George, chuckling.

'Shut the fuck up!' said Martha. George thought it best to comply. 'Can't you see I'm working here?'

'Sorry, Martha,' George mumbled into his chest. She shook her head and sighed. Poor woman. She hadn't been given her due and she only had George as an accomplice. Really, she was much put upon, when you think of it. Just a woman trying to make her way but surrounded by idiots and arseholes. But there you go; such was her lot in life, I suppose.

Martha and Marina looked each other in the eye. I looked from each to each. George looked at the floor.

'Who pays you, love?'

'Never seen them.'

'Never?'

Marina clamped her mouth shut. This was not lost on Martha. She released her grip, cocked her head and studied Marina a little more.

'Come here, Georgie.' He did. 'Georgie boy – ahh, look at him, just a big teddy bear our George – well, I reckon he's taking a bit of a fancy to you. Don't blush George! It's only natural, lovely little thing like her. All neat and petite. Sure he'd love to get to know you better, wouldn't you George? How would you like that, love, eh? Get to know George a little better?'

'Cash in an envelope, once a week,' said Marina, not taking her eyes of Martha.

'Never a cheque?'

'Never.'

'Postmark?'

'Hand-delivered.'

'So who delivers it?'

'Middle of the night, so I've no idea.'

'Never seen him?'

'I've already told you that.'

'Don't get lippy.'

Now I am not one to cast aspersions on anyone, let alone Martha, but it seemed to me to take her a long time to assess this information and to figure out how to proceed. It can't be easy trying to make out if someone is telling a lie, to be fair.

'So,' said Martha, 'it's back to you, in't it?'

Marina and I did as instructed and I replaced her on the chair. I think she may have grasped my hand for a moment as we passed.

'Sorry about the mess,' said Martha, picking up a large volume from the floor. 'Thought I might find something, but no luck!' She flicked through the pages as she walked back and forth in front of me. 'I really should read more, you know. Say it's good for you. For the mind. Expand your horizons and all that. But, really, whose got the time, eh? If it's not one thing, it's another.'

She slammed the book shut.

'Now. Here's the rules. I ask; you answer. If you lie, you get a smack.' She demonstrated the motion to be applied in this eventuality, swinging the book through the air. 'If you give me a daft answer, you get a smack.' A further demonstration. 'You understand?'

'I do.'

'And you?' turning to Marina. She nodded.

'Good.'

'Martha,' said George. 'What about that "getting to know her better" bit?'

Rather than replying, Martha leapt at George and brought the book down on his nose with all her force. A reply of sorts, I suppose. She regained her composure as George crumpled to the floor, clutching his face.

'Right then, everybody ready? Good. Off we go.

'Where is Paul?'

'I don't know.'

'Where's his wife?'

'With him.'

'Not that one. The other one. The posh one.'

'Abroad.'

'Right. Who comes here?'

'George,' which earned me a thwack. I was going to say that she, Martha, was also now something of a feature in the house but as my head rang and my nose ached I managed to consider this was probably not the information she was after. People don't like to be told what they already know, it seems.

'Apart from George and the mousey cow, who comes here?'

I thought it best to consider my answer. It was a delicate balance. I wanted to give a satisfactory answer, which would mean some thinking time, but I didn't want the thinking time itself to become an annoyance, despite the fact that duration had not been mentioned in the rules, which had been very clear in themselves but not as comprehensive as one might wish. I had been on the verge of saying 'Postman', but thought better of it. Not that the postman didn't visit, because surely he must have done to deliver those cards from Cass, unless it was a postwoman, but I felt that, whilst true, this wasn't the sort of answer Martha was after. I wish I could have said 'the man from the bank' or 'Paul's lawyer', even though he hated lawyers for reasons unknown, or even 'that bloke from number 10 down the road', but all of these would have been equally untrue and I didn't trust my ability to dissemble whereas I did trust Martha's ability to smell a rat and deal a solid smack with a book. I think it was an encyclopaedia of sorts; it certainly felt like. I was even more certain of this as Martha, her patience thinning, raised the book aloft.

'Mr Samuels,' I blurted. 'He used to come.'

She lowered the book.

'Who the fuck is Mr Samuels?'

'Mr Samuels is Mr Samuels, but he hasn't been for quite some time.'

'Now we're getting somewhere. Tell me about this Samuels fucker.'

thirty-two

Mr Samuels did not feel the scorching of the sun nor the sweat running down his brow. The sky remained indifferent. A single crow, mouth agape in the heat, eyed him from a nearby tree.

The youth that Mr Samuels then was had only been allowed to wear short trousers.

Mr Samuels Senior found the boy at his desk applying himself to building a small model of a Messerschmitt. The main body was already complete, and one wing was affixed. The shutters were closed against the heat and sun so the boy worked in the pool of his desk lamp.

'How is the bf109 proceeding?'

'Well, Father.'

The young Mr Samuels had really wanted a Focke-Wulf 190 but none had been available when he had had enough pocket-money saved up to indulge himself.

Mr Samuels Senior did something he rarely did. He sat upon the youth's bed, placing a parcel wrapped in brown paper and string beside him.

'Could you not find a Hurricane?'

'No, Father. Only a Spitfire.'

'The show-ponies of the skies, Son.'

'My thoughts exactly, Father,' as he applied glue to the edges of the second wing.

'Glamorous does not equate with good.'

'Precisely, Father.'

'A lesson not to be forgotten, be it in fighter aircraft or any other facet of life.'

'Such as, Father?' he turned to face him, eager to know.

His father avoided the gaze and stroked the package beside him.

'Facets, Son, of which you are not yet aware, but will soon become so, I fear. Facets that – ahem – men find themselves acquainted with, in due course. Facets that – ahem – might take a man off-guard, or lead him astray, or obscure his proper focus.'

'Which must always be the work, Father.'

'Always. Always the work.'

The young Mr Samuels could not imagine what could be so alluring as to obscure his proper focus; a focus that his father had never failed to maintain, as far as he could tell.

'But Father,' said Mr Samuels, 'how can one be distracted from the work?'

'Men are weak, Son.'

'Of course, Father. And I think I know how to identify and exploit those weaknesses.'

'True. I have taught you that.'

'And I have learned, Father.'

Was that a sceptical look that man gave boy?

'The glue is becoming dry.'

Quickly, the boy pressed the wing to the fuselage and held it there.

'Be that as it may,' said the Father, 'it is one thing to identify and exploit the weakness of others, and quite another to identify and avoid the weakness in oneself.'

Despite his care, Mr Samuels saw the glue bulge out from the join and threaten to smear both fuselage and wing. He took a piece of tissue paper and removed the excess.

Mr Samuels Senior seemed strangely drawn to the package. He kept his attention fixed upon it. He cleared his throat.

'Are you sickening, Father?'

'Why do you ask?'

'You seem to have a frog in your throat, as I understand the expression is.'

'No. No. In the prime, Son, in the prime.'

Boy and man were quiet for some time. Boy bent over his model; man hand resting on his parcel.

'Is there anyone – ahem – at school to whom you pay particular attention?'

'Seeing as you mention it, Father, I think Mr Irons has been behaving in a slightly concerning manner.'

'The Physical Education teacher?'

'Yes, Father. When we are playing hockey or rugby, he stands with his hands in his shorts.'

'And what do you surmise?'

'That he is keeping his hands warm.'

'Yes, Son, that is probably it. I was rather more enquiring about your fellow students.'

'I watch and learn, Father, whilst keeping my distance.'

'As it should be, Son. But do you find yourself watching and learning from one particular child?'

'I don't think so, Father.'

'Any particular female, for example?'

'Why female, Father?' The wing now seemed quite secure, so Mr Samuels let his grip go and turned to his father who was still bent over the package.

'I think I have told you on numerous occasions that categorisation aids clarity of thought.'

'Indeed.'

'So, we are breaking down the student – ahem – body into its constituent parts the better to – ahem – get to grips with the – ahem – issue.'

'Can I bring you a glass of water?'

'No. So, in the spirit of categorisation, I repeat the question,' although he didn't.

'Well, Father, I have noticed the behaviour of one female more than the others.'

'You have?'

'Yes. She has the habit, in class, of sucking her own hair and staring out of the window.'

'Nothing else of notice?'

'No. Oh yes; she is a fine athlete. Running and jumping and such like.'

'Is she?'

'Oh, yes. Quite the fastest girl in our year.'

'Quickest,' said the father, 'rather than fastest.'

'Noted,' said the boy, whilst not really seeing the distinction.

A further silence.

'Do you mind my asking, Father, what is in the parcel?'

'Ah, yes.' He stood, the parcel in his outstretched arms. 'Don't misunderstand. This is not a gift. This is just something it is now time for you to have.'

The boy took the package, began to tear at it enthusiastically but then checked himself and unwrapped it with care.

'Trousers, Father?'

'The finest corduroy. Take care of them and you will not need another pair until it is time for your suit.'

'When will that be, Father?'

'You have permission to wear them outside of school hours only, of course. They are sturdy, but they breathe well enough. Fashion has not been a consideration.'

'Of course not, Father.'

'Nor has – ahem – allure.'

Mr Samuels did not reply, not knowing how to.

It was September the 8th of his fifteenth year.

The crow fixed Mr Samuels one last time, cawed, and flew off, unnoticed.

Mr Samuels Senior sat in the same seat he had occupied for days on end, a blanket wrapped over his knees. His rheumy eyes stared impassively. His mouth was slack. His grey cheeks sagged to his ragged neck.

'Father,' said Mr Samuels, now a man and dressed for work in the brown suit that was already a uniform, 'I have a mission which will take me just a couple of hours.'

Mr Samuels Senior lifted his hand from the folds of the blanket and slowly beckoned him to come closer. Mr Samuels bent down to him, cocking his ear towards the mouth that was already trying to form a word.

'Pre-gasp-cision.'

His eyes closed with the effort and his hand dropped once again to his knees.

Mr Samuels took his notebook from the inner jacket pocket, consulted and replaced it.

'A preliminary estimate would be no more, and scarcely less, than two hours thirty-five minutes, Father.'

Mr Samuels could see the patch of dry, flaking skin on his father's scalp. His father let out a low, brief hum that hovered between satisfaction and suspicion.

'You have a glass of water to your right, Father, should you need it. Is there anything else before I go?'

Again the father raised his hand and beckoned. Again Mr Samuels bent down to him.

'Mic - .'

'Mic, Father?'

'- turate.'

'Of course.'

Mr Samuels took the blanket from his father's knees, folded it and placed it on the floor. He then took himself to the right of the chair, gripped his father under his arm and gently began to raise him to his feet. There was no strength in his father's legs; they buckled and they began again, this time with Mr Samuels bracing himself a little more and applying a little more force. His father's arm would soon no doubt show a livid purple bruise where the pressure had been applied. His father stood with Mr Samuels still supporting him but with his knees at such an angle that it was clear no load was being borne. He tottered and swayed as Mr Samuels unbuttoned his father's trousers with his free hand; the trousers of the suit Mr Samuels Senior had habitually worn.

'Lean on me, Father, on my shoulders.'

Mr Samuels barely registered the weight. With both hands free, he lowered his father's trousers, inch by inch, and, inch by inch, bruised, slack and greying skin was revealed, rippling down from his loins.

'Hold on, Father. We are nearly there.'

He could feel his father trembling with effort.

Trousers at ankles, Mr Samuels then lowered his father's undershorts. He averted his eyes. He took the thick cardboard flask from the table beside him and introduced it to his father's penis, necessarily having to watch what he did. His father's testicles, wasted, hung low between his thighs. He averted his eyes again as his father groaned in pain and relief, turn and turnabout, and the flask echoed with the drips of effluence.

'Done?'

Still with his father's slight weight on his shoulders, Mr Samuels placed the flask on the table and the reverse operation was begun. The undershorts were drawn up, then the trousers and then, with Mr Samuels once more taking his father under the arm, the lowering into the chair. He took up the blanket, unfolded it, and placed it once more across his father's knees.

'If you are sure there is nothing else, Father?'

His father's pupils were dull in the yellow of the iris, traced by delicate veins. Father and son held the gaze. Mr Samuels' eyes were clear; his father's opaque with the gathering rheum. They looked on still.

Mr Samuels Senior once more beckoned his boy. Once more, he lent down.

A whisper.

'Nothing. Nothing.'

'In that case, Father, I must be going if I am to keep to the schedule. You are sure there is nothing more?'

Mr Samuels raised his hand. He did not beckon; he dismissed.

After two hours and thirty-three minutes, Mr Samuels returned and the house itself told him there was nothing alive within.

Mr Samuels could bear the sun no longer. Out there in the garden, rapt in memory, he had not felt the merciless sun, but then, all of a sudden, he felt it keenly. Slowly, he made his way back into the house. He did not think where he was going. In; that was enough for now. He poured himself a glass of tepid water and sat at the kitchen table. He pictured the boy opposite him, his mouth open, egg and toast mashing together inside, noisily.

The boy's room was almost intact. Only the computer had been removed. The boy's shirts still hung in the wardrobe. The books still remained on the shelves. Books on local geography, geology, fauna and flora; books on local history, ancient and modern; books on cryptography, sapping, scouting and rudimentary survival techniques; an atlas of the world and an atlas of the stars.

Mr Samuels sat on the boy's bed. It had been his bed when he had been a boy, as this room had been his. It was in this bed that Mr Samuels had listened for the sound of his father returning from some late night mission, night after night. It was in this bed that the boy had slept on unknowing as Mr Samuels had watched him from the doorway, night after night.

The woman in charge was briskly efficient. This gained Mr Samuels' approval. She sat behind her desk, which was clear save for an official stamp, a line of pens and a single framed photograph of herself and a young girl. She perused a small, brown file detailing the suitability, or otherwise, of the applicant. The shouts and screams of playing children reached them through the open window from the courtyard below.

She neatly closed the file that she had been reading, removed her glasses and clasped her hands in front of her on the desk.

'Mr Samuels,' she said, 'I will be frank.'

'That would be appreciated.'

'You are far from being an ideal candidate.'

'Madam.'

'No,' she raised her hand, 'please let me finish.' She stood and crossed to the window. In silhouette, her features became hawk-like as she watched over her charges. 'Those children might not have been blessed with a life within a family – brothers, sisters, parents and so forth – but that does not make them any less deserving of a family life.'

Mr Samuels did not object. He knew what he was offering.

'That, at least,' said the woman, 'is the ideal. But times being what they are.' Turning to him, she noticed Mr Samuels raise his eyebrows as if to enquire. 'Times are hard, Mr Samuels. The biological imperative has been so aided by modern medical science that the pool from which we draw our applicants has been reduced to a mere puddle. That, and the sad rise in the rate of those drawn to a solitary life – for whatever reason, it is not for me to judge – has further eroded our store of suitably stable couples wishing to begin a family.'

'Madam, it does not say within the file because the question was not asked on the application, but I think it best that you know that I intend to raise the boy as an only child.'

'As you were raised,' she said, returning to the desk and flicking open the file to check. 'And by an only parent too, I see.'

'As my father did for me, so I wish to do for this child, should that be acceptable.'

The woman let slip a thin smile.

'Well, the times being what they are and your impressive application – the home check report was excellent I see – your financial position and your references – yes, they are most gratifying, Mr Samuels; most gratifying indeed.' She looked up from the file to fix him directly. 'And, of course, your profession is one which we favour, when all else allows.' Again the smile. 'Yes, all in all, I'm inclined to look at your application in a favourable light, pending further investigation and validation, naturally.'

'You're most kind.'

'Did you have a child in mind?'

'Joseph,' said Mr Samuels, 'file number X451 – slash – D.'

Her eyes crinkled as she tried to recall the child. She crossed to a cabinet and rifled through the files. 'X451 – slash – D; Joseph. Mother deceased. Father unknown. No family extant.'

'Precisely, Madam.'

'Oh yes! Now I remember. He has just had his second birthday. We try to mark the occasion, if we can, in our own small way.' She placed the file on the desk, next to that of Mr Samuels. 'Would you like to visit the boy now, Mr Samuels?'

'Very much so.'

The woman called out, 'Miss Smithers!' A small, impeccably neat woman entered. 'Please take Mr Samuels to room 6. He is here with a view to adopt young Joseph.' She checked her watch. 'Perfect timing, Mr Samuels; he'll have just had his nap. Bright boy, if I recall. Great potential.'

She offered Mr Samuels her hand.

'Thank you Madam,' he said, before leaving with Miss Smithers to see the boy he was already thinking of as Samuel.

Alone in the office, the woman took the official stamp from her desk and applied it first to the boy's file and then to Mr Samuels'. She closed the office door. She closed the window on the cries of the children and then let down the blind. She crossed to the desk, took the back off the framed photograph and took from it a small key. From the desk drawer that this opened she produced a second stamp, which she applied first to the file of Mr Samuels and then to the boy's.

She allowed herself a few moments of quiet satisfaction.

Mr Samuels, alone, sat unmoving on his boy's bed.

thirty-three

What I told Martha about Mr Samuels was perhaps not all that she had hoped, as the application of the encyclopaedia told me. That she didn't repeatedly apply the encyclopaedia hinted that she thought nothing else would be forthcoming. She was particularly irked by my being unable to supply an address. Dragging George to his feet, she left, swearing that she would track the fucker down herself.

She locked the door behind her. I never knew the door had a lock, but, there you go, it did.

This new incarceration was so much better than the last one. For a start, I could see. I didn't see too well for a while, but eventually I saw well enough. Then, of course, I was not alone this time. As soon as Martha and George had gone and the door locked, Marina set about sorting things out. First, she put my cot to rights. Then, taking me under the arm, she gently helped me from the chair.

'Are you okay?' she said, straining a little under my weight, which is not great, but still a weight when all said and done.

I couldn't yet answer.

She sat me down on the edge of the cot and then eased me into a prone position. 'Lie down,' she said. 'Take it easy.'

I was more than happy to comply.

'But don't fall asleep!'

This was a little more tricky, but I did my best. She brushed my hair out of my face and gave me a heartening smile. She only managed it for a second or two, but it's the thought that counts. Even I could see she was struggling. In many ways, she was the worse off. She was, after all, in her full senses and mine came and went in a haze of colours and the odd surge of nausea, which thankfully I didn't act upon. For her, the full weight of our circumstance must have borne down on her. She crumpled a little by my side, her shoulders dipping and her head dropping so her hair fell over her face. If I could have patted her on her back I would have done.

'This is no good,' she said and got to her feet. As an assessment it seemed about right. 'Seeing as we're stuck in here, might as well tidy up.' I didn't see the logic.

She began gathering up the books strewn across the floor and putting them back on the shelves, not caring about height or colour, but I didn't mind, there would be time enough to set that right, hopefully, I thought, and then lost the thought almost as soon as it had appeared.

'I know people look down on cleaners like me,' she said, brightly, albeit with a forced brightness, perhaps, 'but I've always kind of liked it. Not as a job, as such. I mean the pay is awful and people treat you bad. I don't mean that. I mean, just getting rid of mess. Getting things in a bit of order, know what I mean?' She checked I was still awake. 'Even if I was the richest woman on earth I think I'd still clean and tidy. Silly isn't it? But I think I would. I'd miss it. Maybe,' and now her voice seemed less forced, 'I'd have one room in the house that would be the dirty room. I'd hire someone to come in once a week and make it really messy and then I'd come in and give it a good going over. So I still get the kick of cleaning, of putting things straight, without all the hassle. It'd be like a hobby, see?'

I was just about following all this as she bustled about the room. She came over and gave me a gentle shake, just to make sure. 'Stay with me,' she whispered.

'I do my best thinking cleaning, too. I know it's my job and all that so I suppose it's the only time I can think, but I think that cleaning up a room kind of helps me sort out my mind; get rid of the clutter in here' she tapped her head, 'whilst getting rid of it out here.' She paused, then shrugged. 'Seems that way, anyways.'

I wondered how much cleaning would have to be done for her to think how to get us out of the mess we were in.

She surveyed the room. 'Getting there,' she said. 'Everything will be back in its place before you know it.'

I became aware of a cobweb in the corner. She would need a duster on a pole to sort it out, I thought. I vaguely remembered that there was something useful to be learnt from cobwebs, but I had no idea what it might be. I must have been rapt in this for some time because next thing I knew was Marina sitting back down on the cot once more.

'There,' she said. 'At least that's them sorted.'

She had rallied, but now, with the tidying done, she relapsed. I could almost feel the weight descend. A delusion due to concussion, no doubt.

'What's going on?' she said, almost without breath.

I thought I should reply. I had heard the words distinctly and knew what they meant. This didn't do me any good. Perhaps it is never too late in the day to know what's going on, but I had neither the strength nor the inclination. I could have made something up, I suppose.

Somewhere in the house, the dog yapped then yelped.

The door shook as it was unlocked, and Martha stormed in, George in her considerable wake. Without a by-your-leave, which was hardly to be expected, or an act of random violence, which was, she headed straight for the desk over which my papers were scattered.

'Fucking goose chase!' she said, a sheaf of papers clutched in her hand, 'but the Samuels bastard is all over this, in't he?' as she shook the pages in our direction. She skimmed through them. 'Mr Samuels. Mr Samuels, and here, Mr Samuels, every bloody page; Mr Samuels. Mr Samuels does this, Mr Samuels does that,' in a mincing voice that, to my battered ear, reminded me of Paul.

She ran over to us, pushed Marina to the floor and dragged me to the chair once more. This allowed her to shove the pages under my nose.

'Every fucking page!'

'Every fucking page, Martha!' George echoed from the door, before sidling over towards Marina as if to drag her to her feet.

'Back off, George! You fucking randy old goat. We might need her yet.'

Apparently, George backed off.

'There I was,' said Martha, 'thinking "how do I get hold of this Samuels bloke," even got in the car to look for the bastard, not with the first fucking clue where to look, when it hit me, right here,' she pressed her forefinger between my eyes, 'that name, that name,' she ground her finger into my head a little, 'where have I seen that name before?'

She broke away from me and let out a little laugh.

'Oh, Martha! You poor, stupid cow! Even a git like this gets the better of you. And what have I done, eh?' to George, 'eh?' to Marina still on the floor, 'eh?' to me, lolling in the chair 'what have I fucking done not to get a bit of a break? A little bit of luck? One fucking day when it all goes okay? One fucking moment when I get what I want; no hassle, no bother, just what I want when I want it. Is that too much to fucking ask?'

The question was asked of no one in particular, it seemed; of the gods, perhaps.

'Now, git-face', which was a new and welcome addition to her lexicon, and apparently meant me, 'I can't be arsed to read through all this shit,' I could quite see her point. 'I mean, what is this crap anyway?' She applied herself to the page, squinting at it, cocking her head this way and that, trying to make sense of the scrawl. 'This: Mr Samuels woke before dawn in order to super-what the fuck?' and she squinted still further, ' su-per-vysss-eee, supervise, yeah, supervise the coming of the day, as always. Seriously, who talks like that?' She gave me a bang with the back of her hand, almost absent-mindedly. 'Blah, blah,' scanning the page once more, 'blah, blah, blah, he fucks about in his house for a bit, has breakfast, as if anyone gives a shit. But here's the thing! You know all this and you don't know his address? D'you think I was born yesterday?'

'No,' I said, after some little time during which she loomed over me, her hands on her hips, her breath hot, her mouth hanging open in angry expectation.

'So, if I weren't born yesterday I think it's about time you coughed up the address, don't you? Or,' her eyes swivelled in the direction of Marina, 'do I need to give George the say-so?'

The truth and I have never been on the best of terms. The truth was that I didn't know Mr Samuels' address and had never known it. But it seemed that this truth was not an acceptable one, to Martha's mind at least, and her mind was the only one that mattered. My head hanging to my chest, my mouth agape, and, I fear, drooling slightly, unless it was blood, I was perhaps not in the best position to assess the situation, but I tried. If the truth was unacceptable, then perhaps a lie might prove useful, at least to buy Marina and I a bit of time. Yes, I could make up an address and Martha and George would dash off, all excited that finally they were getting somewhere, and Marina and I would be left to come up with some plan of escape. I think I might have even tried to raise my head to put this idea into action but I was stopped by the realisation that I had no idea how to make up an address that would be convincing. I had no idea what any of the streets in this town are called. I've never needed to know. I wasn't even sure I knew the name of the street on which I lived. I had seen the name on the post-cards from Cass, but I didn't read the address as such, my mind focused on the words of Cass above all else and what was going on with her spiritual quest, if that's what it was. Even now, in full possession of my so-called faculties, I am not sure I could make up an address. No doubt there are streets named after local worthies, but as I don't know any local worthies that's no good at all. No doubt there are more generic things: freedom, independence, that sort of thing, and they'd do, I suppose, to convince someone who had no idea of what the streets and squares were actually called. But would they convince a Martha who might be more than willing to go along with a Freedom Square but would instantly know that Freedom Boulevard was just so much nonsense?

I admitted the truth.

'I don't know his address.'

'All yours then George,' she said.

George didn't need telling twice. He made straight for Marina.

'Wait,' I shouted through a bubble of spittle that had formed on my lips. Yes, a thought had struck me. 'I know where it is.'

Martha held up her hand towards George who stopped in mid-stride. His head drooped. Marina took the chance to inch herself into a corner of the room.

'So you do know the address?'

'No. I just know where it is. Its off a square with a big tree. An old house. Near the river.'

We have squares, we have big trees, we have old houses and we even have a river that is still called a river even though there is never any water in it.

'Well my little lovely, it's time we took a trip then isn't it.'

Martha patted me on the cheek so gently that I could feel the callouses on her palm. I had neither expected the pat nor the trip. The callouses were not a surprise.

'George!' He perked up at the sound of his sister's voice. 'Get him cleaned up. Missy,' meaning Marina, 'you're with me. Insurance.' She gave me a wink before grabbing Marina by the arm and dragging her out the door. I can't be sure, but Marina might have looked back at me over her shoulder as she was bundled out. I'd like to think so.

George was not a happy man. He rubbed his face with his massive hirsute hands for a moment then looked at me with something like disgust. It must have seemed to him that this would forever be his lot in life, clearing up after Martha had had all the fun. He ripped me from the chair and pushed me towards the bathroom. Yes, he had a job to do. The mirror told a sorry tale of what my face had been subjected to. The water I dashed onto my face was not unpleasant and the mixed blood and water swirled in the sink very prettily.

He pushed me into the kitchen. There was an odd feeling to the place; as if it was at once strange and familiar. Marina stood by the door with the puppy in her arms. Martha was slumped over the island, her head resting on a large, open file. She raised her head, dashed it down on the file with a sickening thump and then repeated the operation.

'Madam, this is no time for histrionics,' Mr Samuels, resplendent in a white suit, eased the file from beneath Martha's forehead. 'Naturally,' he said, 'everything has been copied and kept in a secure location.' He neatly placed the file under his arm.

Were there tears in Martha's eyes? Perhaps. There were tears in Marina's eyes, certainly; of relief, I fancy. I felt my own eyes moisten, in truth.

'Might I suggest you and your accomplice now leave, Madam, or must I action some of the options I laid out to you?'

She stared at Mr Samuels, her nostrils flaring. 'You fucker,' she said, true to form at the very last. 'You fucking fucker.' She seemed to weigh her options. I can only imagine she found them wanting.

'Martha!' cried George. 'What's going on?'

The poor man was rooted to the spot, his head shuttling between Martha and Mr Samuels in turn.

'You and your sister are leaving, Sir. Isn't that correct Madam?'

One final glare. She pushed herself off from the island and stormed through the open door into the sunlight of the day. George could only slouch after her. He seemed to have shrunk.

Mr Samuels let the atmosphere of the room right itself.

'Might I trouble you for a cup of tea, my dear Sir?' he said, lightly. 'My apologies to you both for being so tardy. Events, I'm afraid, somewhat detained me, as events are wont to do.'

Indeed.

ABOUT THE AUTHOR

Paul Stewart is a British-born author and academic. His first novel, *Now Then*, was published by Armida in 2014 and this was followed by *Of People and Things* in 2019. As an academic and Professor of Literature at the University of Nicosia he was published widely on Samuel Beckett, modern, and contemporary literature. *And Other Elsewheres*, a collection of poetry, was published in 2009.

He lives in Nicosia with his wife and two sons.

ALSO BY PAUL STEWART

Now Then

John Matthews is a happily married college lecturer, living in Bristol with his successful wife, Penny. The couple, now in their early thirties, are trying for a baby. All this is seemingly inexplicably threatened when John is stopped short by seeing a familiar haircut on the street. This insignificant encounter triggers a decline over a single week into depression and near insanity as memories and nightmares, all connected to a past repressed relationship, overwhelm him and threaten his otherwise stable life. In this compelling work of contemporary literary fiction, Stewart weaves dream and reality, false and true memory into a challenging psychological drama of one ordinary man's failure to cope with the secrets of his past as they force their way into the present.

Of People and Things

Of People and Things is at once a comic mystery story, similar to the works of Will Self or a comic Cormac McCarthy, but also a strangely unsettling and moving novel as uncanny moments pile upon each other to test the hapless narrator's attempts to understand just what is going on.

Lightning Source UK Ltd.
Milton Keynes UK
UKHW040209110223
416681UK00017B/1911